MR. SO WRONG

R.C. STEPHENS

COPYRIGHT

Mr. So Wrong

*Somewhere over the rainbow skies are blue. And the dreams that you dare to dream come true. – **Yip Harburg***

MR. SO WRONG

Albert Walsh the Third has spent over a decade running away from his past. With no job and nothing to lose, he goes on a spontaneous drive to visit his sister in the mountains of Colorado. The simple trip proves to be more than he bargained for. Samantha Belmont is floating through life. She's cast her dreams aside and now works on her papa's ranch. One night, Sam is driving home in a snow storm after a hookup when she spots a car in a ditch and saves a man's life. She doesn't expect to develop feelings for the hot as hell stranger. Everything about him is wrong from his pointy shoes and fancy car to his age. Pushing him away would be the smart move. Only Al can't be pushed around anymore. Maybe it's because she saved his life or maybe it's because this cowgirl is completely different from every other woman he's been with. Problem is Sam has secrets of her own. Secrets she doesn't want Al to find out because if he did he'd run in the other direction. She pushes him away even though he melts her panties right off—literally. There is more than just her heart that needs protection. Al won't give up fighting for the feisty cowgirl's attention. Tempers will flare and hearts will be broken.

And Sam's plans to never settle down will be torched like the inferno of passion raging between them.

Please stay in touch because I love to connect and talk books.

For the latest news on my releases, cover reveals and sales sign up for my Newsletter **HERE**

PROLOGUE

SAM

2004

"SHE'S GOT THIS, SAM," Mack said, giving my shoulder a tight squeeze.

"She's right, honey," Mom agreed, her tired voice scratchy and weak. "Your mama's a fighter. You know that." She lay in bed, looking frail. She had cut her hair off just before she started the chemo treatments and mostly either wore a bandana on her head or the silly baseball cap Papa gave her when he got back from the rodeo last year. It had *I am a bull rider* embroidered on it. We all thought it was cute because Mama was a fierce woman. She helped Papa with the bulls in the bull barn all the time. She did everything he did around this ranch.

"I know, Mama. You're a fighter. I just worry. I've only had you for nine years. I need more time," I said as my voice cracked. I couldn't imagine this world without Mama in it. I wasn't finished growing. I needed her to take care of me. Love me. Teach me things I didn't know. Sure, we had Papa, but he wasn't involved much. If it didn't have to do with a heifer or Jim Beam, he just didn't care.

"You go to sleep now, Sam. Give me a kiss. You need a good night's sleep so you won't be tired for school tomorrow. I'll make you your favorite breakfast in the morning," she promised. I may have been young, but I still wondered how she would get out of bed tomorrow morning. She hadn't gotten further than her bedroom door for a long while now. I pushed the thought aside. She was my mama, and she never lied to me. Mack gave me a little nudge forward, and I kissed Mama's clammy cheek. "Goodnight, my sweet girls. Dream of rainbows and blue birds. Dream of making the impossible come true," her voice trailed off. Mama grew up watching the *Wizard of Oz*. She always taught us to dream big.

"I'll dream that you will be better by morning," I said, wishing my mama would feel better and finally be able to leave her bed.

"Thank you," she said. My sister leaned in to give her a kiss too. Mack was five years older than me. She took my hand and led me into my room where she helped me choose a pair of pajamas and tucked me into bed.

"Goodnight, Button," she said, flicking the tip of my nose.

"Night," I smiled back to her. Lately she had been acting more like my mama than my sister, and I thought she would make a good mama one day.

"Can I sing to you before I go to sleep?" I asked, pressing out my lower lip.

That trick worked every time. "Okay. One song." She groaned even though I knew she liked to hear me sing.

I grinned widely and took a cleansing breath through my nose. I loved to sing, but I always enjoyed it more when I had an audience. I opened my mouth and began to sing "Somewhere over the Rainbow." My sister took a seat on my bed and looked down at me, her brown eyes filled with a sadness I understood. I noticed Papa leaning against my doorframe, listening too. He wasn't a man who smiled much, but I could tell by the warmth in his eyes that he liked to hear me sing. When I was done my song,

Papa pushed off the doorframe and walked off. He was also a man of few words. Mack caressed the top of my head, brushing some stray hairs off my face. "You sleep tight now, Button."

"Mack!" I called out into the dark, and my sister turned to look at me. "Do you really think Mama will be up in the morning to make us breakfast?" I wanted to hide the hope in my voice because it seemed to make Mack sad.

"I hope so, Button. Sleep now." With those last words, she left my room, and I dreamed about being a famous singer and singing on a stage. It was a good dream.

MORNING CAME FASTER than I wanted it to. I liked to sleep. I liked the warmth of my comforter shielding me from the morning chill that ran through our house. I was fully prepared to give my sister a hard time getting out of bed just so I could embrace the warmth a few moments longer, but then I remembered Mama promised breakfast. She was the best and our only cook in the house ... Well, except if Papa was making one of his steak dinners. I wasn't a fan of steak, though I would never dare admit that to Papa since he was a cattle rancher. I popped out of bed as the smell of warm buttermilk pancakes and sausage links wafted through the air. Mama was making me breakfast. She was out of bed. Everything was going to be fine.

I made a mad dash to the bathroom and scrubbed my teeth in the up and down motion she had taught me. I ran a brush through my short blond hair. I had chopped off a good ten inches the month before and donated it; Mama said it was for a good cause and would make people suffering with cancer feel a little better about how they looked. It sure was easier to brush and didn't tangle much, though some kids at school started making fun of me calling me a boy. Mack told me to ignore them, but it

wasn't easy. Not when their words were so hurtful. They didn't
understand why I had cut my hair and that made me angry too.

Excitement bubbled inside me as the smell of pancakes and
links drifted upstairs. I skipped back to my room, got dressed
quickly, and ran down the stairs straight for the kitchen.

Mama was standing by the stove frying links on a pan. Mack
stood beside her, watching. Mama must have heard me coming
because she turned her head. "Good morning, Sam. Look what I
made for you?" She was smiling.

She was wearing her robe and still had that silly machine that
gave her pain medicine wrapped around her waist, but she
looked much better than she had in a long time. She took a few
plates out of the cupboard and walked them over to the kitchen
table where a stack of pancakes sat on a plate in the center. I
pulled out a chair and felt my mouth water as I reached for the
fluffiest pancake on earth.

"Mmm, this is so good," I said with a mouthful of holy
goodness.

Mama didn't scold me like she usually had when I'd talk with
a mouth full of food. She brought the pan with the links over to
the table and dumped a pile of them on a plate. I took my fork
and stabbed two of them and brought them to my mouth. I hadn't
had this kind of breakfast in a while. Papa started working out in
the barn around 5:00 am, so Mack made us breakfast, which was
either oatmeal or cereal. Since I hated warm cereal, it was cold
cereal and milk for me. It sure didn't warm my belly on a cold
winter morning like Mama's links and pancakes.

Mack gave Mama a kiss on the cheek and thanked her for
breakfast. Then she came to sit beside me, only she wasn't eating
much.

"I packed your lunches too." Mama nodded and Mack looked
just as wide eyed as me. Mama hadn't packed our lunches in a
long time. "You girls need to eat healthy, remember that. And do
your homework. You don't want to get stuck in this small town

like I did. And find the right man to love. Lord knows I didn't. Your papa wouldn't know what love is if it hit him on the head. That's why you girls need to watch out for each other. Mack ..." Mama paused and Mack stopped chewing her food mid-bite. "You watch out for our little button. She's young and vulnerable. And you, Mack, I know you're smart." Her eyes grew sad. "I know you're going to make it out of here and make a good life for yourself." Mama's words sounded firm, almost like she was scolding us for doing something bad only we hadn't done anything wrong. Like she wanted us to remember her every word, so I stopped chewing and repeated her words in my head.

"Got it," I answered.

Mama began to laugh, and a lone tear dripped down her cheek. She swiped it away. "You grow up and get an education. You hear me. This ranch is no place for a lady to work." She pointed her finger between the two of us. "I don't want my girls taking care of heifers. I want you to be the blue birds that fly over the rainbow," she said with the same cool and urgent tone. Her gaze narrowed on me, her tone soft. "You have such a beautiful voice, Button. Do something with it." She winked and turned her head to look at the clock on our old stove. Everything about this ranch was old. "Now hurry up and get your school bags before you miss the bus." She stood from the table and held her robe tight. Mack and I scurried around, gathering our school bags and lunch boxes. We were on different busses now that Mack started high school.

"Bye, Mama." I reached over to wrap my arms around her frail body, careful not to touch the pouch with the pain medicine.

"I love you, Button."

"I love you too, Mama."

Mack reached in to hug Mama. Mama took her by the chin when Mack pulled back. Wetness swelled in Mama's clear blue eyes. "I know it's a lot to ask, but I need you to take care of her."

Mack swallowed hard and nodded. Her arms wrapped so

tightly around Mama's neck, I thought she might choke her. Mama patted her back, and Mack pulled away. "Go before you're late," Mama said with that firm voice that meant business.

We walked out of the front door. Papa wasn't working in the barn like I thought he would be. He was out on the porch, hugging his bottle of Jim Beam. He didn't say goodbye to us or tell us to have a good day as we passed. We walked down the dirt road to our bus stop. Little did I know, I wouldn't be seeing my mama again.

CHAPTER ONE

AL

Present Day

"Colt, I need to call you back. The snow is really picking up," I say to my best friend through Bluetooth as the wind battles with the snow, causing a cloud of white before me.

"No," he hisses. "You take off without warning. You've been acting fucking off and tomorrow's the last day of my governorship. I thought my chief of staff would be here with me to kiss my term goodbye." His tone softens. I hear the hurt. As his best friend and his chief of staff, I should be there for him. My chest tightens. I can't man up and tell him the reason I took off. It's on the tip of my tongue when a truck speeds by, causing the white cloud of snow before me to thicken. I can't see a fucking thing. Lord knows why I decided to take my Porsche on a road trip to Colorado. Oh yeah, I had to give up my Land Rover 'cause I couldn't afford the payments. The Porsche is older, and I own it outright. Sticking around to watch Colt pass off his title would've been like pouring salt into an open wound. Colton and his dad had been planning his ascent to the presidency basically since I met the guy at Harvard my freshman year. I went along on a ride I thought was leading somewhere. I knew better than to put all my eggs in one basket, given my family's business holdings, but I did it anyway. I believed in Colton. He had gone from state attorney to governor within a few years. We could have made it to the White House on the next election. Too bad I didn't get the full memo; Colt had different aspirations, which I knew about, but like his father, I didn't give them much thought.

"Evie can kiss the term goodbye for you," I answer, grinding my jaw as I refer to his girlfriend and love of his life. I internally snort at the idea he fell so in love. He had been Chicago's infamous playboy. I need to get off the phone before I end up in a ditch. I don't mean to be bitter, but my best friend went and fell in love and basically did a one-eighty with his life. I don't want to admit being that guy, the one who's filled with anger and resentment, but it's been bubbling inside me for months now. It's the reason I left town. I had to get away from myself to get my head on straight. When my sister called and asked me to join her at our family cabin in the Colorado Mountains, I saw the perfect escape. A low-cost vacation and a place to clear my head, figure out my next steps.

"I love you, Al, but fuck you." Colton's voice booms through the car, and I sense his displeasure with me. I didn't want to piss him off, but I didn't want to hang around and kiss my career goodbye when he resigned either.

"Sorry, man." I sigh, gripping the steering wheel. "I'm going to hang out with Izzy. Breathe the fresh mountain air. Clear my head before I decide my next move," I explain as I lift my head to look at the sky. I crossed the Colorado border hours ago. The sun has already set and it's getting pretty dark for five o'clock in the evening. The flurries look as if someone has just given a snow globe a harsh shake.

"Okay, you have a place by me on Pine Island when you're

ready," he says, referring to the location of his new home in the wonderful state of Washington on the other side of the fucking country. He and Evie decided Chicago didn't feel like home after a scandal about their relationship flooded all media outlets a few months back. My anger dies as his words ring in my mind. If anything, Colton has always been a loyal friend. Too bad I was too proud to tell him the truth about my financial situation.

"Thanks, man, I do appreciate it." My voice sounds flat. I can't help the selfishness creeping into my thoughts. My life has bottomed out on me. I was at the top. People like me don't crash into nothingness. Fuck, I sound pathetic.

"I think a little time out of the city will be good for you," Colt says, and I couldn't agree more. I can hear Evie's voice in the background. She doesn't send me her regards, that's for sure. I've been a royal prick to her. I just don't get how Colton turned into a lovesick puppy the minute he met her.

"Yeah, listen, I gotta go. Fucking visibility is near zero. I need Portia to make it through this mess," I say, referring to my car.

A snicker echoes through my car. "You drove your Porsche to Colorado in the dead of winter? Are you fucking crazy?" His tone sounds incredulous, and I can't argue because he's not off base.

"Don't dis Portia. We've been through a lot and she'll get us there." I pat my dashboard like a lunatic, my tone a little lighter and playful.

"Sure, man. Whatever. Be careful. We'll talk soon."

"Bye." I hit the button on my steering wheel to end the call. I check my GPS. Arrival time one hour and ten minutes. Fuck. I'm hungry and tired, but I could rough it through the next hour and make it to the cabin tonight, cozy up to a warm fire. The family cabin was probably stocked with the best of the best. I haven't been there since I cut off ties with my family ten years ago. I know how my family rolled. My little sister Izzy is nothing like the Walshes. She's kind, generous, and young. She hates all the material bullshit they represent. She's also keeping the fact that I'm heading up there a secret, even though my parents have been known to avoid checking in with her for extended periods of time.

I turn the radio on, hoping to catch a station and find out how long this snow will last, but I'm met with scratching sounds on every channel. I reach a long, narrow road. The snow blows off the fields. Fuck. I flick my hazard lights on, driving about fifteen miles an hour, fearful I can't even see where the road ends and the ditch begins. My knuckles turn white while I grip the steering wheel, my full concentration on getting to the cabin in one piece. Freezing to death in the middle of bumfuck nowhere is not on my agenda for today. The Porsche shifts from side to side as the harsh winds push against her will. I crank the heat up in the car and check my gas gauge. Half a tank. I should be okay. I want to check my GPS for the nearest inn since the weather is too intense for driving, but I don't have a death wish. I can't look down at my phone long enough to check my route since the road on this stretch is icy and narrow. Not having much choice, I continue to drive. The road curves and I pray my wheels don't lose traction. I slow to a turtle's pace. My expected arrival time at this speed has now changed to three hours. What the fuck. I'm queasy from the excessive heat in the car. I turn down the heat and open my window a crack. Maybe the cool air will help me stay alert. I've been driving too long. My eyes have grown heavy.

A car approaches in the oncoming traffic lane. The person has their high beams on. With the mix of snow and wind, the light is blinding. I hold my breath as the pickup passes and then exhale quickly when I realize I've made it past the lunatic. I continue to drive with a focused stare on the road. The wind howls and I'm fucking tired and exasperated after too many hours of driving. We have winter storms in Chicago; the lake effect snow can be brutal but nothing to the magnitude of this blizzard.

Another car approaches. The driver seems to stick a little close to my side of the road, even though the lines dividing the road are covered in a sheet of snow. I curse, realizing the fucker is definitely on the wrong side of the road and headed straight for me. He's either drunk or high because any moron could see we are on a direct path for impact. I swerve to the right. My wheels skid against what must be a patch of black ice. I brace myself, realizing my breaks aren't going to work. Before I can process what's happening, I'm veering off the road and down into a ditch. My heart slams in my chest as I wonder how deep the ditch is and what waits for me on the bottom. Maybe death. My car hits a few hard bumps before coming to a complete stop. My heart beats so fast I fear it may give out. I take a few slow breaths, trying to slow the adrenaline pumping through my body. The danger is over. I'm alive. Portia is still running. I don't suspect any serious damage. I shift the gear to reverse, hoping to make it back up the hill. As I press the gas pedal, the tires spin rapidly beneath me. I shift the gear into drive and gun the gas. No fucking traction. I get out of the car and brace myself against the cruel winter winds blowing snow in every direction. My teeth chatter as I realize how much colder it is out here compared to Chicago. I'm walking on a sheet of ice. There's no way my car is getting up that hill. I need a tow. I get back in the car and crank the heat since my fingers and toes feel like they will snap off. I forgot to renew my roadside assistance before I left town. I was in Timbukfuckingtu with no help in sight. They probably wouldn't have covered me out here anyway. I sit in the car and wait for what I don't know. Maybe the storm will end soon. Maybe someone will drive by and I can hitch a ride. My thoughts aren't plausible. No one is stopping in this shit storm. I put my chair back, thinking I'll get a little shut eye. I've been driving too long. I haven't eaten in several hours. I should've stopped hours ago when I hit the Colorado border and got a hotel for the night. I'd been anxious to arrive and sick of driving, figuring it was better to push through.

I stare out the window and my mind travels back in time as I think of my estranged family. My need to prove myself always entangled with their treatment of me growing up. Now my failures are public for them to see. I close my eyes and remember my father. My first year of high school I came barreling home one day, excited about career day. I would get to spend my day with the CEO of Walsh Industries. I went to private school so my friends' parents were all rich and some even famous, but my dad made Forbes list of the richest in America. I was proud to be a Walsh. I ran to my father's office and opened the door without knocking. I should have knocked. My dad had my mom's friend lying on his desk, and he was fucking her from behind. When his eyes met mine, he didn't stop. Her eyes were closed, and she didn't notice me. He waved me off and I ran away, feeling sick to my stomach. I thought of telling my mom. Dad got to me before I had the chance. Told me about the birds and the bees. At least his version. He said, *Son, it isn't right for a man to be tied to one woman his whole life. Having fun on the side is important for the longevity of a relationship.* I remember his words made me want to retch. He continued, *If you tell your mom, you will only upset her. She's happy. Let's keep her that way.* And so, I kept his secret. Never told a soul —even as the years passed, and I found out about more women. His secretary at work, another of my mom's friends. When my brother, Derek, was old enough, he learned the truth about Dad —only it didn't bother him. I never spent career day with my dad in his office. He sent me to the family's tractor development plant instead. Derek sat in the office of the CEO for his career day. Thinking back, I should've seen his preferential treatment of Derek. Only I didn't. I did well in school. Played lacrosse. Had too many girlfriends and life was good. By the time I got to junior year my parents thought a year abroad at a boarding school in Switzerland would be a good idea. I went no questions asked. That's where I met Brie ...

I'm too worked up to sleep as I think of my past. I reach over to a carry bag resting on the seat and take out the bottle of sleeping pills my doctor prescribed a couple months back. Things will be clearer once I got some shut eye. I pop a pill and I'm out like a light.

CHAPTER TWO

SAM

"WHERE THE HELL YOU BEEN?" my father's voice booms as I walk through the front door. A gust of wind follows me inside, along with the blowing snow, as I brace myself and close the door. I'm a grown ass woman. He doesn't have a right to take that tone with me.

"Went to Moe's for a drink. Then came home," I reply, my voice dry and flat. My father eyes me like he doesn't believe a word coming out of my mouth. He's sitting in the old recliner in the middle of the family room, a bottle of Jim Beam and an empty glass on the side table beside him. Papa is right to look at me the way he does. I'm not telling him the truth. I'd been over at Austin's house the last couple hours, then I ran into some trouble coming home and got delayed. That trouble is currently hunched over in the front seat of my pickup. I was hoping to sneak him in here while papa was sleeping, but I see that isn't happening now. "Shouldn't you be in bed or somethin'?" I head to the fridge and pull out the Brita water canister and pour a glass.

Papa looks at me like he doesn't understand me at all. At least there's truth in his stare. He turns around and trudges up the stairs. I wait a few beats until I hear his bedroom door close before I head back outside to the pickup. The snow isn't letting up, blowing directly into my eyes, as I open the passenger door. The man is shivering like crazy, looking at me with a blank stare.

"Come on, mister. I don't need us both freezing to death out here." I take his hand and it feels as cold as an icicle.

Normal people don't drive in this kind of weather. News said the storm could go on for days. Normal people also don't fall asleep behind the wheel in a snow storm that's the worst we've had in fifty years. This guy isn't dressed properly for this weather either, and he's a big husky man which makes him hard to lift.

"Buddy, come on. I'm fucking freezing." Snow, my husky, comes up behind me to sniff what's going on. "Go back inside, girl." I shoo her away. She doesn't listen. She loves this weather. Four years ago, I'd found her out here on a night similar to tonight. She was freezing and had no collar on. I placed a few ads around town about a missing dog, but no one ever claimed her. She's been mine ever since. She's a beauty with breathtaking arctic blue eyes. The man on the seat begins to shift toward me, so I grab the collar of his jacket, hauling his frozen ass over to me. He tumbles out of the driver's seat. I catch him and help him to his feet.

"You aren't making this easy." I huff and Snow walks up to him and begins to sniff him. He must have passed her test because she walks back inside the house. I don't know how long he was sitting out in his car, but I know a good portion of it was covered in snow. What kind of idiot drives a fancy Porsche on these roads when the news clearly warned drivers to stay off the roads? For Colorado, that was saying something. I duck under his shoulder and fling his arm around my neck as we slowly make our way into the house. As I drag him toward my bedroom, I think about the few things I know about this stranger: he definitely isn't homeless because he smells of some expensive cologne and his face is freshly shaven; his clothes and fancy car scream money too. I wonder why a rich guy like him is suicidal. I guide him back to my room in the dark with Snow hot on our trail. I can navigate this house in complete darkness, so instead of looking in front of me, I analyze the features of his gorgeous face instead. He looks as if an artist carved him from stone: high chiseled cheekbones, a slightly pointed nose, and his jaw wide and manly. He must be about thirty to thirty-five years old, which is kind of old in my books but this guy's age makes him look refined ... and hotter.

Hopefully Papa won't come back down the stairs right now. I've never brought home any men, even though I'm a grown woman. Papa would shoot them dead. It's a mere fact. Lord knows I still manage to get around—not that I'm proud of it. If anything, sex has always been a feel-good distraction for me.

We finally make it inside my room. He walks like his legs are spaghetti and they're going to give out on him. Shit! I curse under my breath. He looks up to me briefly. His clear blue eyes stare back at me. They're so clear it's startling. "Come on, buddy." I urge him toward my bed. He mutters something incoherent. I know its fucking crazy to bring a stranger to my room, but I'm pretty sure this guy might be suffering from hypothermia and he looks harmless. Not that looks are an indicator of anything. It's always the good-looking boy next door that ends up being a mass murderer on the six o'clock news. I guess that's why I don't watch the news, and I'm not letting this guy die on my watch. Right now, I'm grateful my room is on the main floor of the house because I may be strong, but there is no way I'm hauling this beast of a man upstairs.

He collapses as he falls out of my arms, curling into a ball like a little boy—even though there is nothing small about him—and he begins to shiver. Shit! I need to get him warm. It had crossed my mind to call an ambulance and get him some medical attention, but I don't think that Rob, our town paramedic, would appreciate a call in this storm. Besides, I have it under control. I flip the big guy on his back and began to shimmy off his jacket.

It's a fine wool jacket, but it's not warm enough for the weather out here.

"Come on, darling, help me out here," I coo as I straddle the guy and try to undress him. I pray he's not dangerous, but I figure Papa has enough guns around here that I'll just have to shoot his dick off if he tries anything. I know he's not armed. I also know his license plate is from Illinois. I finally get his jacket off. It's soaked right through. The button down shirt he wears doesn't look comfortable either, so I take that off him too. I leave on the white T-shirt he was wearing underneath. I hiss a little as I take in his broad chest and wide shoulders. This guy clearly works out. The bottom of his pants are wet and soak my bed. If I'm going to get him warm, I have to get rid of these wet clothes. I work his belt and unzip his fly then shimmy his pants slowly off him.

"Geez, darling. What were you thinking driving out there in that mess? You could've got yourself killed. You're clearly a city guy. You had no business being on those roads. You're too young to have a death wish and definitely too young to die." I leave him with his boxers on and pull a blanket over him.

Snow is sitting on the floor by the bed. "Bark if he wakes." I nod to her before turning out of the room.

I make a quick run to the laundry room. I just did a wash and have one of Papa's old flannel pajamas in the dryer. I take them out and dash back to my room. He's still shivering like crazy. I look down at Snow, who has a sympathetic look on her face. Maybe she remembers being cold and lonely like the stranger. I pat her head and give her nose a kiss. She jumps on the bed and onto him. He makes a *humph* sound but doesn't open his eyes. She remains lying on his legs. It makes my heart flutter that she wants to help him and eases my worry about him being a stranger since she has good instincts when it comes to people.

"You aren't cold and lonely anymore." I wave her off him.

I turn my attention back to the stranger. "Come on, honey. Let's warm you up," I say as I slide the flannel pajama shirt under his back. He's deadweight. Once I button all the buttons, I work on the pants. I stand from the bed and head out to the main closet in the hallway. Mama had a thing for quilts, so we have a lot in the closet. I take as many quilts as I can carry and head back to my room to wrap the poor man up. If his chills don't ease up soon, I'll call Rob and tell him he has no choice but to take this poor man to the hospital. After turning him into what looks like a human marshmallow with all the blankets, I notice his teeth still chattering. I figure this is my last ditch effort to reverse his hypothermia before a trip to the hospital ... I unbutton my plaid flannel shirt, take off the thermal top I have on underneath because I know how to dress for this weather. I work off my jeans and shimmy under the blankets with him wrapping as much of my body as I can around him. It dawns on me that I'm risking my safety to help a stranger, but no one ever accused me of being normal anyway.

As I envelop my body around his, I slowly feel his shakes subside and his breathing evening out. It gives me some reassurance that whatever I'm doing is working. It feels weird to wrap my half-naked body around a stranger, but it seems to be helping, so I don't think too deeply about it.

"Good, I think you're doing better now," I whisper in his ear while I caress his forehead, hoping to put his mind at ease while wondering if he can hear me at all. From this angle, I take in the contours of his face. Everything about this man is heart-stoppingly handsome. His inhales and exhales take on the rhythm of my own and before I know it my eyes drift shut.

CHAPTER THREE

AL

THERE'S a loud clacking noise that won't stop. Fuck! Why won't it stop? I lift my hand from beneath the covers and hold my throbbing head. Clack. Clack. Clack. I feel woozy, but I force my eyes open. Only when I turn my head to the side do I realize I'm not alone in bed. Great, another woman I don't remember in the morning. A sour taste fills my mouth and when I try to swallow it away with my own saliva, I realize how swollen and achy my throat is. My vision clears further. I don't know where the fuck I am. My instinct is to look under the covers. Yup, the lady is naked except for a bra and panties, which is weird because I tend to get rid of those articles of clothing before my cock enters her body.

My gaze drifts from her naked form to me. I'm in a pair of old man pajamas; I'm not naked like her. As my confusion registers, I toss off the pile of blankets that smother me and swing my legs over the bed. Besides the throb in my head and the ache in my throat, my whole body feels weak. At least that annoying clacking sound has stopped.

My memory slowly returns to me. I was run off the snowy road last night. My anxiety was overwhelming me, and I needed to get some shut eye. I popped one of the sleeping pills Dr. Scott gave me since I've had problems sleeping ever since Colton stepped down from his role of governor. I figured a few good hours of shut eye wouldn't hurt and I'd have a better solution to my problem. I had the warmth of Portia, my car, and I didn't see a living thing anywhere in sight. I thought it was a good idea. How the hell did I end up in bed with this blonde? I stare at her a moment and take her in. She's young, which gets my heart hammering in a bad way because she looks too young. I hope she's legal. Negative thoughts roll through my mind. I do everything wrong. I can't even drive to a fucking cabin in Colorado to see my baby sister without fucking up.

"Sam, dammit! It's already five-thirty," an old, deep, crackly voice echoes through the house. At least I think it's a house. This room has a large window. I spot a barn in the distance.

The woman begins to shift a little before opening her eyes. I watch her, taking in her features: short blond hair and kind eyes that are the type of blue you'd see on a ship in the middle of the Mediterranean sea—dark blue with swirls of a lighter blue running through them closer to her irises.

Her gaze lands on me and she startles and shoots up to a sitting position. "Shit! I must have slept in," she says to the air in front of her.

She rubs her eyes and looks at me without startling, like she was expecting me here. "Oh thank goodness you aren't dead." She blows out a cleansing breath and holds her heart.

Before I can get a word in she whips the covers off her. Her eyes turn wide as she looks down to her half-naked body, possibly realizing she is in fact only wearing a bra and panties. She quickly grabs the sheet under the blankets and looks up to me to see if I've caught a glimpse. In my defense, I wasn't expecting her to just throw the blankets off herself. Her pale cheeks redden. She stands from the bed as if the embarrassing moment has passed in a flash and begins to move rapidly around the room. I'm dizzy watching her.

"You crazy or something?" She stops suddenly and gives me an expectant look.

"What do you mean?" I ask, clearly confused.

"I mean are you okay in the head?" I've never been asked a question like this before. I don't have an answer for her.

She grabs a new pair of underwear and bra out of a drawer then pauses to look at me. She's waiting for an answer. Was that even a real question? When I don't answer, she drops the bra and panties on the bed and stalks over to me, placing her palm on my forehead. She goes from investigating me to sweetness in a nanosecond.

"How you feeling, darling?" she asks with a bit of an accent. Her voice is sweet and caring. It triggers my memory and details of last night come back to me.

My car must have run out of gas after I took the sleeping pill. Fuck! Of all the stupid things I've done, this one tops the list. She got me out of the car and brought me here. My body felt cold ... I was so out of it I could barely walk, but for some reason I remember that sweet voice of hers calling me darling. She took care of me.

"Shit, you're burning up." She turns to look out the window. "Snow isn't going to let up for the next few days. You should get back into bed and I'll bring you some Tylenol," she says and she doesn't wait for me to answer. Better yet, I don't understand why she'd want to take care of a complete stranger. "You don't say much, do you?" she asks while her blue eyes stare at me.

She holds the blanket up in front of her half-naked body. A body I got a peek of this morning. I now know she has voluptuous breasts, curvy hips, and a fine ass.

"Sorry." My voice comes out scratchy and quiet. "I'm not feeling too well." I hold my throat. "I want to thank you for saving my ass out there last night."

She eyes me as if she's trying to get in my head. "You on drugs or something? You sure didn't smell like alcohol. If it's drugs ...

I'm sorry I'm gonna have to ask you to leave." Her head tilts to the side in an assessing way.

"No, I don't do drugs. I took a sleeping pill. I've had some troubles these last few months and can't sleep. I thought if I got a few hours of shut eye it would clear my head, the snow would stop, and I'd make it out to my sister's cabin," I explain, still holding my throat. I feel weak and woozy.

"It's gonna snow hard for days. We won't be able to get that car of yours out of the ditch until the snow slows," she begins to explain.

Someone is going to steal my car or part her out. She's the only thing I have left that's actually worth something.

"Um ... it was kind of you to bring me to your home. I should leave and figure things out," I say and stand up from the bed. My lightheadedness causes me to sway.

She stands in front of me, and I get a closer look at her. She's beautiful. "You're too sick to go anywhere." Her hand lands on my shoulder and our eyes meet. It looks like her breath hitches and before I can say anything else, she pulls her gaze from me and directs my body to the bed. "Stay in bed. I wouldn't want anything bad to happen to you," she says, and I see a sadness hanging heavy in those blue eyes.

My brows furrow. "You don't know me." Was this girl fucking crazy? She was beautiful, but she must be out of her damn mind to insist a complete stranger stay in her bed.

"So?" She shrugs. Yup, she's a looney.

"That isn't an answer." I scrub my fingers on the morning scruff of my chin. "You're a beautiful woman. You shouldn't allow a random stranger to sleep in your bed. That's dangerous." My tone almost sounds parental. If I wasn't feeling so bad, I would be inclined to laugh at myself.

Her throat bobs and the palm of her hand lands on her chest. My eyes drop to her chest before looking back up to her eyes. "You think I'm beautiful?" she asks and her brows raise. She looks at me like I'm an alien. She's definitely confusing, and I thought I was good at reading women.

"That isn't the point. You don't have any clothes on and you don't know me." I continue to lecture her, unsure where any of my need to protect this girl comes from. Maybe because she looks so young. Fuck! My brows dip together. That's all I need is to be caught in bed with an underage girl. "How old are you anyway?" I ask. My head is throbbing, but I need to get this squared away. Even with sickness, she's causing my dick to harden at half-mast.

"Twenty-three," she says, but it sounds more like a question.

I exhale. "Phew."

"Huh? Look, mister. If you're crazy or want to hurt me, you should leave," she says, still holding that blanket up in front of her body. It makes her look vulnerable and I don't like it one bit.

"And if I told you I was crazy and wanted to hurt you, what would you do?" I ask just to test her. I don't even know why I'm bothering other than her naiveté pisses me off.

"I'd grab the gun I have tucked away and shoot you." She looks me square in the eyes when she says those words, and I swear my dick twitches. Maybe I'm a sick fuck or just turned on by her no bullshit personality.

"Try me," I challenge her. Fuck, what am I thinking? It must be my fever. That, or I have a death wish.

I move slowly toward her because I can't handle fast right now. She moves so quickly I've barely blinked, and she has a shotgun pressed between my eyes.

"Fuck, you're beautiful," I murmur. This is a dream. A sick fucking dream.

"Answer the question now," she says as the cool feel of the gun presses against my clammy skin. "Are you crazy?"

"Do you think if I was crazy I would tell you? I don't think that's how crazy works." I shake my head. "Look, I really do appreciate you saving me and bringing me here. I hope you don't bring strangers home often. I'm safe. I swear to you. I am the ..." I pause. "I assure you, I would never hurt you." I hold my hands up in surrender. I'm about to tell her that I'm the ex-chief of staff to the governor of Illinois, but I don't because the idea of being in a place where my family name and old job don't hang over my head is refreshing.

She looks down at me and slowly withdraws the gun. "Okay," she says, and it looks like too many thoughts are rolling through her head now.

"Look, I'm really not feeling well. Could I get that Tylenol from you?" I hold my neck.

"Yeah, sure, sorry. Let me just get dressed." She smiles sheepishly.

She turns away from me and drops her sheet, giving me a view of her fine ass. The panties she's wearing drop to the floor and she puts on a new pair. She releases her bra strap and her bra meets the floor next. I gasp. She clearly isn't shy, and if she isn't crazy, then she is one fearless woman.

"I'm pretty sure you were suffering from hypothermia last night. I was trying to keep you warm that's all. Don't get any ideas. I live with my papa, and I wasn't about to walk out in the hall draped in a sheet," she explains. My mouth gapes open. My half-mast dick turns to a strong, stiff morning wood. Thankfully it's covered by these enormous flannel pajamas. She dresses in a thermal shirt, a pair of snug blue jeans that hug her fine round ass, and finishes the outfit with another plaid flannel shirt. She takes long, assured strides back to me and lifts her chin. She's over a head shorter than me. Her chin only reaches the top of my chest.

"What's your name, darling?" She smiles gently, and I wonder if people call each other darling around here or if that's what she calls me specifically. Either way, I like the word rolling off her tongue.

"Al." I cough. My throat feels like I've swallowed a pineapple whole. It hurts so badly. "Albert Walsh the ..." I stop myself. "Just

Al," I murmur, not wanting to throw her off with my high society name that means shit anyway.

She chuckles. Her brows draw together, clearly confused by my name introduction. "Well, Al Walsh, nice to meet ya. I'm Sam. Short for Samantha Belmont. I live on this ranch with my papa, Joe Belmont," she explains.

"I'm on a ranch?" I should be at the cabin with Izzy. My eyes widen as I add this fuckup to a long list of fuckups.

"Yup, come on." She waves for me to follow her out of the room. Her movements are quick and efficient where mine are slow and straggling. I follow her down a hall to what looks like the main area of the house.

"Um, does your dad know I'm here?" I mutter.

She turns to look at me, a small smile curving her lips. That isn't an answer. My body aches as I follow her down a short hall to a main living area that has a bunch of couches and armchairs and a medium sized TV on the wall. She heads toward a kitchen area and opens the fridge. It's one of those older style fridges that has the freezer on the top and fridge on the bottom. She sticks her ass out and even in my sickly state, my dick twitches again. All I can think is, *Down, buddy, she's too young and clearly too kind for you.*

She straightens and turns to me. "What would you like for breakfast, darling?"

Before I can answer, the front door opens. A blast of cool air shoots into the kitchen. A shiver rolls up my spine and spreads through my entire body. It must be the fever. An old guy, who is just as tall as me, strolls in wearing a cowboy hat and a corded jacket lined with white fur. His white hair peeks out of the sides of the hat, and he has the craziest white mustache I've ever seen. He looks like an older, albeit intimidating, cowboy.

"Who the hell is this?" he barks, looking between us.

I remain rooted in my spot. He looks like he has a shotgun close by.

"Papa, this is Al. He was stranded out by Route 68 last night. I helped him out."

"Nice to meet you, sir. I would shake your hand, but I fear that I'm under the weather."

He looks to Sam and a slow smile erupts on his lips. "Where did he come from, Sam? Is he for real?" Then he goes on to imitate me ... "I fear I'm under the weather." He gives me an incredulous look as if I just told him to fuck off and shakes his head then laughs to himself. "That's Sam. She brings in the strays, and I apparently have to pay to feed them." His voice is deep and monotone with no hint that he is friendly or pleased to see me here. I stiffen and when I look down, a dog is smelling my feet.

"Sorry? Strays?" I'm not following. Probably the damn fever. My legs feel weak, like I need to take a seat before I fall over, but I don't feel comfortable doing that now that her father doesn't approve of me being here.

I look down at the dog. It's a beautiful husky with the clearest blue eyes I've ever seen.

"Meet Snow, our other stray," her father says in a curt tone.

"Ignore Papa—" Sam begins to explain, but then he cuts her off.

"Don't ignore Papa. This man is in my pajamas, Sam." He gives her a scolding look like a parent would their small child. "And he's too damn old for you. Did you notice that?" Now his tone drips sarcasm too.

"It's not like that, Papa," Sam begins again.

"Oh, *it's not like that, Papa* ..." He imitates her voice, and I'm beginning to really dislike him to the point that my fist clenches and I want to knock him out.

"Sir ..." I clear my throat, feeling the need to explain or maybe protect her from him, even though it makes no sense because he's her father.

Sam gives me a look that says shut up, so I do. I also drop into a chair at the kitchen table so I won't fall over.

"His car got stuck in the snow off Route 68 last night. He was passed out and freezing to death. He would have died out there," she explains, and I cringe at how idiotic it was of me to take a sleeping pill in that situation. Especially when I know they hit me hard, and I turn into a zombie.

"I'm not having sex with him, Papa. He is too old." She pauses and looks at me apologetically. It makes me uncomfortable that she just spoke so openly about sex with her father.

In my family, anything that has to do with sex is very discreet and done behind closed doors. My family is prim and proper at all times in public. What irks me above all else is that she says I'm, "too old." I'm fucking thirty-five. That's hardly over the hill.

Her father turns his attention to me, a smug smirk on his old face. "Where you from? I pretty much know everyone in this town." His voice is gravelly and sounds very much like John Wayne —and just because I made that connection doesn't mean I'm old. Dammit. His eyes drop to my wrist where my Rolex shines.

"From Chicago," I say with a scratchy voice. "I was on my way to my family's cabin when that storm hit. My car didn't handle very well, and I was forced off the road by a crazy driver." I cough at the end of the sentence and hold my throat, which feels a lot like I have rocks being scraped across the inside of it.

The old man throws his head back, laughing. It's a hearty chuckle and it pisses me off that he's so amused by my misfortune. "What kind of car you drive, City?"

I actually didn't want to answer his question. And did he really just call me City? He looks at me with intense brown eyes that say I'm a guest in his home and he expects an answer. I relent and with a sigh. "Porsche Boxster." This makes his laugh intensify.

"Papa, leave him alone," Sam scolds and comes around the

table to check my forehead. "You're burning up," she says her lips turning into a frown. "Let me get you that Tylenol and then back to bed, mister." I want to smile, but I don't because her old man is looking straight at me with what seems to be an assessing look, and I don't want to piss him off.

"I should really go. I've taken up enough of your time and you're too generous," I say because clearly her father doesn't want me here, and I know when I'm not welcome. What I don't understand is why I feel disappointment over leaving Sam and that removed look in her eyes.

Her father cuts in. "Like I said, she likes to pick up strays." His eyes drop to the dog lying on the floor.

"Papa, stop it now. I work this ranch same as you. This home is as much mine as it is yours. Now please respect my guest," she snaps at him, shocking the hell out of me. I begin to understand why she isn't scared of a stranger. Her frustration is written all over her face. "Your car is still in a ditch. You aren't going anywhere. I can't call the tow company to help because conditions are still really bad out there. You need to stay put and get well," she insists. "Then you can leave." She gives her father a look that says she means business. Who am I to argue? Even with the John Wayne lookalike piercing me with his stare.

"Maybe you should wait in my room? I'll bring the pills there," she suggests, and I hear her father mutter something along the lines of fucking great under his breath.

I shrug my shoulders and make my way back down the hallway that leads to her room. I climb into her bed and cover myself with the pile of blankets. I stare up at the yellowing ceiling. Another fuckup. Now I'm stuck on a ranch in Nowheresville.

I hadn't realized I dozed off when a nudge on my shoulder startles me awake. Sam's sweet voice and breath are close to my face. "Hey," she whispers, concern etched on her face. I look into her warm blue eyes that carry a heaviness that irks me.

"Brought you medicine, some tea, and toast," she says, waiting for me to clearly sit up. "Tea, isn't too hot. I don't like drinking it really hot when I'm sick. I popped a few ice cubes in it. You should be able to swallow the pills. Plus, I added some honey to your tea so that should help with your throat. I don't think Dr. Stu is around today. Hopefully this tides you over until he's available."

"Thank you." I swallow the pills. She waits, watching me like she wants to make sure I'm okay. I never even got that kind of treatment at home from my mother. Usually the nannies or maids brought me stuff when I was sick, and they weren't this sweet or pretty that's for sure.

I take a few small sips of tea. It hurts to swallow. Sam looks down to the toast like she's expecting me to eat it. I can't imagine swallowing crunchy toast with my throat being in the state that it's in, but I eat the toast not wanting to disappoint her. I pause. "You never did answer my question. Why are you helping me? And why aren't you scared of me?" I was a big, strong guy. I would never hurt her, but she didn't know that. It makes me angry for some reason that she's so naïve.

"I'm a good judge of character, and my mama always taught me to help people in need. If I would have left you out there last night, you would have died," she explains. Well shit.

"How can I repay you for helping me?" I ask, looking up to her. Where I come from bottom lines are all about money.

Her brows crease together and her nose crunches up with distaste. This girl is adorable and too good. "I don't need you to repay me ..." She looks down at my watch and her face scrunches up further. "You think just because you have a nice car and a nice watch that us simple folk need what you have? Well shit, City, you are dead wrong." She huffs and turns to her closet where she takes out a heavier jacket.

Did she just call me City too? And how had I managed to anger her? I have to fix this. I blow out a breath. "I'm sorry, it's just where I'm from, people don't take in complete strangers and nurse them back to health."

"Well, it sucks to be where you're from, then. Here in Holston, we take care of people. It's a town of one hundred and forty-five people. We all know each other, and we pretty much take care of one another," she explains with a defensive stance and a snap to her voice.

"It sounds like it's better to be from Holston than Chicago. Where I'm from, people cheat, lie, and stab you in the back. Well, except for my best friend, but he's an odd case. Will you forgive me?" I push out my bottom lip out for extra effect.

A smile breaks through her anger and lights up her whole face. Even her eyes. "Okay, City, I forgive you as long as you eat that toast and get some sleep. I got some cows to feed in this shit weather."

"You're going to forgive me if I do things essentially to make myself better?" I'm so confused I can't help but push a little. Maybe I want to get to know her better. This woman/girl is a conundrum.

Her face scrunches up, and she gives me a look like she thinks I'm slow.

Before she can get her two words in, I say, "Sorry, Sam, will do." I take a large bite of my toast. I've known her all of maybe twelve hours, and she has me wrapped around her crazy little finger because I tell myself she's clearly crazy. She gives me a wide smile for eating her toast.

"That's good, Al." She leaves the room wearing that hefty jacket that makes her look like she's a lumberjack from behind. After I have completed her orders, I fall asleep. I'm pretty sure I dream of the prettiest woman in the state of Colorado.

CHAPTER FOUR

SAM

"GLAD YOU COULD JOIN ME," Papa chides. It's freezing out here in the barn. I'm dead tired after saving Al last night, and I'm in no mood for his usual sarcasm this early in the morning.

"Don't start," I snap and grab a bale of hay.

The rest of the morning we work quietly side by side. No talking. No interaction. We've been working together long enough to know what each of us has to do. By noon I'm exhausted and hungry. I quickly check on Al. His forehead is warm and clammy, which means his fever must be going strong. He's also sleeping like the dead. I watch his slow breaths as his chest rises up and down, so I know he's alive. I look down to the pile of his clothes on the floor, figuring I should wash the clothes he was in last night. Before I take them to wash, I sift through his pockets to see what I can learn about him because although I was always taught kindness, I'm not a complete idiot. His driver's license says Albert Walsh III, so I know he wasn't lying about his name. His wallet has a lot of platinum credit cards and a wad of cash. I'm not surprised. His gorgeous blue eyes hold a loneliness and sincerity that pulls at something deep inside me. He doesn't have any pictures in his wallet of any significant others. I didn't see a wedding band on his finger. He did mention that he was on his way to meet his sister. I wonder if his family is looking for him right now. I'm tempted to pull my cell phone out and do a quick Google search on Al Walsh, but if I don't get my work done soon, Papa will be on my case. Lord knows why I put up with him but I do.

I'M GETTING my ingredients ready to fry up some eggs when there's a loud rasp at the door. One of my best friends, Kelly, has her nose pressed to the glass window. Her nose looks bright red kind of like Rudolph. Snow blows in circles all around her. I rush to open the door. "Kell, what on earth are you doing out of your house in this weather?" I chide. Kelly married her high school sweetheart, Gage, straight out of high school and works at the local supermarket. They have an eighteen month old son, Theo. Kelly is my age. It seems everyone in this town marries young and has kids young. I'm the exception.

"I heard you found a strange man out on the highway last night and brought him home," she says holding a pan of something in her hands. She places it on the kitchen table and rubs her hands together. "Heard he drives a nice car too." She looks to me expectantly. It takes a lot of self-control not to roll my eyes at her and half the girls in this town, even though I love them all. Everyone is always looking for a way out of Holston; the population is minute, which means the economy sucks. If you're not exporting out of state, you're not surviving so well. Our ranch has always fared well, but with the lack of rain these last number of years, we're struggling too. It's hard enough to feed ourselves let alone a bunch of cows.

"He was passed out in his car, Kell." I huff. "I couldn't very well leave him out there to die."

"Is he hot?" She looks at me wide eyed and a little too

excited. My head moves from side to side as I ask myself if Al is hot. Hot would be an understatement. His body is rock solid and gorgeous, and he has the face of a model. Not a skinny fashion model either, but that rugged kind of model that cologne commercials like to use. Al was all man that was for sure.

"Fucking gorgeous." My cheeks turn hot at the thought of him.

Kell claps her hands together, all excited. "I brought warm apple pie. I hope he likes apple pie," she says as if apple pie is the solution to me having a hotter than hell man passed out in my bed.

"Let me remind you that you are a married woman." I smirk, just playing with her. She and Gage are tight. She's been trying to play matchmaker for me since at twenty-three I'm the equivalent to old maid around here. I return to beating my eggs in the bowl before plopping them into a fry pan.

"You don't need to remind me. You know I got you in mind. What does he look like?" she waits expectantly.

"Keep it down," I hush her.

"He looks like a movie star, thick muscles, gorgeous face, eyes that burn your skin when he looks at you," I say, frying my eggs. When I turn to Kell, she looks flushed.

"Holy shit." She waves a hand in front of her face.

"You hungry?" I ask her.

"Hungry?" she repeats in a daze.

"Kell?" I call to snap her out of her daze.

"Huh? Tell me more," she insists, not answering my question.

"I think he has a massive cock," I add, and she melts into the chair at the kitchen table.

"Why can't that shit happen to me?" she says, waving a hand in her face like she's fanning herself.

"Kell," I chide.

"How do you know he has a large cock?"

I walk toward her and whisper that I caught a glance at his morning erection when I was standing in the corner of the room.

"And you weren't scared of him?" she asks.

I nod my head. "Trust me, if you see him, your first reaction won't be fear."

Her eyebrows raise and lower as she gives me a knowing look. I return to frying eggs. "You hungry?" I repeat my earlier question, which received no response.

"I'm always hungry lately," she sighs.

My eyes turn wide at that comment. "You're pregnant?" I gasp.

I can see the excitement dancing in the depths of her brown eyes before she answers. "Due this summer."

"Aww. Isn't that sweet," I answer, hoping it doesn't sound too sarcastic. I'm truly happy for her, but I don't understand the people in this town either. We are all fighting to put food on the table, and they just continued to procreate.

"Don't sound too excited for me." She scoffs, albeit playfully.

"I'm happy for you, sweets." I wink and begin cracking more eggs.

"I'm happy for you too, sweets," she answers with the same mocking tone. "You got a hot man staying here. Maybe he'll be the one," she says it with such hope I actually feel bad. I know she wants good things for me. I've grown up with the people in this town; we are more like close family than friends. I just don't want the same things they do.

"No man is the one for me. I'm happy on my own. I'm not settling down. I'm gonna have fun until I die." I finish toasting some Texas toast and then join Kelly at the kitchen table. It's an old worn in table. Everything here is old and worn. Sometimes I feel like I could relate to the old things here because at twenty-three I feel washed out too.

"You gotta be sick of hooking up with Blake and Austin. Besides, you are driving those men crazy. Although I feel less sorry for Blake." She gives me a look that says he's an asshole—

and she would know because he's her brother-in-law. She stuffs her mouth with fried eggs like she hasn't eaten in two weeks. Kelly was always very hungry when she was pregnant with Theo. She's adorable now too in her pregnant state. Kell's kind of filled in for Mack since she went away to law school then moved to New York City with her partner.

"They keep me satisfied. I don't get bored of sleeping with the same guy with this arrangement. They understand me and I understand them. What's wrong with that?" I place my eggs on my toast and bite into it.

"Nothing." She shrugs. "I could never imagine my life without Gage. I love him. He and Theo are my life. I just want you to love, just once," she says sadly. Almost every woman in this small town has been here at one point or another, explaining to me what it means to love. *Give this guy a try, honey. Date this one, Sam. Fall in love, darlin'. Follow your heart. It won't lead you astray.* The list goes on and on. I'm pretty sure I'm not capable of love. Maybe my heart broke when Mama died and it can never be put back together again. For sure, not by a man. I like men. I find them attractive. Heck, I enjoy a good orgasm if the guy knows what he's doing with his dick; Blake and Austin know exactly how to get me off. I don't need more than that.

"I love you for caring, Kell, I do..." I place my hand on her arm "...but I'm good."

That's a lie. I hate working with my papa. I love him because he's my papa, but that's it. We don't have a sweet, loving relationship. He never hides the fact that he had hoped for boys. Instead, he has two girls. Calls us Mack, short for Mackenzie, and Sam, short for Samantha. It doesn't fly past anyone that we have boy names. Mack went off to college, so Papa needed me to work the ranch. When the ranching economy went downhill a few years back because of the lack of rain, I gave up a scholarship to college and stayed in Holston. It's the one promise to my mama that I broke.

"I know, darling." She gives me a sad smile.

I reach my fork out to dig into her warm apple pie because I can smell the cinnamon wafting in the air and it makes my mouth water. Kell smacks my hand. "Don't you dare put a fork into that pie," she says, looking mean. I laugh. She wants me to cut a nice slice and not butcher her pie.

"Okay." I get up and get a knife to cut a slice for the two of us.

"No way, Sam. We are waiting for the gentleman to wake up. I made that pie for him." She winks.

Really? No words.

CHAPTER FIVE

AL

I DON'T MEAN to eavesdrop, but the ache in my throat wakes me and it screams for liquid. Sam's sweet voice and her conversation with another woman drift toward the bedroom. I can't help but listen because I'm more than curious about her. My sense of relief over the fact that she thinks I'm hot is worrisome; I went away to clear my head, not fuck off some more. I can't think about burying my face between her thighs, which is my exact thought when she mentions my large cock. Still, I'm amused that word traveled so fast about me staying here. It's been what? Twelve hours at most. Even with treacherous weather, there seems to be no stopping town gossip. I'm not sure I like the idea of everyone knowing my business. I think it would get annoying fast.

Once they begin discussing relationships, my stomach sours listening to Sam's words. It sounds an awful lot like a conversation I'd have with my best friend Colton back in Chicago. Colt would try to convince me to give up my philandering ways, and I'd tell him there was no way.

For some reason I hate hearing that Sam enjoys hooking up over a relationship. I don't know why it irritates me, because hell, my DNA is made of the same cocktail of "incapable of settling down." It just seems sad that a young girl like her, who is good and kind, wouldn't want to share her goodness with a man and child. Not me, of course, because I have nothing to offer. Well, except getting her off. She said that those guys knew how. I want to show her how much better I would be ... I give myself an inner punch to the face. She's been nothing but kind to me. She saved my life. I can't fuck her and leave even if that's all she wants from me. I owe her more than that.

I get out of bed and make my way to the kitchen. I'm pretty sure the room is spinning and I'm guessing I have a flu virus. My thirst pushes me forward. That and the need for some ibuprofen. The pill Sam gave me earlier isn't cutting it. As I walk up to the kitchen, I watch the two ladies I overheard eating lunch. Sam's friend, I think her name is Kell, pauses mid-bite and her eyes almost bulge out of their sockets as she knocks her elbow to Sam's arm, tilting her chin forward in my direction.

"There is a very good-looking man standing in the middle of your family room," she says to Sam but stares right at me. It's kind of awkward, but the woman doesn't care. She chews a mouthful of food while she speaks. It isn't gross, though. She's cute and friendly. Sam turns her head and her eyes go round at the sight of me.

"Are you okay? Do you need something?" She shoots to a standing position and brushes her palms over her thighs.

"Sorry to interrupt. I'm parched." I hold my throat. Sam is fixated on me for a few beats as she looks at me with a confused look. "I'm thirsty," I explain, but it sounds more like a croak. I look between the two women. Kell is just sitting in her chair staring at me as if I'm some kind of wonder.

"Sure, I could make you more tea," Sam finally offers, walking toward the kettle.

"A tall glass of cold water would be perfect."

She opens the fridge and takes out the Brita container. I haven't seen one of those since I was a small boy. She pours me a glass and passes it to me. "Thank you." I take it from her hand. She stands beside me and watches me drink like I may evaporate into thin air. I'm still very interested in the thought that she finds me hot. "Can I get another?" I'm pretty sure I'm overheated from the fever. I'm also in need of a doctor.

"Do you need more meds?"

"Yes, I think I better get myself to a doctor," I rasp. I look to the chair and table because standing requires too much effort. My legs slowly carry me there. I fall back in the chair.

"Is there Uber around here?" I ask, figuring I can get a ride and get checked out, get my meds, and be on my way. Both ladies continue to stare at me while eating their lunch. Then they look at each other. Both of their eyebrows dip in the center as they place their attention back on me. I feel like an art exhibit at a museum.

"A what?" they ask in unison.

"Uber. You know, it's kind of like a cab but it's an app and it basically consists of people using their own cars to get other people to places," I begin to explain, but it's useless. Clearly, they don't have the service in Holston.

"Like a taxi?" Kell chimes as if a light has just gone off in her head.

"Yes, exactly. Like a taxi." I smile, even if it's weak and tired.

"None of those around here. Weather is still pretty bad, but if you are feeling like you need a doc, I can ask Stu to try to come by. Maybe I can offer to pick him up," Sam says then pops a slice of cucumber in her mouth.

"Stu?" I require clarification.

"He's the only family physician for about thirty miles. We have a small hospital, but it's a ways out. The drive will be tough," she explains.

"I can take your car and go to Stu. I don't want to put you out." I realize I just assumed I'd take her car. That isn't a good thing. She will think I'm taking advantage of her, and why would she give a complete stranger her car? I also remind myself that I'm staying in her home and I don't know her.

Both of Sam's brows lift, and she lets out a giggle. "No offence, City, but I'm more capable of driving these roads than you are." I don't think I like the fact that she's calling me City like her father. And she's mocking my driving too. I remind myself that this woman/girl saved my life. I don't call her out on her sass. Even if I'd like to kiss it right out of her.

I tilt my head from side to side. "You're probably right. May I use your shower? Maybe after that you could give me a ride?"

"Sure, thing darling." Sam nods and a pang of lust or maybe yearning spreads through my chest when she calls me darling, even though I realize she probably calls everyone darling.

"Wait, would you like some apple pie?" her friend asks and shifts the apple pie toward me. It smells heavenly. "Sorry, what was your name?"

"My apology. I'm Al Walsh. I'd shake your hand, but I don't want to give you whatever it is I have."

She waves me off. "No problem, darling. You should have some apple pie. It's still warm and it'll make you feel good."

Sam stands to grab me a plate from the cabinet.

"I can't refuse fresh apple pie." I smile to her friend. These people really are too kind.

Sam passes Kell a knife, and she cuts me a very generous slice.

"Here ya go. Hope you like it." She smiles and watches me, clearly waiting for me to try it. My taste buds feel messed-up from my sickness, but the taste of the fresh apples mixed with cinnamon and something else tastes heavenly, and truth is my stomach is pretty empty. The toast Sam gave me this morning wasn't much for a guy my size. Even in my sickly state.

I groan as I chew the first bite. "This is very good." I point the fork at the pie as I chew. Then I dig in for more. Kell's smile stretches from ear to ear.

"That's good, Al. I bake stuff all the time for Sam. If you hang around, you'll get to try my other cakes too."

Sam laughs as her friend giggles and gives Sam a shrug. The look in her eyes holds many words I don't understand. Sam does, though, and she sighs.

When I finish with my plate, I stand up. "Thank you very much. That hit the spot."

Kell's eyes roam over my body, unabashedly. "I'm glad it did."

I head over to the sink to wash my plate because I don't see a dishwasher.

"That's fine, Al, I will get it. You need your rest." Sam shoos me away.

"If it's alright, I wouldn't mind that shower."

"Yes, of course. Go ahead. It's just down the hall past my room." I notice she doesn't look me in the eye.

I walk back toward her room. From a distance I hear Kell mutter, "They sure don't make them like that around here."

I laugh internally, not wanting Sam to know I heard. She clearly wants me to think I'm too old for her, and it's better off anyway.

I take my shower. My folded clothes rest on a chair in Sam's room, and they look clean. I put my old clothes back on sans boxers; I'd been wearing them when she took my clothes to get laundered.

Sam drives me to the doctor. I try not to stare at her too much on the drive because I don't want to freak her out. One thought replays in my mind: if I ever were to fall for a woman it would be a kind, caring, beautiful woman like Sam. I wish I knew how to make those sad blue eyes of hers look happy.

CHAPTER SIX

AL

Past

"Hey, man. We're having a party in the forest tonight. You coming?" my roommate, Hans, asked. I'd been in this school a whole of two weeks and never attended the almost nightly parties. Although one didn't need to venture far; some students were doing coke in their rooms. I was doing my schoolwork.

"Yeah, I'll head out soon," I answered. Hans nodded and headed out. I quickly opened up my English binder and finished an assignment that was due on Monday. My relationship with my father had become strained over the years. I didn't understand why, but I thought it had to do with me telling him to his face what I thought of all his floozies. He was never going to get a father of the year award, but after I confronted him last year, the tension between us got so bad that Mom began to ask questions, and my mom had always been very self-absorbed so that was saying something.

As much as a part of me wanted to grow up and work at Walsh Industries, my gut told me I was getting a world-class education out here. I should use it to make something of myself just in case.

Tonight, I figured it'd be okay to indulge a little. It wasn't like I didn't party back home. I shut my English binder and got dressed. The dorms were empty except for a few students who I noticed were either doing work or not interested in the opposite sex. I snuck away from school grounds, knowing if I got caught the first time I'd probably just get a slap on the wrist. Hans filled me in on all the dos and don'ts, and this was his third year here. He knew the place inside out. His father was a German diplomat, and he confided in me that the reality was our parents were paying a shitload of money for us to attend this school, so it was in the administrations best interest to look the other way. That was why I felt relaxed as I left school property and headed toward the forest where the smell of bonfire led me to the party.

I approached the crowd, and a few guys from some of my classes spotted me.

"Al, man, come get something to drink," Stephan called to me.

I walked over to the group. Stephan passed me a beer from a cooler. There were many coolers lined up and filled with all kinds of alcohol. "Pick your poison," he said.

"I'm good with beer." I took a long swig.

I hung around the guys awhile, chatting and laughing. A little while later, a bunch of girls showed up and the partying began with some drinking games. The drugs came later. Besides taking a few drags of a joint, I stayed away. I played lacrosse and drugs just weren't for me.

The party grew and groups formed and separated. Day turned to dusk and the air grew cold. I went to sit by the fire. As I stared through the flame, I thought of my home. The Walshes portrayed themselves as the perfect American family, but behind closed doors my parents were self-interested people who didn't know what family meant. The one I missed the most was my little sister, Isabella. She probably wouldn't even remember me when I got home.

"Hey." A girl pulled me from my reverie with a smile as bright as sunshine. "Mind if I take a seat?" she tilted her chin to the tree trunk I was sitting on.

"Go right ahead." I smiled. I was well acquainted with the opposite sex. Girls were attracted to me. I was tall, athletic, and apparently had good genes.

Her mouth curved at the corners. Her blond hair swished past her shoulders as she took a seat beside me. She smelled of strawberries and looked like a breath of fresh air.

"You look like you have a lot on your mind," she said, staring at me and waiting.

"Ah! Not really."

"You look like you have the weight of the world on your shoulders," she insisted.

My lips twisted in a wry smile. "I look that bad. Huh."

She grinned. "Oh, I didn't say you looked bad. I just ..." She paused and her cheeks flushed.

"I'm Al by the way." I extended my hand to her.

"I'm Brie." She smiled and for the first time ever I felt a warmth in my chest and a pang in my heart.

"Brie. That's a pretty name." I looked her straight in her warm chocolate brown eyes.

"Thanks."

"So, is this your first year here?" I asked.

She nodded. "Just arrived a few weeks ago. My parents are getting divorced. They thought it was best for me to attend school here since they are in all-out war."

I scrunched my nose. "Sorry."

"Yeah, it is what it is." She shrugged her shoulders.

"Where you from?" I inquired. She looked American but I wasn't sure.

"L.A. My parents are famous actors."

I nodded. "You look like a Cali girl."

She laughed. "What is that supposed to mean?"

"Nothing, just your sun kissed skin and blond hair." I shrugged. "You're beautiful."

Brie from California blushed again, and my attraction to her grew tenfold.

"I don't really know too many people yet," she admitted.

"Yeah. Me neither. I wouldn't worry about it. Seems like this crew is easy to get along with."

"Yeah, if you're into sex and drugs." She huffed and then she pinched her lips together like the words slipped from her mouth.

My brows drew together as I waited for an explanation.

She waved me off. "Sorry. Just my dad ... he's famous, and I don't know, maybe it comes with the territory of being a movie star, but he cheated on my mom a lot and did drugs and now our lives are a mess."

"Shit! I'm sorry." I sighed. I wanted to hug this girl like something fierce. "My family aren't movie stars, just plain rich. The first time I caught my dad cheating on my mom I was fourteen."

Brie hissed. "That's awful."

"Yeah, saw it with my own eyes." I shook my head, trying to erase the memory.

Brie took my hand in hers. Her hand was warm and soft. She smiled at me and her eyes dropped to my lips. It was like gravity pulling us together. I drifted toward her and we kissed. Little did I know that things would never be the same again.

CHAPTER SEVEN

AL

Present

"WELL, YOU'RE LOOKING MORE HUMAN." Sam opens her eyes and smiles at me. It is very strange to be staying in a house with complete strangers. I'd say it's strange sharing a bed with a strange woman, but that isn't anything new to me so the argument wouldn't hold. What makes this experience different is the fact that for three nights Sam and I have shared the same bed and no sex was involved. Yes, we were both fully clothed for two out of the three nights, except when she tried to use the warmth of her skin to warm me while I was probably suffering from hypothermia. What's even stranger is that despite our clothed state, I like spending time with her. Not that she gives me a lot of her time. It's mostly her making me meals and nursing me back to health, but what I've come to know I like. I even like that she calls me darling with her long drawl, and I wasn't the type of guy to get stuck on sappy name calling.

"Antibiotics will have that effect." Her sweet voice pulls me from having naughty thoughts about her.

Turns out I had a strep throat and the hypothermia just wore my immune system down even more.

"Stu is one of the good ones." Sam yawns and stretches her arms above her head, pressing that ample chest of hers out. I'm glad I'm tucked under the covers. She seems to be completely oblivious to her beauty. She's unlike any other woman I know because she also doesn't do anything to pamper herself. She's a natural. I watch her climb out of bed. It's 5:00 am, but I don't mind getting up with her now that I'm feeling better.

"You want to tell me that you usually don't sleep in a bra and panties?" I ask, teasing her. I've learned I like to get a rise out of her. She picks up her pillow and throws it in my face.

"No, dumbass. I did that so you wouldn't die." She smirks and her lip quirks on one corner.

"Right, you saved me. How can I repay you for saving my life?" I ask with true sincerity. She pauses and her lush pink lips press together to form a thin line. I forgot about her whole she doesn't want my money spiel. From a brief look out the window, it appears the snow has finally stopped falling. Thank goodness too because the snowbanks were already five feet high two days ago when she drove me to Dr. Stu. I couldn't imagine what it's like out there now. Not that I'm complaining. I like being stuck on this ranch with her. Even though I could do without her dear old dad. I reach for a glass of water on the side table and swallow the antibiotics Dr. Stu prescribed. I sure as hell haven't needed my sleeping pills these last few days.

"I hope Portia fared well through the storm," I murmur to myself, deflecting my last question. Sam is up and rummaging through her drawers. She walks over to the corner she usually dresses in and does her best to keep her body parts covered while changing. I want to say that I'm a gentleman and look away, but I don't. I try to take in every ounce of her exposed skin. When Sam drops her pajama pants to the floor, my thoughts of Portia fly out the window.

"I need to work this morning. I'll probably be done early, though, so I can take you back to your car," she answers, and I know her words should excite me, but they don't because it means my time with her is up.

"Right, thanks." I'm not ready to leave. Even though she doesn't want monetary compensation, I feel on edge knowing I owe her big time. I want to get out to a supermarket and restock her fridge with food. Her father isn't the most subtle guy, but I can't say I blame him. They are running low on money, and I'm a big guy to feed. I also feel like maybe I need to help out around the ranch now that I'm feeling better as a form of repayment since she won't talk money. I've seen how hard she works. Her father doesn't cut her any slack. She's completely exhausted every night. What I do know is that her father inseminated a bunch of cows yesterday, hoping to get them pregnant. I thought cows did things the old fashion way, on all fours, but apparently not.

"I'm coming out there to work with you," I say, getting out of bed slowly. I pat Snow on the head. She's been keeping me company while I lie here sick in bed. I begin to unbutton the top buttons of the same flannel pajamas I've been wearing the past three nights. I watch her throat bob, and she pulls her attention away from me like I'm doused with acid. "I need a quick shower and I'm good to go."

She turns her attention back to me and gives a look that says she thinks I've lost it before she finally bursts into hysterical laughter. Her palm presses against her belly as she falls forward, laughing.

"What is so funny?" I feign being offended. My tone is deep and demanding, my brow cocked.

"Well, there's the fact you just offered to work on the ranch, and who the hell takes a shower before going to work in a barn? My papa had me shoveling shit yesterday," she says and my smirk fades.

"Shit."

"Yeah, real shit," she answers.

"I'm still coming out there. Sans shower and sans boxers. You haven't scared me off." I place both hands on my hips. I may not be up to full strength, but I'm in good shape. I can handle whatever her father has to dish.

I notice her eyes flare with heat and her gaze drops to my man package—for the briefest of seconds. I'm beginning to think I affect Sam. I like the thought of that, and I hate the thought of that all at once. It really just confuses the shit out of me. I want to bed her. I can't bed her. I'm leaving. She's too good for me to mess with.

"Well, good. We could use the extra help. Papa had to lay off the two farm boys we had in the summer. Now it's just me and him doing the work of four people. I won't say no to an extra set of hands." She nods and does the final button up on the plaid flannel shirt that seems to be a favorite style of hers. *Oh, Sam, my extra set of hands can help a lot ... like set that body of yours on fire.* The thought pops into my mind, sending a wave of heat through my body before reason kicks in and I shove the thought aside.

"Good then." I gulp, and she leaves the room just as I take off the flannel pajama shirt I'm wearing. I need to get to my car and suitcase fast because I'm in desperate need of clothes. I head over to my cell phone. It's dead and the charger's in my car. I don't know if Izzy is worried that I haven't shown up or if she figures I simply got sidetracked. I know Colton's probably busy handing his power over to the new governor, so I don't need to touch base with him.

All dressed in the clothes I arrived in, I exit Sam's room and head for the main area of the house where the kitchen is located. I'm in desperate need of coffee after drinking lemon water and tea these last few days.

Sam's father spots me first and at first glance he spits coffee out of his mouth and begins to laugh so hard I fear he may cause an avalanche nearby. "You ain't coming to work in my barn dressed like that." He looks at me like I'm insane.

"What?" I glance down at my clothes. Blue Hugo Boss jeans, dark wash. Gucci button down shirt in this season's eggplant color. My usual black leather belt and my Prada shoes, flat black with lace ties. I'm dressed well. I've been told I have impeccable taste in clothing from more than one lady. I walk over to Sam, who is standing by a coffee pot.

"Ignore, Papa. He's in his regular mood of being an ass." She cuts him a steely glare, but he doesn't care. He just continues to laugh. They have the oddest relationship. They call each other names and no one seems to get truly offended. It's a weird banter I don't understand.

"Coffee," I say like it's my last breath.

"Sure. How you take it?" she asks sweetly. My eyes drop to her full chest for a brief moment.

"Milk and one sugar," I answer, pulling my gaze up to her eyes. She brushes past me to get the milk. Her shoulder makes contact with my chest and my dick twitches. I swear in my head because without the boxers, it will be damn hard to hide a hard on.

"Let me do it," I take the milk from her. I don't want her to feel like she has to serve me or take care of me now that I feel better. She gives me the milk and sugar, and I make my coffee.

"See you two out there and hurry." Her father stands from the table, puts on his large cowboy hat, and exits the house.

A few minutes later, I've devoured a breakfast biscuit with a piece of cheese, and I'm out in the barn waiting for her father to tell me what he wants me to do.

"Hi, sir," I call from behind him. He turns to look at me, his eyes raking down my body to my shoes, and he bursts into another fit of laughter.

"I've never seen a rancher wear pointed shoes like that. What are they, girl shoes?" He's laughing so hard he can barely catch his breath. I begin to laugh with him, figuring it's better to join the laughter than be laughed at. Out of the corner of my eye, though, I see that Sam isn't too impressed. I hate that she lives here with her jerk of a father, doing everything she can to please him.

"Hardy har har." I nod my head. Okay, we get it. My shoes are funny. Now let's move on. I should be the one crying that my seven-hundred-dollar Pradas are going to get ruined. "What work do you want me to do with my fancy shoes?" I ask, standing tall and looking him right in the eye.

He stiffens and his features turn serious. "Alright. Here." He walks a few feet and picks up a shovel then passes it to me.

Sam cuts in. "Papa, no. I'll do it. Al is our guest," she says so softly I can barely hear her.

"No." I lift my hand. "It's fine."

"Yeah, sunshine. You heard him. *It's fine*. He's practically moved into our home, eating our food. I should be charging him room and board." Her father continues, and he's absolutely right. I should and I would. I keep that to myself though because any talk of repayment seems to piss Sam off.

"What should I do with the shovel?" I ask.

Her father points to the piles of shit on the floor. "Does it require an explanation?" He's mocking me now. Sam looks like she wants to crawl out of her skin.

"I've got this," I whisper in her ear. I can't help but take in the floral scent of her hair when my nose makes contact with it, or the brief goose bumps that pebble along her skin. All I know is that I'm in deep trouble with her.

CHAPTER EIGHT

AL

I'm FREAKING EXHAUSTED, and I smell like shit—literally—as we take a break for lunch in the middle of the day. I'm scrubbing my hands in the kitchen sink as Sam makes us all ham and cheese sandwiches. I really need a change of clothes, which I don't say out loud. I overheard Sam speaking with her father outside the bull barn, and they are worried that they might not have enough food for the cattle to get through the winter. A few of the cows aren't gaining enough weight, which is apparently a problem. All this work and talk of not having enough makes me realize what a spoiled asshole I really am.

I take a seat at the table next to Sam, and she pushes a plate with a sandwich my way.

"Thanks." I smile, realizing I still have my jacket on, but I'm still shivering from the cold outside.

Her father walks in and washes his hands then grabs a beer from the fridge.

"Tractor ain't working again. Got to drive that thing down to Slim," her father says to her. "Going to meet Tim for lunch. Just wanted you to know," he says, tipping his beer into his mouth.

"Okay." Sam nods. Her dad walks out the door with his beer.

With him gone, I breathe easier. She turns to me and smiles. "I can call the tow for your car if you'd like," she offers, and her closeness sends a spark of electricity through my body.

I swallow. "That would be great. Thank you. I need my suitcase for a change of clothes more than anything right now." I scrunch up my nose as the smell of cattle shit wafts up my nasal passages.

That comment buys me giggles. "Yeah, it isn't the best of scents. I'm pretty used to it by now." We continue to eat in silence.

We finish eating and Sam grabs her keys off a hook on the front door and with her head motions for me to follow. I do even though I literally smell like shit. As I follow her outside, I wonder why she works here on this ranch with her asshole father. She seems to have a good head on her shoulders, and she's a hard worker. She should be able to find another job anywhere, but I'm digging deep now. I have to stop.

She drives me back to my car, which is still sitting in the same ditch. Thankfully she remembers the exact location because the only distinction that I remember that night is that everything was white around me, which isn't very distinct at all.

"Louis beat us here. Good," she says as she pulls up to the tow truck at the side of the road. She puts her truck in park. I hate sitting in her truck, smelling the way I do. I can't get my suitcase fast enough, and I crave a shower like there's no tomorrow. I know those thoughts alone make me a bad rancher.

We both step out of her truck. My feet are frozen as I walk through the snow in my Pradas. They are already ruined and even if they weren't, I'm not getting the shitty smell out of them.

"Hey." Louis gives me a strong hand shake then smiles at Sam.

"Hi, thanks for coming out here." I shake his hand back

"I need to get my truck on an angle and then hook up the ropes. We are going to have to pull the car up," he explains.

"Sure, Lou. What can I do to help?" Sam asks.

"Nothing. I got this." He winks at her. I don't like it.

He trudges back to his truck to park it sideways. He gets to work on some motorized ropes, extending them behind his truck and toward Portia. I begin to contemplate how on earth Sam got to me the night she found me. I was in zombie mode. It couldn't have been easy for her. She's tiny, but I know she's strong after seeing her work the ranch. Those bales of hay are heavy.

Portia is hauled out of the ditch. My face falls and my stomach sinks when I see my rims are all missing as well as the special nineteen-inch sport tires. Motherfucker.

"Looks like you're going to need to order in some parts. Not sure my uncle has these kind of fancy rims in stock," Louis explains.

"Shoot, Al. I'm sorry." Sam lifts her hand and caresses my arm. I bite the inside of my cheek, thinking of my next words. If this were last week and I was in Chicago, I'd be seriously fucking pissed because my car is my baby. Now, after shoveling shit all day and being exposed to how the other half lives—and I don't mean it in a bad way—I'm acting like a stuck up jerk. I'm the first to admit my own faults, but I feel like I need to tamp it down around Sam. Or maybe I just want to behave like a nice human right now in front of her and not the spoiled asshole I truly am.

"It's fine. It's only a car." I don't choke on my words.

"Al, it's a beautifully expensive car. I don't know who could have done this, but there are so many different towns feeding off this route," Sam explains, biting her lip. I like that she sticks up for her people in Holston, insinuating they could never be responsible. As much as I don't understand why she would work on a ranch with her shithead father, I'm beginning to sense her connection to this town and people runs deep.

"It's no big deal. Really," I answer softly while looking into her kind blue eyes.

Louis's deep voice breaks through my fixation on Sam. "'Kay, folks, let's get moving. It's fucking freezing out here."

"Yeah, he's right."

"Okay, we'll meet you at Slim's shop," Sam calls out. I follow her back to the truck.

"IT MIGHT TAKE two weeks to get the parts out here with the weather the way it's been. Calling for another storm tonight," Slim, who is Louis's uncle and also the mechanic, explains. His two hands rest on his hips as he evaluates my Portia. "I need to test the battery too and check to see if any other parts are missing. The brakes on these babies are expensive. Looks like the thieves knew what to take."

I don't know shit about cars. He could tell me the radiator is missing and I'd believe him. I have a wad of cash in my wallet, which probably adds up to a few grand, and a good thirty grand more in the bank. That was it. No more money and no job in sight to replenish my funds. The rent on my apartment is super high and will be coming out of my bank account the first of the month. I've never had to deal with money issues before. Everything I'm experiencing was a first for me. Life is relative. As bad as I think I've been faring, it seems that Sam and her father are faring worse. They not only have themselves to feed but a bunch of cows who they need to fatten up and survive the winter so they can sell them come spring and make money.

"So how much?" I ask.

Slim scrubs his fingers along the scruff of his pointed chin. "Not sure. Need to call the supplier."

"Okay let me know." I smile.

I grab my phone charger and suitcase then follow Sam back to her truck. I notice she has a little bounce in her step when she walks. I can't help but notice her fine ass slowly swaying.

"At least my clothes weren't stolen." I grin. I place my suitcase in the small backseat. We drive off. She's quieter than she has been with me. We head back on a main road. She pulls into a small building on the side of the road that says Ruby's Supermarket.

After I pay for a shopping cart filled with groceries, we make it back to the ranch. I carry the large paper bags into the kitchen. Her father isn't home, which is a relief. After we unpack the groceries, she turns to me and says, "I ride a bull. I mean I compete. I got some practicing to do. So ..." She twists her heel.

"You ride a bull? Like a wild bull?" My eyes widen, even though I shouldn't be surprised.

"Yeah." She chuckles. "Why don't you take it easy or something for a couple hours," she suggests.

I scratch my head. "Okay. Sure." I'm a little speechless. She's a bull rider. I've seen movies about bull riders. That's intense. She leaves through the kitchen door, and I get a better idea than just chilling for a couple hours. It will either get me shot or it will buy me a really big smile from Sam. I follow her out the kitchen door and see that she's walking to a barn a little ways out. This ranch is huge. I don't know how many acres it sits on, but I'm guessing around the hundred range. When she's out of sight, I do something really stupid.

CHAPTER NINE

AL

ONE OF THE businesses my family owns is a tractor development plant. It was the place I spent my career day freshman year. I took an interest in the mechanics of the tractors and on occasion found myself back at the plant hanging out.

I'm on my back outside on the frozen ground when I see a pair of boots. "Fuck, City, what are you doing?" It's Farmer Joe's voice. He must be back to take the tractor in for repair.

I slide out from underneath. My hands are frozen and my back aches, even though the tractor is parked in a large barn type structure. There is no heat out here. "I'm fixing your tractor."

He chortles deep and hearty. "Fuck, that's the funniest thing I've heard." He holds his stomach.

Truth is I just finished up. I want to test the part one last time. "If it's so fucking funny, why don't you get on and try it out," I say with a challenging glare.

He stares me down for a moment, until I think he realizes I'm not kidding. "Okay." He turns the key. The tractor roars to life. He gives me a curious look. "Where did you get parts?"

"I took Sam's truck back to Slim's shop," I answer. I paid attention when Sam drove us there earlier, but I don't mention I didn't ask her permission to take the truck.

"Problem was the transmission," I start and he cuts me off.

"I knew that."

"You haven't had an inspection on this in a long time. You got a lot of problems with maintenance," I explain.

"Maintenance costs money I don't have," he retorts.

"Fair enough. I fixed the problem you were having with the shaft too," I say, and he eyes me curiously.

"How much do I owe you?" he asks.

"I wanted to do this. Sam won't take my money," I explain.

"How did you learn how to fix a machine like this? If you don't mind my saying, you really don't look like a mechanic."

I smirk. "Definitely not a mechanic, sir. Just a hobby I learned when I was younger," I say, knowing it isn't much of an explanation.

He nods his head, accepting my explanation. "I appreciate what you've done," he says, extending his hand for me to shake. It takes me a second to realize what he wants. I shake his hand, and he turns and walks away. I figured it's the best I'm going to get out of him. At least he didn't shoot me for taking Sam's truck. Speaking of which, I haven't seen her in a couple hours. I walk toward the house to look for her.

CHAPTER TEN

AL

It's late evening by the time I make it back to the main house. Sam's truck isn't parked in the driveway where it usually is. I trudge inside, feeling worn and achy. I take a warm shower, relieved Farmer Joe isn't around either. Every bone in my body feels broken as I scrub my body down from head to toe. I want to turn the water to the hottest it goes so that it will scald my body and relax my muscles, but I opt for a quick rinse. Water costs money. Suddenly, I'm aware of the simple things I've never given a second thought to. I get out of the shower and dress in fresh clothes: a fitted, gray, long-sleeve Hugo Boss T-shirt and a pair of designer jeans. I trudge back to Sam's room, barefoot. She still isn't back from where ever she went. With my phone charged, I call my sister. She picks up after one ring.

"Thanks for ditching me close to Christmas," she chides.

"Hey to you too," I answer. "I didn't ditch you, although my car ended up in a ditch. I didn't have my phone charger. I didn't remember your number by heart."

"Shit," she hisses. "You okay?"

"Yeah, I guess. My car needs some repairs ..." I pause, contemplating telling her the whole story.

"I shouldn't be mad at you, then. Where the hell are you anyway? I was expecting you days ago."

"Right." I scrub at my chin. "A woman saved my ass when the car went in the ditch and I've been staying with her."

"Of course," she answers, resigned. I may not have the best big brother reputation since I tend to fill my free time with women in my bed.

"It's not like that, Izzy." I exhale. Here goes nothing. "I took a sleeping pill and fell asleep in my car in the middle of a snow storm. I was tired of driving and frustrated and I decided sleeping was a good idea."

"Shit. That is messed-up."

"I know. I didn't mean to not show. I also got sick, so I was in bed. Don't ask. It's been one big mess."

Izzy sighs. "Sorry, big brother. Sounds like you had a bad go of things. When should I expect you?"

I pause, not sure how to answer the next question.

"Is the woman that saved you pretty as hell?"

"Uh ... yes ... but ... there is more to it. I'll fill you in soon," I say, not wanting to add that my stomach is grumbling from the manual labor I did on the ranch today.

She groans. "Yeah sure, okay. You take care."

"You too," I answer and end the call. It's only after I hung up that I realize she seemed a little off.

I walk back out to the main area of the house and notice Farmer Joe sitting in the same chair he usually sits in with the Jim Beam by his side. "Do you know where Sam is, sir?"

"She went to Moe's. It's a bar on the edge of town." He does me a favor answering.

Fuck! I want to go meet her. Uber or even a taxi aren't available around here. I clear my throat and take a deep breath because Farmer Joe is kind of fierce and even though he's old, he has one too many guns lying around.

"Sir, would you mind if I borrowed your truck?" I hold my

breath as I finish the question. He gives me a look that says he thinks I'm nuts—and I probably am to think he would lend a complete stranger his truck.

"You mean my Ford?" He cocks a brow.

I've dealt with all kinds of criminals and assholes while working for the state prosecutor, but Joe Belmont practices a different kind of intimidation. Maybe it's all the guns he has lying around. I don't really know. I take a big gulp, swallowing hard, expecting him to lash out. Only his dark eyes soften for a brief moment when he says, "Ford is one of America's greatest accomplishments. Take care of my truck." He may have even cracked half a smile under that thick mustache of his, but I'm not sure. He may have just been passing gas.

"Huh?" I feel confused. Did he just give me permission to drive his old beat-up truck? It seems like he's trying to trick me with his answer.

"What are you, deaf, City?" he snaps and of course the moment of kindness passes. "Bar's at the corner of Route 68. You should know it. Your car was in the ditch a few miles out from there."

I'd paid a little attention when Sam and I went to fetch my car earlier; she had hung a right turn out of here. I don't fully remember, but I also am not about to ask Mr. Grumpy for directions. I'll find it on my own. Still in shock he's even letting me borrow his truck, I run back to the room I was sharing with Sam put on some socks and a pair of Hugo Boss running shoes. I grab my wool peacoat since my other jacket now smells like shit, and I run back toward the door to get the keys from the hook, half expecting him to pull a shot gun on me. They're the last set of keys on the hook, so I pray it's the right set. Any words I exchange with Farmer Joe are on a need-to basis.

The truck doesn't start up immediately. On the second try, it roars to life and I'm off hanging a right then heading down a long dark two-way street. While driving in silence, I think of Sam. Did she happen upon me that night because she was coming home from being out at the bar? Did she just finish hooking up with someone when she found me? What was she doing driving in that treacherous weather anyway? I can't stop thinking of her, and it's disconcerting to say the least.

About five minutes later, I pull up to a barn that looks like it's been converted into a bar. It has a big red neon light on the roof that says Moe's. I spot Sam's pickup parked out front along with another twenty or more cars. This place must be the local hang-out. I turn off the ignition and step outside, locking the door with my key. The last thing I need is for Farmer Joe's truck to be stolen.

"Hey, nice to meet you. I'm Leslie." A lady who just pulled in beside me comes over with a bright smile and extends a hand for me to shake.

"Al." I shake her hand as a shiver rolls through my body from this crazy cold weather.

"You're driving Joe Belmont's truck." It's a statement.

I nod.

"You're his houseguest, right?" she continues.

"I am." This is so weird.

"This is Riley, my boyfriend." She points to the tall brooding man beside her.

I extend my hand to her boyfriend, and he shakes it, not saying a word except for a small grunt.

"Don't mind him. He needs beer," Leslie explains, waving off her boyfriend's anti-social behavior. He kind of reminds me of Farmer Joe. I'm pretty sure he grunts more than he speaks actual words. Maybe it's a cowboy thing or a rancher thing. "Let's head on in. It's freezing out here."

I follow them, hoping Leslie will lead me to Sam.

As I enter the front door, I take the place in. It looks like a barn with lots of tables scattered around. All the tables are full. There is loud country music playing in the back ground. Can't say I'm a fan of country music, but I can put up with it for a night. There is a small dance floor and some billiard tables off to the back. My eyes stop on Sam as I watch her dancing in front of a juke box with a beer in her hand. She looks different tonight, wearing a tight white shirt with the shoulders cut out and a form-fitting pair of jeans. They're the ones she usually wears, but with that tight top it gives a whole different look. Her short blond hair is down and she's wearing a hint of makeup. She looks gorgeous. My eyes rake up and down her body unabashedly, and as if sensing my stare, she looks up and makes eye contact with me. Her throat bobs as she stills for a beat before she pulls her gaze away and looks over to Leslie. At that moment both women shriek and run for each other. Leslie's boyfriend follows. Leslie and Sam give each other a long hug, which involves the two of them swaying their hips from side to side.

When they pull apart, Leslie points to me and says, "We picked this stud up along the way." She winks at Sam. Her tone crackles enthusiasm.

"I can see that," Sam answers, her tone even. If I didn't see her throat bob when I walked in, I would think I'm the last person she's interested in seeing here tonight.

"You guys want to join us for drinks?" Leslie asks, referring to me and Sam as if we were a couple. Sam looks up to me then back to Leslie, her mouth slightly open as if she wants to say something but no words come out.

"Um ... you guys go ahead. I'm starving I need to get a bite to eat."

"Don't be silly, Al. You can order food and we can get our drinks. Come on over to the booth here." Leslie waves us over. Her boyfriend Riley hasn't said much, but he climbs into the booth after her. Sam climbs in on the opposite side. I notice she looks a little tipsy.

A waitress comes up to our table. "Usual?" she asks, looking around. They all nod. Her gaze pauses on me. "Don't know what your usual is handsome." She gives me a flirtatious smile. Sam shifts in the seat beside me.

"Do you have a dinner menu?" I ask.

"No, just a menu. What are you in the mood for? We got burgers, chicken sandwiches, nachos ..." She stands, waiting for me to answer. A nice charbroiled steak with steamed vegetables would be nice, but that isn't going happen.

"I'll have a burger," I say since it's the closest thing to steak. Not.

"Would you like fries with that?" She waits, chewing some gum.

"Sure."

"And cheese?" she asks.

"Sure."

"And to drink?" Riley looks on edge with all the questions she's asking me. He probably wants his beer.

"Whatever they are having." I smile.

"You got it, handsome." She nods and puts her order pad into her apron.

After she walks away, Leslie starts to tell us a story about her younger brother who just deployed. We all listen intently. The waitress returns with my food and the drinks. I say drinks because she has placed two beers each in front of Riley, Leslie, and Sam, who is just about to finish the one in her hand. She places something amber in a shot glass in front of each of us.

"Thanks, Crystal," they almost say in unison.

"Ready?" Sam asks, lifting the shot glass and looking around the table. Both Riley and Leslie have theirs ready in their hand. I pick mine up too, even though I'm not in on this ritual.

"And go," Leslie says, and then everyone tips the shot glass into their mouth and downs the liquid. It stings going down, and I learn its tequila. They place the empty shot glasses on the table and pick up their beers.

"Need something to warm us up," Riley says, looking more relaxed.

I nod and eat the large half pound burger on my plate. At least it's big because I'm starving.

"You got a healthy appetite there, Al." Leslie grins.

"Papa had him shoveling shit all day," Sam chimes in, and Leslie's eyes turn wide.

"You don't seem like the rancher type," Leslie responds. "I took you for a city guy. Maybe a businessman."

"I'm a lawyer," I respond and take the last bite of my burger.

"Mr. Belmont can be tough," Riley finally speaks. "When we were kids, we brought Sam home late one night after a party, and Mr. Belmont was waiting outside on the front deck with a rifle in his hand." Riley laughs, clearly more relaxed now than he was earlier. I guess he would be after the shot, and now he's on his second beer.

"Riley, we don't need to hear stories about Papa." Sam eyes him like she wants him to shut up. "Besides, he's already threatened Al with his gun collection." Sam rolls her eyes. And the conversation shifts to Leslie. I sit back and watch them chatting. It's nice to have childhood friends around that you share history with. These friends seem to be close-knit. The waitress comes around with another shot. I've already had one shot and two beers. I may drink regularly, but I like a mild buzz. By the looks of it, this group drinks to get drunk.

"Um ... how are we driving home if we drink all this?" I ask Sam. I'm responsible for her father's truck.

"We can get a ride with one of our friends and pick up the trucks tomorrow. There is always someone that can drive," Sam explains, just as Kell walks up to the table with a guy that I presume is her husband. "Like Kell for example. She can't drink so she can give us a ride." Sam starts to slur her words. I can tell she's pretty wasted.

I decide to pass on the shot. I need to get the truck home.

"Hey there, Al." Kell smiles. "This is Gage, my husband," Kell says, introducing us.

"Hey, man. Welcome to Holston." Gage extends his hand. He comes off as a little friendlier than Riley.

"Thanks," I answer when the girls start shrieking something about the song playing in the background.

"OMG! This is the best song. You have to come dance," Sam says, pulling me by the hand.

"I don't know how to dance to country music," I protest. Leslie and Riley and Kell and Gage have already headed over to the dance floor and are dancing and shouting the words to the song.

"It's Garth Brooks for Christ sakes. Just come dance," Sam yells above all the background noise. I allow her to guide me to the dance floor. I have no idea what I'm doing. I sure don't know the words to the song, but Sam sings it to me. The whole group is shouting the words, and she's dancing with me up close, moving her body against mine. I may not like country music, but I like watching her body move. I wrap my hand around her waist because that is what I watch the other cowboys on the dance floor doing, and I move my feet. At least I have rhythm. When the song ends, another song starts up it's a slower pace. I wrap my arms around her waist. Her arms come up around my neck and we move. Our eyes lock together as heat licks through my body, leaving an inferno in its wake. She moves in closer and her breasts make contact with my chest, her warm breath lingers too close. I drop my head even more.

"You're beautiful," I whisper. She doesn't answer me, but she moves closer and her lips brush mine. Any reservations I've had about keeping my hands off her fly out the window, including the fact that she is way past drunk, because we've been playing this little dance for days, flirting, getting to know one another. She wants this as much as I do. There's no denying it.

I crash my lips to hers and her hands come up and cup my head. The kiss is hot and hungry. Our mouths move, our tongues come out to play, and she tastes heavenly. We don't stop and my next thought is we need to get the hell out of here and take this somewhere private like the truck. Thoughts of her riding me in the front seat of the truck make my blood boil to dangerous levels.

I am so wrapped up in Sam, I don't realize a man is standing behind her with a crossed look on his face. "Excuse me," he booms placing his hand on her shoulder like he's claiming her.

He pulls Sam away from me. My breaths are ragged and my lips taste of her when I try to regain my focus. My gaze lands on him.

CHAPTER ELEVEN

AL

HE'S WEARING A LEATHER JACKET, his dark eyes look blood shot, and he has tattoos running up his neck. He looks like the kind of man that doesn't answer to anyone only now he's going to answer to me.

"We're busy," I answer, my tone clipped. *Who the fuck does he think he is?*

"No, you aren't," he scoffs and blows out air with a twisted smile that tells me he doesn't give a shit if Sam and I were in the middle of something.

His dark eyes rake over Sam's body then snap back up to her face and a million words pass in that gaze. Words the two of them seem to understand. I remind myself that Sam had a life before I came barreling through it.

"Stop it, Blake. You don't own me." Sam pulls out of his grasp and turns back to me.

"You're drunk dammit and hanging all over this fool. I don't like it." He bites while his jaw clenches so tightly I think it might snap.

He's big but not as tall as me. I figure I can take him if I have to, not that I'm a fighter. In my social circles, fists aren't raised. My acquaintances use other means to stab each other in the back. Fucking someone's wife, stealing a company. Suddenly a bar brawl over a woman seems so simple. Only I'm the odd one out. Sam has known these people since childhood. The name Blake rings a bell. She mentioned him to Kell. He's one of her hookups. I don't want to stir shit up. Not when she's gone out of her way to be kind to me.

He pulls her away, not giving a second thought to what she thinks. They stop in front of a jukebox at the far side of the bar. I've been abandoned in the middle of the dance floor. Gage leans over and whispers, "That's my asshole brother, Blake. They've been off and on for years. Don't let it get to you," he whispers then returns to dance with Kell.

"Yeah, man," I murmur, but my head is spinning and it isn't from the alcohol I drank because I barely have a buzz. I stalk over to the bar and order a beer, taking a seat on a stool. I don't know what's going on in my head or my heart. My reaction tells me I like Sam more than I realize. I'm irate that this Blake seems to be staking a claim on her. My attraction to Sam irks me. I don't only want to have sex with her. I want to get to know her. Out of the corner of my eye, I notice Sam and Blake arguing. He's got her arm in a hold and my blood turns hot.

His lips press into the side of her neck, and I'm seeing colors. I jolt up from the barstool ready to stalk over there and state my own claim. My movements are faster than my mind's ability to catch up with my actions. His mouth remains glued to her nape and from this vantage point, it looks like his tongue has darted out to take a taste. I cringe as he pulls her hips against his and begins swaying with her. My body turns rigid, anger bubbles inside me, pumping through my veins like poison. I'm a glutton for punishment, and I can't look away. Sam turns her head and the man kisses her on the lips. Fucking hell. I should look away. I need to leave. I can't leave. Instead, I battle the storm in my mind and try to focus more on Sam, her features and her reactions to the man kissing her. Her brows are dipped, and her mouth forms a thin line. She looks flushed as she tries to push him away. He takes a step back, and she holds a hand up, preventing him from taking another step. They're arguing as she sways back and forth. I know for a fact she's had one too many drinks. He tries to kiss her again, and she shoves him hard. He doesn't seem to want to back away. Before I register my own actions, my feet are moving me across the old wooden floor of the bar and straight toward the jukebox Sam is standing beside.

My jaw ticks and my fists ball at my sides. I'm going to rip him apart for manhandling her. My breaths are haggard as anger pulses through my body. I'm ready for a fight when out of nowhere Leslie gets in my face, and the look on her own face tells me that she knows what my plan is and isn't on board. She places a palm on my chest.

"Hold up handsome," she says with a worried look.

"Give me a minute, Leslie," I ask without making eye contact because I can't peel my eyes off Sam and that asshole.

"That's it, Al, you don't need a minute. You need to look at me down here and listen." She grabs hold of my arm, halting my charge toward Sam. I look at Leslie, hoping she has a good reason for stopping me from saving Sam. "Don't do it. Don't go there. Sam's been with Blake off and on a long time. Whatever it is, she can handle herself. You pounce on him and you'll have this whole bar to fight off." She reminds me I'm the outsider here. She's telling me that I need to know my place. Problem for me is that I've never known my place. My jaw clenches and my adrenaline pumps hard, spurring me forward.

"Thanks for the advice, Leslie." I walk around her before she can get out another word.

"Sam," I bark, and Blake whips his head around to look at me.

"Mind your own business asshole," he snaps and returns his attention to Sam, placing his hand firm on her behind.

Sam sways. And I know that these two have a history. I get it. It still doesn't give him the right to treat her badly.

"Never been good at that," I answer as I stand straighter and puff my chest out wider. I'm in full-out alpha mode, and I don't give a shit about repercussions. What I do know is that I don't like how this guy is treating Sam. She's piss drunk and clearly can't defend herself.

"That's too bad. Sam and I are busy." He furrows his brows and gives me a look that tells me he thinks I'm an idiot, Sam is his, and to bug off. He's a couple inches shorter than me but just as built, only he probably got his muscles from working the land where I have mine from a gym. Not that it makes a difference.

"Stop being a jerk." Sam steps out from under him. "This is my houseguest be nice," she slurs.

"Houseguest?" he repeats but it's a question. His jaw tenses and his brown eyes narrow to slits. "Not sure I like this guy staying in your house," he says like he owns her. I wonder what kind of past they share that he would be acting like this.

"Well, it doesn't matter what you think because you don't own me," she answers him back, and all I can think is good girl. She's not the type of woman who should be subservient to a man. She is strong, smart, and any idiot should know she deserves to be treated like an equal.

He cuts Sam a look I don't understand. "Not for lack of trying, Sam. I've tried to make you mine for a while now."

Another young guy walks up to us. Also, tall and built. He's wearing a hoodie, a pair of jeans, and his baseball cap is flipped backward. "Everything good, Sam?" he asks. He looks her up and down as if he wants to make sure she's okay. The tight white shirt she's wearing reveals just how full her breasts are, and I watch the heat in his eyes grow. I know what he feels. It pisses me off that he's probably her age and maybe more suited for her than I am.

"Oh for crying out loud," Sam shouts. I'm lost because Blake gives the guy a look that says he wants to rip him to pieces, and the guy doesn't look too pleased with Blake, and all the while they both look like she belongs to them. I remember Sam's conversation with Kell in the kitchen while I was still sick, and I figure this must be her other hookup.

"Sam, baby, if you need a ride home, just say so." The younger one smiles sweetly at her. He doesn't seem to be as angry as Blake.

Sam baby? I want to hurl at his term of endearment. The three of us stand and stare each other down.

A few beats pass as tension dilutes the air around is. Kell steps between all of us. "Hey, darling." She hugs Sam. Sam looks worn out as she curls into her friend's arms. "Come with me," Kell says, but it's almost a whisper.

"Hey, Al." Kell beams at me as she guides Sam away from our ring of fire. Another beat passes, and Kell turns her head and says, "Shows over, boys. Disperse."

Blake grunts and knocks into my shoulder as he walks past me. The younger kid gives me a weird look and walks away. I turn and head back to the bar to reclaim my seat and order another Bud. It takes everything in me not to follow Kell and Sam, but I don't like the scene that just went down. I don't fully understand what it means, but I dislike it nonetheless. As I take a long gulp of beer, I notice Leslie has taken a seat on the barstool beside me.

"Hey, darling, you okay?" she asks with a soft smile. I wonder why I shouldn't be. What does she know that I don't? I'm guessing a lot, and I'm guessing her lips are sealed too.

I draw my brows together. "I think so," I answer. Truth is I don't know what on earth is happening. I left Chicago because I wanted to clear my head. Now I want another kind of therapy, and it comes in the form of a too-young-for-me rancher that's about five-five with short blond hair and a nice rack.

Leslie gives me a sympathetic look. "Sam has a lot of admirers in this town, looking the way she does, and she has a heart of gold," Leslie explains, giving me information I already knew. Sam has a big heart. She saved my life and nursed me to health, and I was a complete stranger. I wonder what she does for those she loved.

"I know that. She saved my life."

"Yeah, and you're okay now. Looking healthy and yet here you are, still living it up at the Belmont Ranch." Both her brows raise. She waits for me to argue with her possibly. I have nothing to contest. I could have called Izzy and told her to pick me up. I could have arranged for car parts to arrive faster, but I didn't because I was in no rush to leave.

"I should go. Sam probably needs a ride home." I point my thumb to the door and throw a twenty on the bar. Leslie looks up and places her hand on my arm, stopping me.

"Uh uh." She nods her head, and I'm thinking what is up with the people in this town? "Kell and Gage will get her home safely. It's better you don't follow her out." She tilts her chin to the right corner of the bar. My eyes follow. Blake is sitting at a booth by himself, looking at his bottle of Bud like it has all the answers to life. "Blake is very protective of her, and you being new to town and all..." she shrugs as if I should take the hint "...better not to cause any trouble. We got Sam's back. You don't need to worry," she says and again, I have no clue what all that means. I also don't think Leslie is going to give me any answers either.

"I still think I should call it a night," I say.

"Stay a little while longer," she says and it isn't a request, but she's a nice woman and means well. I stay rooted on the stool.

"What do you do?" I ask because it's clear Leslie is stalling me, and I'm sick of being shut down where Sam is concerned.

"I'm in college. Studying education." She smiles. "I come home on weekends. Holston may seem like a boring little town to you, but it's our home. It's what we know and there are good people here," she explains. I was beginning to understand what she was saying. They may be up in each other's business, but I could see they had Sam's back. That they cared.

"I can see that. I may have grown up in the city, but Holston has its own kind of small town charm." I'm done making small talk. I want to leave. I don't want my leaving to end in a fight, even though I'm burning for one. I know my negative energy is the result of months of frustration and tonight that all bubbled to the surface. It wouldn't be fair to Sam though. I know better than to cause a shit storm for her. Besides, as worked up as I am, I'm more overcome with the need to protect and take care of Sam like she took care of me.

Leslie's lips spread into a thin smile. "I know you know that I'm keeping you here, and I appreciate you staying and hanging out. It says something about you." She eyes me like she's impressed, like there has to be more layers to me than my good-looking face. Something about the way she looks at me unnerved me. It makes me think of my family. Growing up, my younger brother Derek has always been jealous of me. It never made any sense to me because he was smart. Smarter than me. I had to work for my grades in school, but everything came easy to him. We are only two years and nine months apart. I got a lot of attention from the opposite sex. I'm tall and built, and he's thin and average height. I never paid much attention to how different we looked. I never noticed a lot of things that I should have noticed. Derek wasn't oblivious though. Derek was competitive and mean. I don't realize my mind drifted for long, but when I refocus, I see Leslie looking at me expectantly. I blame the drama that just went down.

"Nothing to say? Well that's okay." She sighs.

"You can get back to your man, Leslie. I'll hang out here awhile longer and nurse this beer slowly." I grin. She's a good friend to Sam. It's a far cry from the environment I grew up in. Colton's probably the only person I know that isn't competing with me or trying to hurt me. That says a whole lot about me. I don't have people to count on like Sam does. The thought twists my stomach and that self-loathing I've been feeling for months begins to resurface.

"Sure." Leslie gets up from the barstool and pats my back. "Hope to see you around, Al." She walks away. Her words tell me she's okay having me around. I don't know if Farmer Joe or even Sam feel that way, but I hope they want me around awhile longer. I'm not ready to leave.

"You too, Leslie." I take another long pull off my beer, and my mind pulls me back to my childhood. I've been thinking of the past a lot lately, wondering where I went wrong, pondering how the family that raised me doesn't want to reach out and fix things. As usual, I have no answers. In the decade that passed, nothing has changed. Well, maybe that isn't true. I've changed and I am changing. I'm not happy being the person I am and being here in Holston and watching how the whole town is coming up to bat for Sam drives that idea home even more. Deep down I know I'm at a crossroads. I just don't realize what it all means.

CHAPTER TWELVE

SAM

Eight years ago

"Sam, wake the hell up." Mack's voice sounds loud and intrusive, so I take a pillow and cover my head. "For crying out loud, get up. I need to drop you off at school. I can't be late. You're being so unfair right now," she whines. It's darn annoying.

"Just go to school and let me sleep," I manage to croak out.

"No chance, darling." She huffs.

The blankets are thrown off me. A cold chill runs over my body, and I curl into a little ball. My bed sinks beside me as Mack sits right next to me.

"I don't know what to do. I know you've had a hard time, but I can't let you just throw your life away." She sounds completely resigned and it makes me feel bad. She basically has taken on the role of being my mother, and she's only twenty years old.

Instead of going away to college, she attends a college in Grand Junction. It's a far cry from her first choice, but she didn't want to leave me here alone with Papa. I'm grateful for Mack, I truly am, but I'm completely exhausted. She leans forward and before I can move out of the way, she presses her nose into my hair.

"Dammit, Mack," I growl. I don't mean it, but she puts me on defense.

"You smell like pot." She sighs. "I told you Blake was a bad influence. I saw it from the minute he walked in here. I wish you could see it. Mama wouldn't want a guy like that for you," she says, and her words burn through my heart because I know they're true.

Problem is I like the way Blake makes me feel. We get high a little and laugh a little. He makes me forget my life for a while and makes me feel good. That can't be a bad thing.

"Don't start. I'm not marrying the guy," I bark, and it's not a lie. I won't ever marry a guy like Blake.

"Why don't you date the Neumann boy ... what's his name?" She taps her chin with her pointer finger.

"Austin, and he's not my type."

Her lip quirks on one corner. "Right. What was I thinking?" Her tone is full of sarcasm. "Why would my baby sister want to date a nice boy from a good family? One that isn't two years older than her and smokes pot and who knows what else? Yeah, that would be so bad, Sam." She shakes her head at me and the gesture drips with the disappointment she feels.

She made good on her promise to Mama and is attending college. She wants to be an attorney, and she's told me numerous times that once she gets into law school, she's leaving no matter what. That's over a year away, so I've just pushed it to the back of my mind.

"Well, you should make Austin your type. His brother has gone off to Yale. Do you know what that is, Sam? That's an Ivy League college. That's big time. A kid like Austin could be a good influence on you," Mack continues. It seems like the only thing she does these days is lecture me. I wish she could just act like my sister.

"I'll think on it," I answer just to appease her.

"Great. Now get your butt up because I don't want to be late for class and neither should you. Your math teacher left a message that you failed the last math test. I need you to do better, Sam," Mack berates me.

Since Mama died, all I feel is sad. She was my world. My sun and moon. When she died the sun stopped shining and even when the moon came out it was dark without the sun. I just couldn't seem to find myself without her. I don't know why. My marks in school have been affected. My whole darn life is affected.

"I know, okay." It comes out a lot snarkier than I'd like. Mack is trying to follow through on her promise to Mama that she'd take care of me. I don't mean to be difficult. I truly don't.

"Please come home after school and do homework this afternoon. No Blake. Okay?"

I have a hard time saying no to Mack. "Okay," I relent. Problem is the follow-through later on.

After we're all dressed and have eaten a quick breakfast, Mack drops me off in front of my high school. By second period, I bump into Blake. He's a junior and I'm a freshman, so we don't have any classes together. When he asks me to come over to his house after school, I agree. His mom is a single mom who works at the Walgreens, and she won't be home. His older brother Gage will be working too. The thought of being alone and kissing Blake causes my blood to pump hard, making me feel alive. I just want to make that feeling last. Is it so bad to want?

CHAPTER THIRTEEN

AL

I WAIT at the bar a whole half hour, pondering my life in the process. Blake's glare bores into me the entire time. My mind has sucked me into thoughts of my family, so I'm too busy to pay him much attention or feed his anger. I wonder if that's what I've done with Derek. Did I somehow feed his anger unintentionally? Could I have been a better brother to him? Things have always felt so strained between us, I didn't know he had it out for me so bad.

After wallowing in my life's mistakes for a while, I find my way back to the Belmont Ranch and pull up to the long drive out in front of the main house. Sam's truck is already parked along with another truck, also a Ford, which I assume belongs to Kell and Gage. I lock Farmer Joe's truck and walk up to the door, which I've noticed is never locked. I figure thieves know not to mess with Joe Belmont. I wouldn't be surprised if he shot a few people in his lifetime. Stepping through the dark kitchen, I'm relieved Farmer Joe isn't around.

I trudge back to Sam's room, figuring she's passed out in her bed. I come to an abrupt stop when I hear a commotion. I remain quiet and still in the dark hallway, listening to the voices quarrelling. I should feel bad for eavesdropping. This drama-filled night has left me with too many questions about Sam and what the hell I'm still doing in Holston. Maybe I'm still here because I don't have a place to go. I'm thirty-five fucking years old and lord knows to a certain extent I've made the bed I sleep in. Or maybe I'm still here because I like Sam.

"Come on, honey." Kell's soothing voice radiates down the hall from the bathroom.

"Kell, just give her a quick rinse," Gage shout whispers. "I did the best I could with her front seat. We need to be gettin' home," Gage says and it sounds like he's in Sam's room. I gather Kell has Sam in the shower. He also said he did the best he could with her front seat, meaning Sam probably vomited all over the front seat of her car.

"Gage, you damn well know I'm not leaving her like this," Kell snaps back. "Even though I feel really nauseous now watching her hurl all over the place," she whines. I remember her mentioning she was pregnant.

"If you're going to throw up, make sure you get it in the toilet," Gage shouts back. Shit this was one weird situation I walked into, and Gage sounds like a real charmer.

"Fuck you," Kell screams out. Can't say I blame her.

The bathroom door swings open. Light floods into the dark hallway. I wince, squinting my eyes. I can't turn around now or act like I didn't just hear their entire conversation. Sam has a towel wrapped around her body. I don't cover my eyes, though, because she's walked around in a towel since I intruded on her life and even gave me the privilege of showing me her fine backside.

"Uh ..." I stutter. "You need some help?"

Kell jumps in the air and loses her grip on Sam as she palms her heart. "Fuck, Al, you just scared the living shit out of me."

"Sorry," I answer because I'm a little stunned myself.

Sam loses her balance and bumps into the wall, falling into a fit of laughter.

"Guess you heard she vomited in her truck. I hate the smell of vomit. I couldn't put her to bed like that," Kell explains. "Maybe it's best you sleep on the couch tonight," she says sweetly.

"Uh ... sure, yeah." I run a hand over my buzzed hair that's grown since I arrived. I was hoping to sleep beside Sam. I want to take care of her the way she took care of me, with sweet words and a warm touch. I see that isn't going to happen. I follow the two women into Sam's room.

"Hey." I nod to Gage, who is sitting at the edge of Sam's bed, looking at something on his cell.

"Hey, man." He nods back but the conversation ends. The whole situation makes me uncomfortable. I move through the room swiftly, grabbing a pair of sweatpants and T-shirt out of my suitcase and head into the bathroom that Kell and Sam just came out of. Once I've changed, I head over to the couch in the family room and grab one of the throw blankets and lie down. I'm too worked up after everything that happened tonight to get any shut eye.

Twenty minutes or so later, Kell comes toward the door, holding Gage's hand.

I stand and rake a hand through my hair. "Hi. Uh ... is she okay?"

Kell waves her hand. "She'll be fine. She sometimes drinks a little too much. That's all. I placed a garbage bin by the bed. There shouldn't be any more mess. You have yourself a good-night, Al." Her tone is saccharine.

"Yeah, you too," I mutter, feeling numb and useless. Once they leave, I head back to Sam's room to check on her. When I reach her door, I hear singing. I pause and listen to the most magnificent voice I've ever heard. She's singing "Somewhere over the Rainbow." Her voice sounds sweet with a hint of sultry. It's beautiful and heartbreaking. I wait until she stops, but then she starts another song, and I take a seat on the floor and press my head to the wall and drink in her angelic voice. When she stops singing, I get up and open the door to check on her. I'm pretty sure she's sleeping.

Only her soft voice says, "Hi."

"Hi," I answer a little breathless, although I'm not sure why I would be.

"Would you come lie down with me?" she asks, and all I can think is that she could ask me for anything right now, and I would never say no.

"Of course." I slide into bed beside her.

"Hold me," she says into the dark.

I wrap my arms around her and my nose presses into her wet hair that smells like a floral shampoo. I inhale and exhale her scent and it relaxes me.

"You okay?" I whisper into the dark.

"Better now," she answers. Her breathing slows, and I am pretty sure she passes out. Her sweet voice and words ring in my head. *Better now.*

"I feel better now too," I whisper back.

"Sometimes life turns out in a way you don't plan," she says, breaking the silence.

I huff, even though I don't mean to. "I know all about that."

"Oh yeah?" I hear the interest in her tone. "How's that?" she asks. She clearly isn't as drunk as before.

"It's a bunch of messed-up shit with my family. I haven't spoken to them in a long, long time," I say and my heart feels heavy. Maybe because hanging out with the Belmonts and the people in Holston reminds me of family in general. I can see they have their own problems, but there is love and dedication beneath the craziness.

"I'm sorry. That isn't easy. Being separated from your family," she says, and her sweet voice carries a heaviness that pierces my heart.

"No, it isn't easy, Sam. It isn't easy at all. A part of me is sick of feeling so alone," I admit, surprising myself because I don't share intimate parts of my life with a woman. Or anyone for that matter. Sam is easy to talk to. She's is drawing me in like a fish on a line and all I want to do is swim in her sea.

"Yeah." She sighs, and I feel her breath evening out. I press a soft kiss to the back of her head, and I fall asleep, holding her in my arms, feeling a fierce need to never let go.

CHAPTER FOURTEEN

AL

Past

FEBRUARY IN SWITZERLAND is fucking cold, which meant no more sneaking off to the forest for parties. Well, except to smoke an occasional joint with a buddy. Tonight, was Brie's seventeenth birthday. We'd practically been inseparable since the night of the bonfire. She was my girlfriend, but she was also my best friend because we just got each other.

I went home over Christmas, but there wasn't anything that stood out about my trip. My father still kept me at arm's length. Derek has really taken on the role of favorite son. His grades in school were high. He was taking business courses and was even hanging out at the office with my dad. He mentioned coming here to school next year, but Dad didn't give him a real answer. Izzy was still sweet and loving. She really made my trip home bearable. I spent most of my time taking her Christmas shopping and hanging with friends.

Brie's mom came to town and whisked her off to London over the holidays, claiming that things were too intense with the paparazzi back home. Brie said it was her first Christmas without her dad and the worst one ever.

I continued to prepare everything for my night with Brie. It wasn't easy sneaking into the girls' dorm, but Hans and a bunch of my friends were helping me slip through the cracks. My heart beat fast as I used the back entrance to the girls' dorm and slithered through a receiving area. Getting caught in their dorm could lead to suspension. For some reason, it was more frowned upon than the parties we had in the forest. Probably because sex could lead to babies and the school didn't want that kind of liability on school property. Brie and I were both virgins, and it was crazy that we'd lasted this long. Neither of us took sex lightly after what we'd seen with our parents.

Brie's roommates were in on our plan to spend a few hours of private time tonight together. As they slipped into their neighbor's dorm, I sneaked into Brie's.

She charged me the moment I entered her room, wrapping her thin arms around my neck. "I knew you'd make it." Her grin was wide, and I wrapped my arms around her waist and pressed my nose into her silky hair. Ah! The scent of fresh strawberries.

"Of course." I smiled down at her. "Brought you something." I released her and took the backpack off my back. I pulled out a Tiffany's jewelry box.

"You know I don't need gifts. I'm just happy we could spend my birthday together."

"I know." I gave her the box. "Open it." I waited expectantly, wanting to take in her features when she sees the gift.

She opened the box and took a sharp intake of breath. Her round chocolate brown eyes glistened in the dim room. "It's perfect. How did you ...?"

"I got it over Christmas break when I was back home. Here, let me help you with it." I put the necklace around her neck and fixate on her fingers playing with the heart. I wrapped my arms around her waist. "I love you, Brie." I looked into her eyes and waited. I'd never said it before. My heart beat fast and sweat broke out along my forehead, waiting for her to answer.

Her breath caught for a moment and my stomach sank. "I love you too."

She smashed her lips to mine and we kissed passionately. It was hard to stop once we started. Heat furled down my spine, making my cock hard. We'd done just about everything but sex. I walked her toward her bed, and when the backs of her knees connected with the mattress, I lifted her thin frame in my arms and laid her on the bed.

"You need to eat. You feel too thin," I said through our heated kisses.

"Jeez! How can you think of food now?" She was wearing a T-shirt, and I pulled it over her head.

"I don't know." I gave her a quizzical look and laughed at myself before returning my attention to undressing her.

She laughed and the sound swirled through the air. I loved her laugh.

We continued to make out.

I broke the kiss again. "I know we said we'd take things all the way tonight, but we don't have to." I lay above her painfully hard. I was still determined not to turn into my asshole father who couldn't keep his dick in his pants. Maybe that was why I stayed a virgin until now. I hadn't cared for any of the girls I made out with before Brie. She was special.

"I want to. I love you. This is love. This is not what they do," she said, and it was the things she said that made me love her more.

"This is love," I agree.

I made love to Brie that night for the first time, and my world came apart. Everything I understood about my family made even less sense because I only wanted her.

CHAPTER FIFTEEN

AL

I WAKE up to find I'm spooning Sam. Her butt is in my crotch. Her short hair brushes against my face. My arm is draped across her body. I'm pretty sure our feet are entwined under the blankets. This is usually the point I realize I have had another insignificant hookup and take off. Not now. Not with her. I want to stay right where I am with my arms wrapped around her and hold her tight. Protect her from this big bad ugly world. There is something that haunts Sam. I see it so clearly in the depths of her blue eyes that at times they seem lifeless. Like she's given up hope. She may only be twenty-three years old, but she's seen the hardship of life. That much is clear. And me, well I want to make it all go away. She shifts in my arms and turns her head to look at me.

"Good morning, darling," I say because I've grown to like the fact that the folks around here call each other darling.

Sam groans and holds her head. "Oh! What the fuck did I do?" She covers her face with her hands, and she won't look at me.

"Hey, what's going on?" I ask softly, trying to hide the alarm from my voice. We had a hot kiss followed by a very intimate conversation. That's it.

"I fucked up is what happened. I made a fucking scene kissing you last night. Or should I say shoving my tongue down your throat." She snickers as if it was a bad thing.

"You don't hear me complaining, Princess." I sit up in bed and look at her. She eyes me out of the corner of her eye.

"I'm no princess." She gives me a look that says she thinks I'm crazy. "I shouldn't have kissed you like that. Don't go getting any crazy ideas." She turns to me and lifts her pointer finger close to my face.

"Um ... okay then. You're a grouch in the morning. I get it." I stand up from the bed. "I'll go get you some juice and pills." I hate seeing her feel sick, but I'm glad to have the chance to take care of her. I quickly adjust my morning wood because having her pressed up against me doesn't help my situation. She turns her head and her eyes drop to my crotch and both her eyebrows raise. Let's just say that I'm well endowed. "Sorry." I apologize, figuring it's the polite thing to do.

"Don't apologize for that," she answers and a laugh bubbles out of my chest. I nod my head and leave the room.

Trying to understand Sam is pointless. She's filled with mixed signals. I wonder how many women have had that thought about me.

Farmer Joe isn't around. I rummage through the fridge and pull out the orange juice. I grab two tall glasses and fill them to the rim. I gulp my own glass down fast. As I place my cup on the counter, I see a note addressed to Sam.

Sam,

Gone hunting. Be back before Christmas.

Dad

Farmer Joe is a man of few words, and his note isn't any different. Christmas is a week away. Which means Sam and I have this place all to ourselves for an entire week. I grab the bottle of ibuprofen sitting on top of the fridge and head back to her room with the orange juice in my other hand.

I pass her the glass of OJ. "Drink up." She nods and takes the glass from me. She swallows two pills with the juice then groans. "Shit! This is the worst part of drinking. I hate being hungover. You'd think I'd learn my lesson by now." I stand quietly and watch her. I'd like to get in her head and figure out why she does this to herself. She puked all over her truck last night. It doesn't seem like a first either. She looks up to me, waiting a beat, then says, "Aren't you gonna say anything?"

I cross my arms in front of my chest. "What is it you want me to say?"

Her lip quirks at the corner. "I don't know. Give me a lecture about drinking too much ... something."

"Sorry, babe." I shrug. "Nothing to say. Why would I want to lecture you? I don't know you all that well. I don't know why it is you drink the way you do. My best friend back home used to be on my case about drinking too much, hooking up too much. I just found his lectures annoying."

"So, you didn't stop?" She looks up to me and an emotion passes over her face. I don't know what it means.

"I'm not proud of it, but no," I admit. "You found me in a car in the middle of a snow storm, completely comatose because I took a sleeping pill. That doesn't say much about me, now does it?" I look down at her and say, "Get up. I'm going to make you breakfast." I get ready to leave the room when I remember I put the note her dad left in the pocket of my sweats. "A note from your dad. He's gone hunting."

She scoffs and crumples the note in her hand. "Look, Al, I don't want to give you the wrong impression. I'm fine if you stay here, but that kiss last night was a one-time deal."

"That's fine by me, Princess. Rest a little longer. I'll go make us some breakfast." I wink and turn out of her room. I get a week with Sam. The thought makes me happy. I just don't know what's going to happen once the week is over. She may think she's immune to my charm, but she isn't. I want to bed her, I want my face buried between her thighs. She may think last night was a one-time deal, but it won't be if I have anything to do with it.

CHAPTER SIXTEEN

SAM

WHILE AL GOES off to make breakfast, I head to the bathroom. I bring my cell phone with me since I noticed I have messages from Blake, Austin, and Mack. I listen to my voicemail first.

"Hey, babe, I wanted to make sure you're okay," Blake's raspy voice comes through the phone. I erase the message and send him a text.

Me: All good. Got a headache. Comes with the territory.

Blake: We need to talk.

Me: Soon.

Blake: Okay.

Now that Blake knows Al is staying with me, he isn't going to be pleased to say the least. He's tried to get me to commit to him many times since he came back from his short stint at college. I don't want commitment. He has no choice but to accept that.

I glance over at Austin's message. He's always been more laid back and less demanding, more supportive.

Austin: How you feeling, sunshine?

I smile, thinking about the Texas drawl he's picked up living there these past number of years. He was always a good friend. He never pressured me.

Me: Rough morning. All is good. How long you in town for?

I wait a few moments, but he doesn't answer. He probably isn't awake yet.

I read the message from my sister.

Mack: How are you? We need to discuss Christmas.

I place my phone on the counter, get undressed, and step into the warm shower.

As I recall the events of last night, I remember Austin, Blake, and Al coming face to face. That was seriously messed-up. Both Blake and Austin know about each other. I began hooking up with Blake in high school. Austin and I began hooking up after high school. Blake went off to college by then, and Austin and I had become good friends as per Mack's request. Austin is a good guy. He comes home some weekends to visit his family since they're tight-knit. He's pre-med at the University of Texas. We still hook up on occasion when he makes it home. As I rub soap all over my body, I can't help but think that none of those men get my heart racing like Al.

As I run my hands over my tired body, I get turned on thinking of Al. The shirt he wore last night was casual and fit snugly over his arms and chest, showing how defined his muscles truly were. I spotted Al at the bar before he saw me. Then we were dancing together and even though he danced like a city guy, our bodies shared a rhythm all its own. And when we kissed, I felt like I could combust. I choose the men I sleep with. I choose to stay here on the ranch with my jerk of a father. I choose to drink the alcohol I drink. What I haven't chosen is my attraction to Al. The intensity seems to have crept up on me out of nowhere. It's electric, new, and exciting, but it's more than that. When I look into his eyes, I see a man that has lost his way and it's something I can identify with. There's so much I want to know about him that it makes my head spin.

I exit the shower and head back to my bedroom, slip on a pair of yoga pants, a bra, and a white thermal shirt. The cows don't need to eat since we stocked things up yesterday, and the shit can wait. I run a brush through my hair, which takes a whole of ten seconds with my short hair, and head out to the kitchen.

Austin messages me back.

Austin: Heading back out tomorrow. You take care and try to stay out of trouble. If you need me call.

Me: Thank you XOXOXO

Austin is sweet. A part of me wants to be madly in love with him, but it just never came.

Smoke is rising from a frying pan as Al works frantically to contain it. I wrap my arms in front of my chest and a slow smile curves my lips. I figure I'll let him squirm a little before offering some help. Besides, it's a mighty fine view with him in a simple white T-shirt and dark sweatpants hanging low on his waist. He must work out a lot to have such a defined round ass.

"Oh, hey." He turns his head. "When I offered to make you breakfast, I should have mentioned I'm a terrible cook," he chuckles.

I walk over to the stove and look down at the pan. He's frying the sausages we got in the supermarket. "That doesn't look half bad, but I think they're ready." I head over to the cabinet and grab a plate. He pours them on the plate along with globs of oil.

"I tried making pancakes, but fucked up." His lips twist in a wry smile, and he shows me the plate sitting on the opposite side of the counter. I swallow hard like I have an apple lodged in my windpipe. As a little girl my favorite breakfast was links and pancakes. It's the last breakfast my mother made me the day she died. I eat pancakes and sausage but never together. I can't. Al wouldn't know any of this. He holds the charred pile of pancakes in front of me, and I don't know what happens ... I choke up. I try to hold back my sniffles. Mack knows never to give me sausage and pancakes together for breakfast, but how could Al have known? Tears begin to fill my eyes. Al is just trying to be kind and make me a nice meal. I take off toward the bedroom like a crazy girl.

I hear Al mutter to himself that he needs to learn how to cook. He thinks I'm upset he burned the pancakes. I run to my bed, throwing myself on top, as I sob into the blankets. What is wrong with me? Enough time has passed for this wound to have healed over somewhat and it has. I get by. I don't spend my days crying, that's for sure. There will always be a part of my heart that misses Mom dearly, but days go by, and I don't even think of her anymore. For some reason that thought saddens me too. A soft hand at my back pulls me from my thoughts. He's hovering above me, his presence soothing.

"I'm sorry. I'm usually not such a flaky mess," I apologize. How do I explain my reaction?

"Hey, what just happened?" he asks. "I know I need to learn how to cook better. I'm just glad I didn't burn down the kitchen because Farmer Joe would shoot me."

It dawns on me he just called my father Farmer Joe. I lift my head off the bed since I had it buried in the blanket and give him a questioning look. He looks a little wide eyed and embarrassed.

"I said that out loud didn't I?" His hand runs over his morning scruff along his jaw. It's a beautiful manly jaw.

I nod my head and burst out laughing. If Papa ever heard him calling him a farmer, he would have the shotguns out because he's a rancher not a farmer. Big fucking difference. I laugh so hard I curl into a ball, holding my belly. Al starts laughing too and comes to lie beside me on the bed. We both laugh so hard the tension releases. I finally catch my breath, and Al turns to face me on the bed. He takes a finger and swipes at my tears.

"Do you normally laugh and cry at the same time?" he asks, and his small smile is so sexy it warms my chest.

"No, I'm sorry. I'm usually not emotional at all." I pause because an awkward feeling runs over my body. I want to tell Al the reason I am so emotional. Something is wrong. I've never wanted to spill my secrets to another human the way I want to spill them now. I don't know if it's his penetrating gaze or the lonely looks we seem to share, but something hangs between us, giving me the worst case of verbal diarrhea I've ever experienced. "That was the last breakfast my mother ever made me. Pancakes and Sausage. Together," I finally croak out.

"Shit." His head drops for the briefest of moments before he picks it up and wraps both his arms around me. "I'm so sorry, Sam," he says, holding me close.

His words breathe life into my broken heart. I don't know why. I've been held by a man before, but this feels different, and it's not just his heavenly manly smell of cologne and his distinct scent. It's something else too.

"Has she been gone long?" he asks.

"Since I was nine," I answer, and he stays quiet, but I can see the balls rolling in his head. He's probably wondering how a man like Papa could ever raise a kid. "I have an older sister. She took care of me," I explain. He nods like he understands now. "Papa was the breadwinner. Mack made sure I showered and brushed my teeth."

"My nannies made sure I brushed mine. My parents didn't actually parent," he responds. It wasn't the response I was expecting, but I appreciate the fact that he doesn't pity my situation.

"They were too concerned with their social standing. Mom was the lady of the house. Her job was to look pretty and host dinner parties. My father is a business mogul. He runs a very big company." I can't help but notice that he looks away from me, moving his gaze to the window, when speaking of his father.

"That explains the fancy clothes and pointed shoes." I laugh because it's fun to play with him.

"Hey." He tackles me and begins to tickle me under my ribs. It makes me crazy, and I begin to squirm. We begin a little wrestling match.

"My pointed shoes are Prada and very much in style." He laughs, trying to pin my arms over my head.

"Whatever you say, City."

"Stop calling me that. Your father gave me that name, and I don't like it." He huffs and he finally pins my arms above my head. Somehow our wrestling match goes from playful to heated when he pauses, hovering over me. His light blue eyes hold mine. I swallow hard and his gaze drops to my lips. *I want him to kiss me, and I want to push him away all at the same time.*

"Sam?" he says my name like a question. I know he's truly asking for permission to kiss me.

"Yes?" It's a question too.

"I'm leaving soon."

"I know."

His Adam's apple bobs, and the warning look he gives me makes me think he's trying to get in my head. Good luck.

"I don't do relationships," I assure him. I told him last night wasn't going to be a repeat. Just because we tend to drift together, and there seems to be this magnetic pull between us, doesn't mean we need to pursue anything.

"And why's that?" he asks. My hands are still being held above my head. He is still hovering close. He isn't putting his full weight on me, but we are both breathing hard.

"I've never wanted to be attached to one man."

"I say the same thing about women," he retorts, and it makes the air in the room shift because in some ways I'm looking at a male version of myself.

Silence follows. He releases my hands and rolls off me to my side. I'm disappointed and relieved all at once.

"Come." He stands up from the bed. "I'm throwing those pancakes in the garbage and making you a spinach omelet." He extends his hand to me to help me up.

I don't give him my hand just yet because I need to get my

emotions in check. I try to remember what he just said. *Spinach omelet.* "Ew. Gross. That sounds too healthy."

"Don't diss it until you try it." He winks.

"You can make me a plain omelet," I concede and give him my hand. He gently pulls me up off the bed and straight into his body. He wraps his arms around me in a hug and his nose brushes into my hair. *For fuck's sake, he's wearing me down.*

"I can make you an omelet, but you need to teach me how." His voice is so deep and husky when he says it that I replace his words with *I want to fuck you till you're sore.*

I shake my head to clear my dirty thoughts. "You'd never survive in the wild."

"That's why I'm thankful you saved me." He grins, looking down at me, and it would help if his gaze didn't bounce back and forth between my eyes and lips. He hugs me even tighter then releases me.

I want to tell him I'm thankful I saved him too, but I don't because I don't want him to know that I like having him here. I don't want to tell him I feel less lonely. Guys like him run at the first sign of a girl falling for them. I know his kind because he's me. Only difference is this time I don't want to run. I want to chase. It goes against every basic instinct in my body. What I truly want is for him to chase me, because if he does, I'd be a goner and I wonder what my life would look like then. Probably better than the shit storm I live with on a daily basis.

I don't answer his comment about saving him. I just run my hand along his jaw and say, "Let's eat some food, City. I'm starving."

He nods for me to follow him, and we leave my bedroom. Our heated moment is left behind.

CHAPTER SEVENTEEN

AL

"What can we do today?" I ask, thinking we'd spend the day together. She stands up from the table and walks over to the coffee maker for more coffee. "Well, assuming you don't have plans already," I stammer because why would I assume she would spend her free time with me?

"No, I don't really have plans. Sometimes I meet friends at the diner for lunch on Saturdays and hang out. I need to take the tractor to Slims and get it checked out. I'm pretty sure Papa didn't have a chance to get it fixed before he left," she says. I would have thought her dad might have mentioned that I fixed it, but he obviously didn't.

"Oh ... uh ... the tractor is fixed," I say curtly.

Her brows dip and she smiles. "What do you mean?"

"I fixed it."

She laughs. "No ... seriously."

"I did. I swear." I lift my left hand.

"No offence but how would you know how to fix a tractor?" she asks, and I contemplate how to answer that. I like being a no one in this little town, being respected for who I am and the work

I do and not immediately judged because of my last name, which I know I should have changed a long time ago.

"Well, my dad owns a plant that manufactures tractors. I know shit about cars, but talk to me about a fried shaft, calibrating, improper maintenance, and lack of lubrication ... I'm your guy."

She cocks a brow, and I realize I said lubrication.

"Get your head out of the gutter," I scoff playfully.

She laughs.

"Okay, don't. Trust me, I make sure a woman is well ready before I enter her." I raise my brows.

"You have a dirty mouth." She laughs and the apples of her cheeks turn a healthy red.

"I do," I admit, enjoying this playful side to her.

"I would say to put your money where your mouth is, but I am not going down that road with you. I've got a full plate." She smiles and pours some milk in her coffee.

"That's too bad." I cross my arms over my chest and smile widely. Sam shakes her head. She thinks I'm kidding around with her, even though I'd be happy to show her exactly how wet I can make her.

"Well, thanks, Al. I mean, you need to tell us what we owe you for the parts and your work," she stammers a little.

"I owe you, not the other way around," I answer.

"Those parts are expensive."

My lips form a thin line kind of like hers do when I talk about repayment. "Sam, not happening. I'm grateful to be of use around here. Let's leave it at that."

"Okay." She smiles.

The phone on the kitchen wall rings, and Sam lifts her pointer finger telling me to hold on a second.

"Hey, Mack," she says into the phone. I know now that's her older sister. "Yeah, that's great ... no he went hunting. Said he'd be back for Christmas ... I know, right. 'Kay, looking forward to seeing you all ... Yup, say hi to them for me and give them hugs." She hangs up the phone and comes back to the table where she sits across from me.

"That was Mack, my older sister. She's coming to town for Christmas with my nephew and her girlfriend, Autumn." She pauses. "I'm guessing you need to be with your family. And your car isn't ready ..." She bites her lip. "We have an airport in Grand Junction. You can always fly out to them and then come back and get your car ... or wait." She shrugs her shoulders, and I know we should have had this conversation already, but she didn't bring it up and I was happy staying put. "You said your sister has a cabin not too far from here. Were you headed there for the holidays?" It's the first time she's inquiring about my plans. She's talking fast too, not waiting for me to get an answer in. Is this her way of getting rid of me? Maybe I over did it with the sex talk.

I run my hand over my hair. It feels like my short buzz is growing out. I'm searching for words right now that basically say I don't want to leave.

"Uh, I hadn't thought about Christmas really," I lie, but I can't come out and say I want to stay right here. "Originally, the plan was to hang with my sister Izzy at the family cabin. She texted me this morning to say she's expecting more company up there for the holidays. Her boyfriend and another couple ..." I pause and let the rest of my sentence sit on my tongue, contemplating whether I invite myself to stay here or leave. The Belmonts clearly have their issues, but they aren't as fucked-up as the Walshes. I bet they know how to do Christmas right.

"Truth is, I thought I'd hang here at least until my car is ready. I understand if I've overstayed my welcome. You've been more than kind to me. I can find myself a hotel in Grand Junction," I continue to mutter while staring at her. She looks uneasy and my stomach feels like it's bottomed out. What the hell am I doing? I don't even recognize myself right now.

"No, um ... I'm sorry," she murmurs. "I don't mean to be

kicking you out. I just figured it would be a full house around here, and I didn't think you were up for that ... I mean, I don't know what your family does for Christmas ... I figured they'd want you around." Her teeth dig into her lower lip as she holds on to her coffee mug. It isn't a full-out invitation that's for sure. I'm disappointed.

"I haven't spoken to my family in over ten years. I stay in touch with my sister because she's young and has nothing to do with the reasons I don't talk to them. Normally, I spend Christmas with my friend Colton and his father back in Chicago ..." I explain, standing up from the kitchen table. I take my dirty plate and Sam's too.

"You don't have to." She begins to stand.

"Please, sit. Let me do the dishes. I want to." I smirk because what is going on with me? What are these words coming out of my mouth?

Her lips turn up slowly and a warmth radiates from her eyes. She exhales softly. "Thank you." She leans back in her chair, looking a little more relaxed. Her small reaction to me helping out tells me that she probably has to do everything herself most of the time.

"Colton ... he's your best friend, right?" she asks.

"Yeah, he's moving to Washington State with his girlfriend. His life is a little hectic right now," I answer, avoiding the small print of Colton giving up his job as governor.

She nods her head.

"And what do you do for work?" she inquires.

"I'm actually out of work right now." I nod and swallow, knowing I'm not being very forthcoming with information about myself. Maybe it's because I want a woman—no, I want Sam to get to know me as a person and not as Chief of Staff or a Walsh.

I head over to the coffee pot, wishing there was something a little stronger to add to my coffee even though it's early in the morning. I spot one of Farmer Joe's bottles of Jim Beam.

"You think your father would mind if I took a little of his Jim Beam?" My lip quirks on one side. I'm hopeful, but by the look on her face, I know it isn't happening.

"It's rare he leaves a bottle just lying around, and he probably has a mark on it measuring how much he has left. I don't suggest it." She's still sitting on a chair at the kitchen table and pulls her knees up to her chest and just looks at me for a moment then asks, "Why do you want to drink Jim Beam this early anyway?" Her gaze practically melts through me, and there's a challenge in her tone. The words she doesn't speak are "You saw me get loaded last night. You know I get loaded sometimes because I have my reasons for doing so, but what are your reasons?" I may also just be reading into her question.

I nod, disappointed, and walk over to the kitchen table and fall back into a chair. "I guess thinking of my ex job and old life makes me want to drink. I have to find something to do with myself." Admitting that at thirty-five, a time in my life where I should be established and I'm not, really hits me.

"Well, it seems like you've got money. What are you worried about?" she asks, and she makes it sound simple. She can't understand that growing up the way I did, in a high society family, means high expectations. When I walked away from my family, I hoped I could show them I would succeed on my own.

"I've got some money, yeah, but if I don't find a job soon, it'll run out." She nods her head like she understands what I've said.

"I keep telling myself all we need is one good year here on the ranch and I'll leave. I just need Papa to make enough money to pay for help. I want to go to school. Problem is the years go by and things aren't getting any better around here." She nods. "I promised my mama I'd leave this ranch, and here I am working just as hard as she did. And for what? This ranch has been in my papa's family going on third generation now. He won't give up on it. I'm not sure why I don't just give up on him," she declares, and I wasn't expecting her to spill her truths to me but she has.

"You're probably scared of failure. I can relate." I huff. "My entire career I've remained in the shadows because I'm scared of failing in front of my family." I look her straight in the eyes, and she looks back at me. I can see my words have resonated.

"It fucking sucks to admit you're scared of failure. Doesn't it?" She pauses. "And I've failed so much, Al, I can't fail anymore." Her voice cracks and her words gut me. I place my hand over hers, and she gives me a small smile.

There isn't much left to say other than we both need to stop being scared but who wants to stop when it's so much easier than putting yourself out there and failing. "Back to Christmas," I say, my palm resting on her hand. "I'd like to stay."

"Why?" she looks at me and doesn't get it.

"Because I like your small town." I swallow hard again, scared to speak my truth. I'm a fucking coward. She looks me right in the eye, and her silence tells me she thinks so too.

"Okay, stay for Christmas," she says, and I think she agrees because she's a good person who doesn't want to put a stranger on the street, but when I look down to her hands they are shaking like she's scared of something. I want to tell her I'm scared too. I'm pretty sure we both look like we just took a plunge and discovered the water below is freezing. It may be frigid, but I won't let her regret this. I'm going to make sure I heat the damn waters for her. Make her feel warm and cozy.

"Good. It's settled, then. Is Farmer Joe going to shoot me?" I ask, trying to keep a straight face. I'm partially trying to break the tension radiating between us and partially trying to figure out if I will truly die.

My comment buys me a huge bout of laughter. "Maybe."

"Let's go get dressed and buy us a Christmas tree, then," I say, and I don't know where it comes from because I've never bought a Christmas tree in my life. My family had one delivered every year. It was a tall massive tree that was professionally decorated and sat in the grand foyer of the family mansion. The only thing I can think of is the Christmas movie I watched in the last hotel I stayed at; the couple went out and bought a Christmas tree together. It seems like something I would want to share with Sam.

"A Christmas tree?" she asks with confusion. "We haven't had a Christmas tree in this house for a long time. We make fun of papa because he's so much like the Grinch."

I laugh. "That's funny. I can totally see why you'd say that. We're on, then? Is there a place you know of to get a tree?" I ask, feeling like a little boy. My excitement surprises me, but my heart is beating fast and my blood is pumping hard. For the first time in a long time my emotions don't feel fucked-up.

"Yeah, I know of a place." Apparently, my excitement is infectious because Sam stands up beside me and rocks on her heels. Her own smile now stretches from cheek to cheek, and that distant look in her eyes is nowhere to be seen.

"Good. Let's go get dressed." I walk toward her room. We take a few quick steps, and I stop. "This is weird."

"Yup," she agrees, like she knows what I'm talking about.

"We've been sleeping in the same bed now for what four nights?"

"Five," she corrects me.

"Now we are going to get changed in the same room," I state the very awkward facts, but circumstance has placed us both right here, right now in this situation.

"I know it's freaking weird. I barely know you. You're living in my house, sharing my bed, and you've seen my backside. Trust me, I've thought about our peculiar situation. I tell myself not to over think it, but how can I not?" She seems nervous.

"Sam?" I ask and she pauses. "I want to kiss you." She already looks like prey ready to make a run for it, but I can't stop myself now. I turn to face her and take her hand into mine. We stare deeply into each other's eyes. The moment is sweet and romantic.

"Al," she says my name, and I stop drifting toward her. "You're too old for me." I pause and my heart misses a beat. Fuck me.

"Al?" she says my name again, but I'm too stunned to answer. "I'm just kidding. Kiss me."

I release a breath, and my heart begins to beat rapidly. I press my lips to hers, slowly at first. A warm feeling spreads through my chest as she kisses me back, her warms lips pliant and welcoming. Our lips move together in an effortless motion. I try to take things slow with her, but she moans as my tongue coaxes her mouth open and her lips part. She tastes heavenly and sweet. My body stirs in an unfamiliar way. This isn't blind passion or lust. There is a deeper connection between us that I'm only just beginning to figure out. As we kiss, I wrap my arms around her waist. Her hands come up to my hair, and she runs her fingers through my buzz cut. When she does, a throaty groan escapes me. She moans into my mouth and the vibration shoots straight to my groin. I have no control over where my thoughts wander, but I need to slow this kiss because I like and respect Sam.

As much as I want to take her back to her bedroom and have my way with her, I can't—even if I believe she'd be willing. The reason I can't take her is not even for my own self-interest, it's more for hers. I think Sam likes to fuck because it feels good. It's the same reason I like to fuck around, but by kissing her, I've realized something new. I like her. I want to get to know her. If I take her to bed now, I may not get the chance. I don't know if she feels the same way, but if she does, then we need to explore it and not ruin it. It's the oddest time to remember something you told your best friend eons ago, but my own voice rings in my head: *Even great men fall.* I made fun of my best friend as he was falling hopelessly in love with his girlfriend. It was a jackass move I know. I'd been in love before but love was for fools. I promised myself I'd never fall in love again which means right now with Sam I'm totally screwed.

CHAPTER EIGHTEEN

SAM

AL DRIVES my truck a good twenty miles over to Groves Nursery since I'm feeling like crap from my hangover and am not in the mood to drive. We don't say much to each other along the drive. It isn't uncomfortable. I'm in deep thought after that hot kiss, which completely rocked my world. He also doesn't mention my car smelling like puke, which is an added bonus because I'm embarrassed. This beautifully broken man, who basically admitted to me he's a player, is getting under my skin. If I were anywhere close to normal, I'd be running in the opposite direction. I'm not normal, though. I use men like he uses women.

But that kiss ... when our lips connected ... just thinking about it makes my heart pump fast, filling my chest with warmth. He knows what he's doing with that tongue. It feels too hot in this truck as I think about it, the way it slowly melted the ice that's been built around my heart and caused ice chips to slowly crack off in small bits, reminding me that just maybe I am capable of falling hard for a man. The sign for Groves Nursery pops into my vision.

"Shit! Make a quick right," I holler as I snap out of my daze.

"Huh? When?" Al looks at me then back to the road. He's

about to miss the entrance.

"Now!" I practically scream it.

He takes a sharp right and the tires slightly skid against the snow on the ground.

"Sorry." I blow out a breath.

Al gives me a look that says I almost killed us.

"Don't look at me like that," I snap, but I'm not really angry. How could I be? He's so handsome, kind, helpful, funny, sexy. Shit, it's a long list. I wonder what Mack, Autumn, and Ethan will think of him. Will he be Mack approved? She might think he's too old for me. And look at me thinking this way ... I've got to stop. He's leaving soon.

He leans in and kisses me. Just like that. I kiss him back. How am I supposed to stop thinking about him when he touches me like this? His thumb comes up and brushes my cheek softly. He has big manly hands, so of course I wonder about the size of his dick. It's a completely normal thought in my abnormal brain. I let out a sigh. He pulls away and looks into my eyes.

"I need to stop kissing you, but I can't." His lips brush against mine, and it takes everything in me not to wrap my arms around his neck and pull him closer. I need control. I stop the kiss, and he turns away and shuts off the truck.

I follow him outside. He takes my hand and we enter the nursery. I didn't take him for a guy that holds a girl's hand. I sure as hell never walked hand in hand with Blake or Austin.

"There are so many trees. How do we choose?" He looks back at me. He's wearing a pair of stylish running shoes and walking through the snow.

"I don't know, but we better choose fast or your toes will snap off," I comment, looking down at his feet. I can see the leather of his shoes is wet, which means it's only a matter of time before the snow soaks through.

My comment buys me a wide smile. It makes my stomach flutter because he's even hotter when he smiles.

"What is it with you and my shoes? After we buy a tree, you're taking me to buy proper winter boots and a pair of work boots too. I plan on working beside you while I'm here."

I love every word that has come out of his mouth ... except the last three.

"Sure thing, City." I wink. He bends down and rolls the snow in his hands. I see that he's forming a snowball. "Hell no. You don't want to get into a snowball fight with me," I warn, reaching down to roll some snow. He whips a ball at my head. It's cool and disintegrates in my hair and my face.

"See, that's where you're wrong. I actually enjoyed that very much," he says with a shit-eating grin. He begins to run away from me. The front of this place is lined with rows of Christmas trees. The place had great reviews on Google. I can see why. They have a great selection of trees in all sizes. My competitive side goes into overdrive as I charge after Al with a very large snowball in my fist. I get within a few feet of him and throw as hard as I can. It hits him in the center of his chest, but he's wearing a jacket so I need to do better. He disappears around a corner. There are people walking around, looking for trees. Some families and some couples. I've never gone to buy a tree in my life. It's actually more fun than I thought it would be. Or maybe it's just Al is making this fun. With a newly formed snowball in my hand, I search him out. My hands are freezing cold from touching the snow, and my fingers are turning purple, but I want to get him back. He declared war when he got me in the face.

I look around but I can't find him. I hear his voice call "Sam." I turn around. Somehow he managed to get behind me. Exactly how is beyond me. As I turn and receive a snowball to the face again, he takes off before I can retaliate.

I run after him, screaming, "Asshole," then think better of it with all the kids running around too. "I'm gonna get you back. You can bet your butt on it," I holler. I finally reach him, and I draw my hand back to throw and bam! He lets me get him square on the cheek. "That isn't fair." I huff and place both my hands on my hips.

Before I know what's happening, he's charging toward me. He wraps his arms around my waist, lifting me up, and then drops me softly into a pile of snow. "Hell no," I scream with my arms flailing beside me as I try to break loose. His cool hands slide underneath my jacket and shirt, and he tickles my warm skin. I begin to wiggle beneath him, but he doesn't stop. He's just lying beside me in a snowbank, tickling me to death. And I'm squirming and laughing. That is until I hear someone calling my name.

"Sam. Sam Belmont, is that you?" the voice says, and I would know that voice because it's the voice of my best friend Kell. Only she's looking at me like she doesn't know me as she crouches down to get a look at my face. She looks between me and Al. "Nice to see you again, Al," she says, smiling wide. Al and I begin to straighten ourselves out and stand up. As we both brush all the snow off our bodies, I realize that Gage is standing in front of us, and he has Theo in his arms. He looks a little dumbfounded too.

"Hey, Theo. Give Auntie Sam a kiss," I say, my chest rising and falling from the exertion of wrestling Al. I blow Theo a kiss. Theo smacks his hand to his mouth and kisses it, which tells me he's trying to kiss me back.

"Sorry. Hey, Gage." Al steps forward to shake Gage's free hand.

"Um, I'm surprised to see you here," I say to Kell as I continue to brush the snow off my pants. It doesn't help that Kell is looking at me like I'm alien, although I can't blame her. I'm usually anything but playful.

"Hey there, little man." Al looks to Theo and gives him a little handshake. It throws me off. I wouldn't expect him to be the kind of guy that's good with kids.

"Nah! We buy our Christmas trees here every year," she answers, giving me a knowing look and then turning to Gage and eyeing him, which seems to be code for something I don't know. He gives her a warm smile.

"We sure do. They have the best selection," Gage chimes in, looking between Al and me like he's pleased. I didn't know this place existed before an hour ago or that this was something families did. I speak with Kell every single day. She never mentioned once, in all our years of friendship, going to buy a Christmas tree. It gives me a sinking feeling in my stomach. Did she feel like she had to hide this from me because my family doesn't do Christmas trees?

"You two are looking comfortable." Kell smiles and nods her head. "Haven't seen my girl laugh like that since grade school." She raises both of her brows, clearly talking about me but looking to Al.

I give her the stink eye, hoping she will shut the hell up, but no, Kell continues. "Glad to see you're putting a smile on her face, and if I might say, you are looking much better too, Al. Smitten in fact." I'm glad the cool air and snow caused my cheeks to turn red because I'm pretty darn sure I'm blushing hard.

My mouth drops open as I wonder when the last time was that Kell used the word smitten. I get that she wants the best for me. I don't know that embarrassing the hell out of me is gonna help.

"Okay ... yeah ..." I mutter. I need to get away from them before they reveal every one of my secrets to Al. "Well ... you guys enjoy your tree shopping. We are going to choose a tree too." I take hold of Theo's little hand. It feels so soft. "Bye bye, Theo." I wave with my other hand. Al waves too.

Theo waves back. I turn and take Al's hand. "Let's go. You all take care," I shout out as I walk away with Al, pulling him in the opposite direction. I can still hear Kell whisper-shout to Gage, "She took his hand. She took his hand." I roll my eyes and act as if I didn't hear, but when I look up to Al, that shit-eating grin from earlier has returned with a vengeance.

CHAPTER NINETEEN

AL

SAM HOPS out of the truck and walks to the back like she's getting ready to pick up this massive tree.

"No way," my voice booms. "I don't care how strong you are."

She gives me a smirk. "I picked you up the night you passed out in your car. Shoved you up that hill. I think I can handle a tree." She continues to open the bed of the truck.

"How about you carry my new boots and I carry the tree." I suggest, thinking compromise is always good. By the look she has on her face, she doesn't think it's a compromise. She looks offended.

She stalks up to me and raises her chin, looking me straight in the eyes. "You don't tell a cowgirl what she can and cannot do." She places both her hands to rest on her waist.

I don't have a comeback. "You're sexy when you're pissed," I say, staring deep into her eyes. I don't know what else to say, and it's the truth.

She huffs. "How about you carry it all into the house." She turns and walks away, and I watch that fine ass of hers sway until she hits the front door, whips it open, then slams it shut after her. I can't wipe the smile I have off my face. She is definitely stubborn. I've never had so much fun spending time with a lady before in my life. After we left the tree nursery, we went to a hardware shop to buy ornaments and a tree stand to decorate the tree. Then we went boot shopping.

I grab the tree and haul it through the front door, grateful Sam didn't lock it. "Where do you want it?" I ask.

She points to a place in front of the fireplace.

"That doesn't seem like a good place."

"Why not?" Her brows dip and her voice comes out as a whine. It's adorable.

"Because if we make a fire in the fireplace, the tree can catch fire," I state the obvious.

"We don't use the fireplace, Sherlock," she answers, as if I should have known this. The fact that she calls me Sherlock makes my blood pump faster, and every feeling I have right now is heading south.

"Maybe we should start. I'm freezing to death." My words buy me a smile. I don't know why. "Are you happy I'm freezing?" I ask, not understanding.

"Well, no one told you to get into a snowball fight with me with no gloves or boots for that matter," she scoffs, but her anger isn't real. She likes to spar with me, that's all.

I place the tree on the floor upright, away from the fireplace to the side of the main living area. "I have boots now," I remind her, lifting one leg in the air.

"Yeah, with that new puffy jacket and those boots, you look like your average mountain man," she snickers, standing off to the side, her eyes raking over my body. Her own visceral reaction is transparent.

"And do you find you're attracted to mountain men?" I wiggle my brows.

She looks at her unpolished fingernails. "Not really. I like my men slick and straight from the city." She winks. Her words make my dick hard, and then she walks off and straight out the front door.

"Where are you going?" I shout out after her.

"To get the ornaments and the rest of the bags." She shouts back. She's too much. A handful, a spitfire, kind and sweet. She's everything. I take my boots and jacket off, more relieved than ever that Farmer Joe decided to take that hunting trip. Sam walks in with the rest of our bags and drops them on the couch. I notice a pile of wood next to the old stone fireplace.

"Mind if I make us a fire?" I ask.

She shrugs. "Sure, go right ahead." She dumps all the ornaments on the couch and sifts through them. I scratch my head a little then place a few logs in the fireplace. I have a gas fireplace in my condo, so I have no clue how to make a fire in a real fireplace. She pauses to look at me. "You don't know how to start that fire, do you?" she asks, but it looks like she already knows the answer to that question.

"How about you start the fire, and I make us dinner?" I offer.

She purses her lips together. "Can you handle dinner? Because you burned breakfast." She starts cracking up. For some reason I feel like we are an old couple with our banter.

"Very funny. I was going to put those steaks we bought in the oven to broil, and I figured I'd throw in a couple of potatoes to bake alongside the steak." Nothing too extravagant but a meal nonetheless.

"Hmm. That sounds very gourmet," she says sarcastically. "Okay. You got a deal." She smiles and gets to work on the fire. Even though I'm pulling steaks out of the fridge, I turn my head and check out her ass as she leans over. She wears these very fitted jeans, and today she has a little white tank top underneath her flannel shirt which shows a lot of cleavage. Especially since she left the first few buttons open.

By the time I have the steak and potatoes cooking in the oven,

Sam has the fire going. It's frigid outside. The house never feels warm and comfy, but with the fire going, my bones defrost a bit.

"Food should take about half an hour," I say.

"You say that like you know what you're talking about." She walks over to the couch and takes a seat.

"I do know what I'm talking about. Popping a steak in the oven is one of my go-to meals. I can actually make it for myself even though I tend to eat most of my meals out of the house."

"Isn't that super unhealthy?" she asks. I take a seat beside her on the couch. Sitting beside her, along with the warmth of the fire, feels nice.

"Not where I dine. Most of the food is very healthy, made by top-notch chefs."

"Of course." She turns her head away from me.

"Hey ..." I tilt her chin toward me. "What's this all about?"

"Nothing. Just a reminder how different we are."

"That's funny, because I always get this eerie feeling that we're so much alike," I say, and I can't help it when my lips drift toward her. I want to have sex with her so badly right now. Spread those fine legs of hers ... have her on all fours with that fine ass up in the air ... I have to stop my thoughts and focus on simpler things, like her lips.

I lean forward, getting into her space, as she leans her head away from me, only she isn't moving further away; she is just lying back on a pillow on the couch. "I'm having very dirty thoughts right now," I say as my lips linger close to hers.

"Would you care to enlighten me?" I sense the heat in her eyes. I take note of her fast breaths.

"I would very much like to. I need to make sure you know that when my car is ready, I need to leave." I feel like I'm repeating myself. A warning to her that truly feels more like a warning to myself.

"Al, I want you now I probably won't want you tomorrow. I

wouldn't grow a conscience about leaving." Her tone is sweet like honey but lacks emotion. Her words irk me.

"Okay." I'm thinking with my dick when I lunge for her lips, and she accepts my hunger, grabbing me by the back of the head with both her hands, running her fingers through my hair and kissing the shit out of me. Our bodies press together and everything moves fast. Her breasts push into me. My kisses linger down her neck as my hands work the buttons of her flannel shirt. When I've opened all the buttons, she lifts up a little and helps me remove the shirt. She's left in a white tank top. Her bra is lace so I can see her rose colored nipples hard and peeking through the fabric. I take one of her breasts in my hand and knead it roughly. She moans and we kiss some more as her hands come to the hem of my shirt and she pulls it over my head. Her breath hitches when she looks at my bare chest. I remove her camisole, and as I do, she works on my belt, unbuttoning and unzipping my jeans and pushing them over my ass. I stand to shrug out of my pants. She stands and gets to work taking off her jeans. Both of our chests heave with the exertion of lust coursing through our veins. While she takes her jeans off her ankles, I toss a few of the throw blankets on the floor and open them up, making a little makeshift bed with pillows around. With the fire burning in the background, the room is warm and the atmosphere oozes sex and romance.

We stand in front of each other and stare for a brief moment before we get tangled up in another hot kiss. I tongue her and ravish her sweetness. I lift her up in my arms and she lets out a squeal. I kneel and lay her head down on the pillow. She looks beautiful and sinful. I try to tell myself to stop all this. She is too young, too kind. She's hurting and if I sleep with her, I'm taking something from her that I don't deserve, but before I can even consider the voice of reason running through my mind, I'm hovering above her and she pulls me toward her and begins to kiss the hell out of me again. This time our bodies line up, the swell of her breasts rubbing against my skin. I reach behind her back and unclasp her bra. She pulls it off and my mouth is on her, suckling her nipples as she arches her back and pushes into my mouth. With my other hand, I knead her breast and she presses her hips into my very hard cock. She spreads her legs and as much as I want to take things slow, there is no chance right now. I remove her panties and throw them off to the side.

"Shit." She lifts her head and her eyes are wide.

"What?" I ask through heavy breathes.

"You just threw my panties in the fire."

"Fuck." I chuckle. "I'll buy you a new pair." Before she has anything else to say, I finger her and her head falls back. Now isn't the time to talk about me melting her panties.

I insert another finger and begin to pump. Soft moans come from her pink lips. She's so wet and tight, clenching around my fingers. Her responsiveness to me drives me crazy. As I continue to pump her, she pushes my boxers down my ass. Her hands cup my ass before she moves to my front and takes my cock in her hand. Her hands stroke torturously, up and down, stopping at the crown. She rubs her thumb over some pre-cum.

"I'm on the pill but considering you told me you get around a lot, a condom is best," she says.

I need to clarify. "I'm clean. I just had a checkup, and I'm always safe. I always use condoms but let me grab one from my jeans," I say, and I know how that looks that I walk around with a condom in my pocket, but I say it like it is. I can't hide who I am.

She places her palm on my chest and says. "It's okay. If you say you're clean, I trust you."

"Are you sure?" I'm trying to think straight, but her pussy is dripping wet and she lies beneath me with her legs spread, and I want in.

"Yes." She nods, and I reach down and claim her lips again. While we kiss the hell out of each other, I reach down and roll her nub to make sure she's still wet and ready to accommodate my large cock. She moans and rolls her hips, so I pull my finger away and decide to tease her with my cock instead. I rub my crown along her opening, slipping in a little then pulling out. It drives her crazy and makes me mad with lust. Her wetness coats my cock, and I can't take it anymore. I slide right in and move. She lets out a gasp followed by moaning. She feels tight and warm. Again, I want to move slowly, but it isn't happening because her hips gyrate against me. I move to her rhythm as she rubs herself along my girth. She curses and squirms, and I pick up speed.

"Fuck yes, oh yeah ... oh ... that feels soooo good." Her voice with that accent makes me blind with lust. I'm a caveman with basic instincts. My purpose is to get us both off. Only it doesn't take much effort because as I pick up the pace, she begins to detonate. Hearing her sweet moans makes me come like a tsunami. I pump into her, hard and fast. Sweat breaks out over my body as I pour my seed into her. Her body is slick with sweat, and her breasts bounce with the force of my thrusts. When I've blown my load, my head falls into the crook of her neck, and I inhale her sweet scent as I try to catch my breath and get my bearings. I've never gone bareback before. Holy hell that was intense. I don't think it's the only thing that made the sex feel off the charts.

"You good?" I ask into the crook of her neck.

"Yeah," she answers softly. I pick up my head and lay a kiss on her lips. Then I fall back beside her, looking up to the ceiling. The fire crackles in front of us. It's dark outside now. With the red glow of the fire radiating over her body, she looks angelic. I take her in my arms and hold her warm body against mine. "Al?" she looks up to me.

"Yeah?" I smile.

"Somethings burning," she says, and it's not what I'm expecting. My eyes go round as I remember leaving the steaks in the oven on a high broil.

"Fuck." I fly up to my feet and Sam does too. We are in the main area of her house, both of us buck naked, as we charge for the stove.

"I'll get the gloves," she shouts as I open the oven door and smoke fills the kitchen.

"I completely forgot about the steaks broiling." Sam reaches into the oven and places the pan on the stove. The whole kitchen is filled with smoke. The steaks look charred and so do the potatoes. "Sorry, your oven must be a lot hotter than the one I have back home." My lip curls on one corner.

"It's just really old. It doesn't cook evenly," she explains. Then she looks to the front door and wraps her arms around her body to cover herself. "We better clean up and get some clothes on. Never know who can drop by."

"Right."

We head back to the family room and gather our clothes. I fold the blankets back up and place them on the couch.

I follow Sam back to her room. "Is there anywhere we can get a steak dinner around here? I'd like to take you out."

"Yeah, there's a nice place in Grand Junction we can go to." She smiles. We get into her room and my gaze drops to her fine behind. My hand follows, and I cup her ass.

"Sorry, I should clean up. That all happened so fast I have cum running down my legs." She chuckles and pulls away.

I shake my head. "Lean forward and put your hands on the bed," I say, and she listens.

Placing her palms on the bed, her fine ass up in the air, I stand behind her and caress her cheeks. I watch as her breathes quicken. I lean forward and curl over her body, using both my hands first to knead her breasts, then I slowly move down her body. We are both a mess from the sex we just had, but there's nothing hotter than dirty sex or seeing my cum running down her legs.

From this angle, I wrap my arm around her waist and cup her

sex. She lets out the slightest of moans just from my touch. I smile, but she can't see it since she's facing the other direction. With one of my fingers, I use the wetness and move it up to her nub and down to her opening. I begin with soft slow strokes, just enjoying the feel of her in my hands. She starts to build, and I continue with the same strokes, only now I finger her too, pushing deep then pulling back and rubbing her nub in a slow, sweet circle. She begins to moan and her head falls as she takes in the pleasure I bring her. She moves back a bit and presses her ass into my cock, and it's my turn to groan. She continues in that little bouncing rhythm as I finger her and rub her clit. She moves against my hand.

"Al," she rasps into the darkness of the room.

I don't answer. I know exactly what she needs. I bend my knees and use my hand to guide my cock inside her. When I enter her, she gasps, and I let out a guttural groan as her sex clenches around me. My body curls around her from behind and my arm wraps around her so I can roll her clit while I thrust inside her.

"Fuck! You feel like heaven," I groan as I pull out of her almost all the way before slamming back inside.

She hisses. She's building fast. So responsive.

Her moans float through the room, filling the air with ecstasy as we move to a rhythm all our own. I don't know what's happening, but I can't seem to get enough of Sam, and it isn't only her pussy. I increase the speed. I rub and thrust into her, deeper and harder, and she curses, detonating like a bomb.

I fall with her, coming hard and fast, as her sweet pussy milks the last drop of my cum. Her hands give out on her, and she falls forward onto the bed.

"Let me grab you a towel," I say, and before she can answer, I leave the room for the bathroom. I take a clean towel and turn the tap on until the water runs warm. I clean myself off then take a new towel back to her room.

She's lying naked on the bed, staring out the window. My chest warms. She must sense me watching her because she turns to me when I enter the room, and I kneel on the bed and spread her legs. She doesn't speak as she watches me take care of her, running the towel slowly from her ankles, moving up her thighs, to her pussy and back down. I fall on the bed beside her and wrap her in my arms, discarding the towel onto the floor. My nose presses into her hair. I take in the floral scent.

"What are you thinking?" I whisper. She looks blissful, but her eyes seem distant like she is in a faraway land.

"Not much," She forces a smile, and it irks me she's closing down. "Come, let's get dressed. I'm starving. You must be too." She shifts off my chest and walks over to her closet without saying a word.

I sigh. I just tried to get closer to her, and she pulled away. We get dressed quietly and head out to dinner. Only Sam isn't present with me like she was when we were buying the Christmas tree. She's retreated somewhere inside her head, and I want nothing more than to bring her back to me.

CHAPTER TWENTY

AL

Past

BRIE STAYED in Europe for the summer with her mom. Her parents' divorce was being drawn out in the courts. Her father hadn't come to visit once since we started school last September. She didn't say anything, but I knew it bothered her. I knew what it felt like to have a parent that didn't give a shit.

I went home for the summer, spending most of it at a sleep-over camp in upstate New York. I'd been hit on a lot. Some of the girls were pretty too, but none of them held a match to Brie. We decided even though we were apart we would stay together.

Now we were back at school and everything went back to normal—except for Brie. She started drinking way too much at the forest parties. I had a feeling she was doing drugs too, even though she didn't admit it to me. As close as we were, I felt her drifting away.

"Hey. How about I come back to your dorm after the party," I suggested, wrapping my arms around her waist. It was October of our senior year. The weather was cooling so the forest parties would end soon. I hadn't made it out to many because I was busy doing school work. Brie had returned to school before classes began in August and was hanging out with some of the students who remain here all year.

"Sounds nice." She laughed. She had a perma smile plastered on her face all night. She kissed me hard and ran away to an area where a bunch of people were dancing to techno music. I didn't really develop a taste for that kind of music even though it was huge in Europe.

I went off to hang out with a bunch of the guys. Brie and I had been intimate since I returned to school. Everything seemed great between us, so I didn't understand why she was pulling away tonight.

By two in the morning I was tired and thinking of classes tomorrow. I went over to Brie, who couldn't seem to stop dancing. She acknowledged me but held out her finger while she chugged down a bottle of water.

"You want to walk back with me?" I asked her.

"Not really." She laughed and bounced out of breath.

My stare narrowed in on her dilated eyes, and I saw it ... She must have taken something. Ecstasy had been popular and I suspected she was high on it. She wrapped her arms around my neck and hopped up on me, wrapping her legs around my waist. I was shocked. Brie was never into PDAs. "Let's go by the trees and fuck," she said into my mouth. We'd done that before at a party when we were both drunk and it was fun and carefree, but this felt different.

She began to rub herself on me and my cock grew hard. "Dammit, Brie. Take it easy," I hissed. We were around a lot of the guys and some of them started to shout out obscenities. I didn't like it. I felt protective of her.

"Why? I need you, Al. Please," she pleaded, and I knew it must be the drugs making her feel hot and heavy. I hated that she took the drugs but knew better than to lecture her while high. I also didn't want her getting off with anyone when she wasn't in her right mind. I took her deeper into the forest and kissed her breathless.

She was unbuttoning my jeans and pulling my cock out before I had a chance to gather my thoughts. She dropped to her knees and sucked me briefly, her mouth suction strong and harsh. I was coming apart at the seams. "Brie, wait." I knew I had to get her off before I lost it. I took off the jacket I was wearing and motioned for her to lie on it so she wouldn't scratch up her back. She lowered herself to the ground, and I took the condom out of my pocket.

"Al, please. Hurry." She began to rub herself and it was the hottest thing I'd ever seen. She was clearly uninhibited tonight because the Brie I knew was shy even when we were intimate.

"Jesus," I hissed. I was going to lose my shit watching her. She began to moan from touching herself. I got on the ground, taking a deep breath, and thrust inside her. "You are so wet." I moved in and out of her. She placed her hands on my ass and urged me to go faster. She came apart screaming my name. When we were done, she wanted me to go again, but I needed some recuperation time. She stood up and started to dance while I lay there watching her.

I didn't take me long to get hard again, and when I did, I had sex with Brie. She orgasmed like a bomb being set off. I ended up staying at the party till the break of dawn just to watch out for her. We fucked three times that night. In the morning I sneaked into her dorm and missed my classes as I watched her sleep and come down from her high.

Something was bothering her and she wasn't sharing it with me. It hurt because we always shared stuff about our families and shit that bothered us. Why was it that she couldn't share with me now?

CHAPTER TWENTY-ONE

SAM

WE'RE SEATED at our table, and the waiter comes up to take our order.

"I'll have the sixteen ounce steak with a baked potato and steamed vegetables." Al smiles, but I can tell he's on edge.

The waiter turns his attention to me. "What can I get you, miss?" He grins, holding his order pad in his hand.

"I'll have the same as him." I tilt my chin to Al.

"And would you like some wine with your meal?" the waiter asks. This is one of the spiffier places in town. I've never been here, but I heard the food is good.

"Yes, can I see your wine menu?" Al asks, and he speaks so proper and fancy. It pisses me off for some reason. The waiter leans over the table and passes him the wine menu. Al gazes over it. "Which do you prefer? Red or white? I was thinking red would pair well with the steak," he says, and I can't help but imitate him in my head. Yes, I'm making fun of him because I need to separate him from the feelings building in my chest. It's better to laugh at him than fall for him. My reasoning doesn't even make sense to me.

"I'm good either way," I answer because to me wine is wine.

"Great, we'll take a bottle of your Napa Valley Cabernet sauvignon," Al says and places the menu on the table.

"Great choice, sir. Coming right up." The waiter grins and moves over to another table.

"What's going on in that head of yours?" he asks me.

"Nothing." I shrug and look around the restaurant. It's a nice place. The lighting is dim, white table clothes adorn the tables, and each table has a little candle sitting in a red glass holder. It gives the place a romantic feel. If I knew the place would be like this, I would have chosen the Chili's down the street.

"You've been quiet ever since we left the house," Al continues, and I don't know what he expects. We had sex twice. That doesn't mean we are a couple or we need to share our thoughts.

"I don't have much to say." This feels like a date, and I don't like it. I prefer hanging out in informal settings.

"Your mood has changed since this afternoon. Why?" He tilts his head to the side and waits. My hands remain on my lap out of fear that if I place my hand on the table, he will take hold of it and that would be an intimate gesture.

"You don't know what I have to say because you don't know me," I snap. Shit. I don't mean to snap. He's a nice guy. I let out a sigh. "Look, you're a nice guy ..." I begin, and he scoffs at me.

"Don't feed me that line. Please." He looks remorseful, and I can't help but laugh.

"I'm guessing you've used it yourself one too many times." I cock a brow and lean back in my chair, crossing my arms over my chest.

"Don't do that." He waves his hand up and down in front of my face.

My brows dip together. "Do what?" I can't help my defensive tone.

"This ... what you're doing ... pushing me away. I see all the signs. We were friends." He rolls his eyes. "I know we've only known each other about a week, but I like you as a person, respect you, and am grateful for you. You thought the same thing about me. I don't care what you say right now, or what you have to make up in that head of yours just so you can push me away and lock your feelings down, because it will all be a lie. And believe me, I know all about living a lie," he says, and my words fail me.

"I told you I don't do relationships. We had sex and now we're sitting for a meal." I pause because the waiter brings the wine bottle and along with two glasses. He sets the glasses in front us and goes on to pour us each a glass.

"Thank you." Al smiles and the waiter leaves.

"You are acting as if this is a date and not two friends sharing a meal." I continue the rant I started before the waiter interrupted.

The waiter sets our meals in front of us. I'm starving and it smells delicious so I dig right in. Al watches me for a brief moment and gets to work on cutting his steak.

After he places the first bite in his mouth, he groans and closes his eyes. "This is a good steak." He points to the plate in front of him. Then he pauses. "Two friends don't fuck like animals in heat, Sam. The chemistry between us and the connection I feel toward you isn't one sided. I saw it today when we went Christmas tree shopping. You were happy and free. That desolate look you get in your eyes was gone. Now it's back," he says and cuts into his steak, pulling his attention away from me ... and fuck him! He thinks he knows me, that he can read me, but he can't.

"What are you talking about anyway? You know all about living a lie ..." I want to call him out on the statement he made only moments ago.

He's chewing a large piece of steak, his sexy jawbone working the meat. I wish he wasn't so darn attractive. And he's right. There's been a strange connection between us. I felt it the first morning he woke up sick in my bed. Maybe that's why I let him stay with us. I don't know.

"That's not how this works." He picks up his fork and waves it at me. "I don't mind sharing, but you need to open up too. Tell me what the hell is going on in that head of yours because I just had the best sex of my life. I could tell you enjoyed yourself too. Now you're acting like I don't exist. Why?"

"You're a bastard," I snap at him, and he stops chewing. He stops everything. Hell, it even looks like he stopped breathing. It freaks me the hell out. He places his fork and knife down and leans back in his chair, but his movements are stilted like he's the Tin Man.

He sits and stares at me for a few long beats before he leans forward on the table and looks me in the eye and says, "You're right. I am a bastard."

My face twists with confusion.

"Let me explain," he says before I can open my mouth again. I sit quietly because I've clearly ticked him off. I nod, showing him he has my attention. "When I was twenty-five years old, I walked into my father's office and told him I was ready to learn the family business. I was fresh out of college. I am the oldest of my siblings. It made sense for me to get involved. Only my father was having an off day." His brows raise as if I'm supposed to know what an off day means. Hell, every day is an off day for Papa. "Some big deal he'd been working on fell through. He was drunk and going on some rant. Then he says to me ... 'You're a lawyer. What do you want to accomplish here at Walsh Industries?' He started to laugh. It was a deep and hearty chuckle. It's been over ten years and it still echoes in my ears at night. I thought it was the alcohol making him an asshole, so I decided to sit quiet. Told him I could head his legal team. That made him laugh some more." He leans forward on the table and folds his hands in front of him, looking me straight in the eye. A shiver crawls up my spine. "He said, 'Your brother walks in here and tells me to teach him to run this place. He wants my seat at the table and you want to run the legal team?' He started to laugh some more and I was lost. I assumed it was the alcohol but then he said, '*No matter how much I tried to make you a Walsh, you were never a Walsh. You just don't have my blood in your veins.*' My confusion morphed into hurt as you can imagine." He cuts me a steely glare.

"I knew my father was an asshole, but his words were plain cruel. I remember saying to him, "*Father, you're drunk. Maybe we should get you home.*" I stood up and came around his desk and took him by the arm, figuring I should get him out of there before he makes a fool of himself in front of someone else, but when I took him by the arm, he pulled it away. He gave me an incredulous look and said, '*I'm not that drunk, boy. I know what I'm talking about. You're a bastard. I married your mother a few days after your second birthday. You aren't my son.*'" Al pauses and the hurt he must have felt that day cracks through the surface, and is etched on every part of his perfect face from his stormy eyes to the frown on his lips. "I didn't know what caused him to say such cruel things to me. I left his office and called my mother right away. I thought maybe he was high on something or taking pills, only my mother corroborated his story over the phone. She didn't even tell me to come to the house so she could explain. I was driving when I found out I wasn't Albert Walsh the Third. I wasn't a Walsh at all." He accentuates and blows out a harsh breath. I don't know who the Walshes are, but it sounds like they are some rich, well-known family. "I was raised to believe I was a Walsh. I grew up with a sense of pride and power because I held the Walsh name and they took that from me. It turns out it was a fluke my mother named me Albert because she had seen my stepfather in the news and developed a crush on him. She thought he was this important strong and handsome man. My mom was born into money. She got pregnant accidentally and never told my birth father I existed. She set her sights on Albert Walsh the Second, and he apparently swept her off her feet."

"Whoa." I lean back in my chair. And I thought my life was dramatic.

"Yeah." He nods. "Turns out my half-brother Derek found out I wasn't my father's son and told him it wouldn't be right for me to get involved in the business with the intent that I would one day run the entire empire. Derek, who was a true Walsh, felt entitled. I walked away. I speak to my mother a few times a year at best. The only family member I stay in touch with is my little sister, Izzy. She's a Walsh, but she doesn't like her parents very much, and she has no interest in the family business. She wants to be a fashion designer, and she refuses to use the family money to help her succeed," he finishes.

Fuck that sounds rough. I sit back and don't know what to say.

"So you see, you're right, I am a bastard, but I'm a bastard that actually cares about you." He exhales and looks like his body deflates.

"Shit," I hiss and drop my head. "I'm sorry, Al. I didn't mean to call you a bastard. I mean, I shouldn't have. You were pushing, and I don't like it. I don't want you to push. I just want to sit here quietly and enjoy the rest of our dinner," I say.

"Fine by me." He pulls his attention away from me and focuses on his meal. I focus on mine and when we are done, he orders desert. A mud pie. He offers me a spoon to share, and who says no to mud pie? I take the spoon and share the delicious dessert with him. We don't speak a word the whole time. He pays the bill and we drive back home. His story replays in my mind, and I don't know what to think. Is he just some rich kid that has mommy and daddy issues? Does it matter if he's rich and I'm poor? Is there really a difference at the end of the day? Everybody's shit fucking stinks, and I feel bad for Al. He was sideswiped. I can't imagine how he must have felt to learn his father wasn't his father. The worst part is that his brother backstabbed him, and his father followed suit. I can't imagine a sibling behaving that way. Mack had stepped up to the plate for me. She would do anything for me, and I wasn't the easiest kid to be around. I definitely understand what having a shitty father entails. I've acknowledged my daddy issues a long time ago. I'm sad for Al, but I don't tell him that. He would hate it if I pitied him.

As we pull into the drive at the ranch, I turn my head and ask, "Hey, Al, does Colton know that story?"

He looks me in the eye and shakes his head. "No one knows that story. That is a Walsh secret that the Walshes will take to the grave."

"Why did you tell me?" I ask because I sensed it was a dark secret. I could see him shaking as he told his story and that it gutted him to his core.

"I don't know," he answers and at least it's an honest answer.

"Okay." I nod and get out of the car and head into the house. I don't turn around to see if he's even following me.

CHAPTER TWENTY-TWO

AL

THIS WOMAN IS PISSING the hell out of me. I tell her my deepest darkest secret. I don't know why I told her other than the fact that she called me a bastard and that set me off. I can't even explain the rise she gets out of me. She's infuriating. After I basically pour my soul out to her, she doesn't even say a word. I want to scream at the top of my lungs, but I will probably just wake up a bunch of cows. I slam the truck door shut and follow her into the house. She's already headed back to her room. I trudge after her and when I get in the room, I kick off my boots and lie back on the bed beside her.

"You want me to leave?" I ask, but I don't look at her. I can't. My emotions are running high, and I don't trust what will come out of my mouth next.

"I don't know," she answers the air in front of her. For some reason her response pisses me off more. I want her to know that she doesn't want me to leave.

"You don't know?" I ask. I stand from the bed. "Fuck this." I walk over to my suitcase. I have a bunch of stuff all over the room, and I think she took some of my boxers to launder them for me.

"What the hell is that supposed to mean?" She flies up from

the bed. "Fuck you, Al," she spits and then whips herself around like she is going to stalk out of the room. I grab her arm strong enough to pull her back to me but not hard enough to hurt her.

"Let go of me." She struggles.

"No."

"Dammit, Al." She wiggles in my arms, but I sense the fight leaving her body. I wrap my arms around her, her back pressed to my front.

"Tell me you at least like me. Admit it, Sam," I urge, holding her in my vise grip.

"No fucking way, you asshole." She struggles some more, and I spin her around so that she's facing me. Our chests heave from the exertion.

If looks could kill, then the one that she's cutting me should murder me. Only as we stare each other down, my gaze briefly drops to her kissable lips and her gaze drops to my lips before coming back up to my eyes.

"Fuck you," she hisses.

"Fuck you," I hiss back. Before I know what's happening, she's kissing me and I'm kissing her. My grip on her loosens, and our hands turn into a wild frenzy raking over our bodies, grabbing and rubbing. We kiss hard and she begins to move me backward, I think, so we can make it to the bed. Only I trip on something and lose my balance, falling with a hard thump.

"Fuck, that hurt."

"Shit, sorry," she says, but she isn't sorry because she climbs on top of me, and we kiss some more. It's feverish, hungry, and angry. I've never angry-fucked before because I've never had a woman cause such a rise out of me. I sense it isn't overrated. She pulls my shirt roughly over my head as I claw her shirt off her. She's unbuckling my jeans at a feverish pace as I work her button and zipper. I'm shrugging off my jeans, and she stands to pull hers off along with her panties. Before I can even get my jeans off, she's back on me, kissing the hell out of me and then she sinks onto my throbbing cock.

"Fuck." I jeer. "You feel so fucking good." She doesn't say anything. She just sits up and begins to move. Fast and angry. I grab her breasts and knead them with the same fervor that she's fucking me. Rough and ...

"Fuck, Al, don't stop," she groans, rubbing herself on me. She rises up and down, up and down. I shift my hips to slam into her every time. We are panting, moaning ... her orgasm building, and I know I can't hold out for much longer. Not with the turbulent rhythm she has set, and before I have time to gain some control, she's coming. Her moans are loud, untamed, and hot. I come so hard heat shoots up my spine and white light sparks behind my eyes. When her climax ceases, she falls on top of my chest. We both work to catch our breaths. After a few minutes of lying on the floor, she climbs off me and says she's going to take a shower. When I offer to join her, she tells me not to. I get off the floor and get into her bed. When she leaves the shower, I go to take a shower. All the while I can't stop thinking I just don't understand her.

The first few days I was here, she was sweet, thoughtful, and caring. Then the chemistry between us ignited and now she's angry, volatile, and sad. I need to know why. I can tell Sam isn't going to make it easy on me. Problem is, I won't make it easy on her either.

CHAPTER TWENTY-THREE

SAM

An annoying buzzing sound pulls me from my delectable dream. My dang alarm clock. I reach out into the darkness, my mind moving further away from dreamland where Al was just going to town on my pussy. Reason breaks through the fog, telling me I have responsibilities I need to tend to. I blink the sleep away from my eyes, my thoughts clearing as I become more alert, and pull myself from dreamland to reality. Turning over in bed, I check my surroundings. Yup! He's still here in bed with me, even though I haven't spoken to him in three days. Three days since we had angry sex, which was probably the best sex of my life. The chemistry between us seems to set off some chemical reaction in my body, which makes me believe I want more with him. It's a deceiving reaction because Al isn't capable of more, and I'm not capable of a relationship. The feelings brewing inside me are a short circuit. Something's wrong with my brain. Signals are firing and sending off the wrong message. There is lust between us, nothing more. He has another week and few days to wait for car parts, so he's here sleeping in my bed, but its only sleep.

I throw the blankets off me and rub my eyes some more, wishing clarity to finally strike. I'll never get used to waking up at

the ass crack of dawn to take care of cattle. Sensing my move-
ment, he rises from the bed, throwing blankets and pillows off
him. He's been sleeping shirtless so when he stands and raises his
arms over his head, stretching his torso and showing me his
strong abs, broad chest, and defined arms, I pretend I'm not looking. Truth is I steal a side glance before heading over to my closet
to grab some clean clothes. The clench in my belly betrays me
since I'm willing my body not to be attracted to Al. As if it's a
possibility. I should never have slept with him from the start. Not
when I know he causes a rise out of me that I've never felt before.
I don't trust it. If my mama were here, she'd probably tell me to
run in the other direction because Al has an invisible sign of
heartbreaker written across his chest. He's playful, honest,
sincere, and freaking amazing in bed. A dangerous formula. It's a
formula that's combustible, and I learned long ago my heart is
fragile.

He walks over to his suitcase and pulls out the Levi jeans that
he bought in town yesterday when he accompanied me once
again to the supermarket. He also pulls out the flannel shirt he
bought. I don't know why he's trying to dress like a rancher, but
it's funny and cute. I don't share my thoughts with him, though. I
don't say much to him. Instead, I grab my clothes and get dressed
in the bathroom after I brush my teeth and wash my face. I may
have been more open when he first arrived, but that was before I
knew he was a thief ... well, in the sense that he stole my heart.

With my teeth brushed, I head to the kitchen for a much
needed cup of coffee. Papa isn't back from his hunting trip. I
figure he'll be back tomorrow just in time for Mack, Autumn, and
Ethan's arrival. The coffee maker drips slowly, and I reach into
the fridge and grab a low fat yogurt since I'm not too hungry this
early in the morning. When I pull my head out of the fridge, Al is
standing behind me, a smug grin on his face. He was clearly
checking my ass out. I don't call him on it. I don't say anything
except for, "Coffee?" I hold up the coffee pot.

He walks around the counter and grabs a mug. I don't like that he feels so comfortable around my kitchen anymore. Before he was a sick stranger I was helping. Now he is more.

"Thank you." He holds his mug out to me with that same mischievous smile, and I pour his coffee. He lifts the cup up to his lips and begins to drink it black.

I eat my yogurt without making eye contact. His gaze bores into me as he slowly sips his coffee. When I'm done, I pitch it into the garbage can. I grab my heavy jacket off the kitchen chair and head outside. He follows me quietly until we enter the barn.

"Got the vet coming in today to see if Papa's inseminations were successful," I explain. "We just need to feed them, load up the water, and clean the shit," I explain very matter-of-factly.

"Sure." He nods, but it irks me the way he watches me like I'm some puzzle he can't figure out.

We both get to work, only I leave for the bull barn because working beside Al makes me hot and bothered. The fact that I'm having fantasies of him throwing me into the bales of hay and having his way with me disturbs me. Maybe because I like having him here and I'm getting used to him.

My phone buzzes in my back pocket. I figure its Leslie or Kell checking in, but when I pull it from my pocket I see it's a message from Blake.

Blake: **We need to meet.**

It's not a request. I hate how demanding Blake can be.

Me: **I'm busy.**

Blake: **Stop being stubborn. If you don't come to me, I'm coming to you.**

Dammit. I do not need Blake coming here. That would be bad news.

Me: **Fine. I'm working now. I'll give you a call later.**

Blake: **Fine.**

A few hours pass and I hear a car pull up outside. It doesn't sound like Papa's old truck, so I head out front to see who's here. I see a rental car with my three favorite people on earth.

I run up to the car. Mack, Autumn, and Ethan are all smiling at me. Mack is driving. She gets out of the sedan first. "Well, look at you, Little Sis." She smiles, coming over to me.

"You don't want to hug me. I was just shoveling shit." I smile. Mack smiles too. She squeezes my shoulder.

"Good to see you, baby girl." Through her smile, I notice her jaw clench. She tries to hide her disappointment that I'm still here in Holston and still shoveling shit. To me she's transparent. Autumn, her partner, comes out of the car next along with Ethan, their seven-year old son.

"Auntie Sam." Ethan runs to me and wraps his arms around me before I have a chance to warn him.

"Ethan." I smile and wrap my arms around him, hugging him back. Autumn leans in and gives me a peck on the cheek.

"Good to see you, Sam." She smiles to me then down at Ethan, who has attached himself to my midriff.

"You too, Autumn." I look down at Ethan. "You know your aunt has been working the barn all morning and now you're going to smell like me?"

He shrugs his shoulders. "I don't care." He looks up to me. "Will you take me to the barn to see the cows?"

"Sure, I got to stay out here anyway. Gus the vet is coming by to see how successful Papa was in getting the cows pregnant," I explain to Ethan. He loves coming out to the country to visit. He basically only knows New York City life since that is where Mack and Autumn live. When he comes out here, he likes to help out with the cattle, which makes Papa happy. Papa has high hopes of him becoming a rancher. I hope he doesn't. I'm banking on Mack won't allow it.

"I didn't know Grandpa knew how to get cows pregnant." He gives me a perplexed look, and I ruffle the hair on top of his head.

"Gross, Sam. You're going to get him all dirty," Mack chides.

She never did like working the ranch. Never wanted to get her hands dirty. Probably explains how she is a junior associate at a prominent law firm in New York and I'm still here.

"Meh, a little dirt never hurt anyone."

"Yeah, Mom," Ethan chimes in. "A little dirt is good." He winks at his mom, and Autumn tilts her chin to Mack to follow her to the house.

I spend the afternoon in the barn with Ethan. I'm kind of relieved they all arrived early because it means Al and I won't be alone anymore, and we won't be tempted to jump each other's bones.

CHAPTER TWENTY-FOUR

AL

I HEAR chatter outside the barn but figure it's better to stay in here and work. Sam says her sister's name, so I'm assuming they arrived a day early. I'm thinking it's a good thing because I want to see what Sam's sister is like. I wonder if she'll give me insight into Sam because I don't understand her at all.

I wait until noon when I decide to walk through the front door, figuring Sam has had enough time to explain who I am. Besides, I need to make myself lunch. I didn't eat breakfast this morning, and the physical labor gives me a big appetite. As I walk up to the front door, which actually lands me right in the kitchen, I see two women cooking side by side. I walk right through the door and clear my throat since they are busy arguing about the very large turkey in front of them.

"Oh!" One of the ladies jumps and turns around.

"Hi. I'm Al." I wave and pull my gloves off. I reach forward to shake her hand. She gives me the once-over before taking a step forward.

"Autumn. Nice to meet you, Al." Her brows furrow together. She is clearly too polite to ask me who I am.

The other lady steps up, and before she says anything, she gives the other woman a weird look then looks to me. "I'm Mack, Sam's sister. This is my wife, Autumn," she says, which I already knew because she introduced herself.

"Nice to meet you both." I nod. I walk over to the kitchen sink to wash my hands. Both ladies have now stopped arguing and are watching me. Both their gazes bore into my back. I reach for paper towel to dry my hands and remove my hefty winter jacket. They continue to watch me as I walk over to the fridge. I take out a bag of ready-tossed salad and the roasted chicken Sam and I picked up yesterday at the supermarket then head over to the kitchen table with a plate, fork, and knife. Both ladies still stand by the counter, watching me.

"Can I offer either of you some chicken?" I ask, my lip twisting on one side. I'm not sure what else to say since they both stare at me awkwardly.

"Oh, uh ... no." Mack blows out a breath, and her brows pinch together. She looks at Autumn then back at me. "Who are you?" she blurts out. There is no embarrassment in her tone.

I pause mid-bite. "I'm Al. Did Sam not tell you I was staying here?" I answer, figuring since Sam told me they were coming for Christmas, she would tell them I was here.

Mack walks around the kitchen counter. Her pace is slow as she takes in the details of the house. "Are you responsible for the Christmas tree?"

I chortle. "Partially. Your sister came to buy it with me."

Mack gives me a look that I don't understand. Autumn walks up to her. "It's great, sweets. We finally get ornaments and stocking stuffers." *Did they not have that before?*

"Yeah." She sighs. "Did my father hire you to work around here?"

"No," I answer.

"No?" she repeats as a question.

"No, I'm a friend of Sam's," I say, figuring it isn't a complete lie. Just because she won't talk to me doesn't mean we aren't friends. A knock on the door pulls everyone's attention off me. Kell walks in, and I'm grateful. She's holding a pan covered in a towel. Bonus. I hope it's one of her pies. She makes the best pie.

"Hey, everyone," Kell's friendly voice chimes.

"Hey, Kell," Mack says, walking away from the tree and over to Kell. She embraces her in a hug. Autumn follows suit, and while the ladies are busy, I take a few good bites of chicken because I'm starved.

When they pull apart, Kell looks down to me. "Brought you more pie." She smiles.

"I was hoping you'd say that." My grin is wide, and I stand up to give Kell a hug. When I turn back to the table, I notice Mack still looks very confused.

"You know him?" she asks Kell. She clearly doesn't have a filter. Mack is the type of woman that says what's on her mind. Surprise, surprise. A family trait.

"Of course." Kell shrugs, still smiling wide.

"How?" she asks, looking like she's working hard to get answers.

Kell looks down at me and winks. I'm not sure what she knows about how I ended up here. I'd be embarrassed if the whole town knew about the sleeping pills.

"Al is a friend of Sam's. He's visiting here from Chicago," Kell explains.

"I'm originally from Chicago," Autumn says cheerfully. I'm relieved Kell doesn't go into detail about me. I blow out a breath.

"Which part of Chicago?" Autumn asks, and she looks straight at me with her eyes wide. Oh shit! I've seen that look before. I'm thinking Autumn likes to read the gossip columns. She gives me the once-over. "You're dressed like a rancher," she says before I have a chance to answer where I am from.

Kell looks me over appreciatively. "I'm liking the new look." She smirks and winks again. Oh boy! I feel like I'm on an after-school special, wearing a cowboy costume.

"New look?" Mack asks one of her brows cocked.

"I knew you looked familiar." Autumn smacks a hand to her thigh. "You were in the news. You were Governor Mathis' chief of staff. My mom was on top of that story," she says, accentuating the word that and story.

Mack's jaw drops. "You used to work for the governor and now you work on this ranch?" She gives me a quizzical look that says she thinks I must be crazy.

"You worked for the governor?" Kell asks, and her eyes are wide as she uses her hand to fan herself.

"Yes," I confirm to the ladies. You would think that I just admitted to being Brad Pitt the way their cheeks flush.

"Um, wow," Mack says. Of the few minutes I've known her, I'm guessing she is way too serious about everything, that she has a very particular personality, and I'm not sure she likes me. "How did you say you know Sam?" she asks.

"I didn't." I shrug. I suddenly just want to eat in peace and quiet. If I thought I'd get any information out of her sister, I was dead wrong. She's an attorney, and she's the one fishing for information. I'm not going to make it easy on her.

"Sam met Al when his car got stuck in some snow. He had nowhere to go, so he's been staying here with Sam. They've become friends," Kell explains, and I let out an exasperated sigh. These people are too much.

"My sister let a complete stranger stay with her in this house?" Mack asks like she's questioning Sam's sanity.

"Well, your dad was home." Kell shrugs, and I want to tell her that her argument isn't a strong one, but I love her apple pie and she keeps bringing them over. Besides, I truly like Kell.

"Well, that's just great." Mack throws her hands up in the air and takes off up the stairs. Autumn gives me a sympathetic look and then follows Mack up the stairs too. I'm guessing her bedroom is upstairs. I've never been up there so I don't know.

A few minutes later, Sam walks through the door with a kid.

"Hey there, little man," Kell says, opening her arms up to the boy.

"Hi, Auntie Kell," the boy says, hugging her tight.

Sam walks over to the sink and washes her hands. "Guess you met Mack," she says, looking at me. Her tone is neutral but still holds an edge of hostility.

Kell looks between us and says, "Did you know Al worked for the governor of Illinois?"

Sam's eyes turn as wide as saucers, but she quickly reins in her emotions and looks to me pointedly, waiting for an explanation.

"I was chief of staff until a few days ago," I explain as if I telling her the cow ate some hay today.

"I see." She nods.

The boy looks between Sam and me. "What is he saying, Auntie."

"Nothing." She waves him off.

"I'm Al, by the way," I say to the kid.

"I'm Ethan," he replies. "Mack and Autumn's kid."

I nod.

"Nice to meet you. I just met your moms. They went upstairs," I explain.

The kid looks me up and down. "Are you a rancher?" I look like one, for what it's worth. I'm just missing one of those cowboy hats and the long drawl.

Sam bursts into laughter behind him. "No, buddy. He's from the city like you. He's just dressed up like a cowboy," she explains.

"I want to dress up too, Auntie," the boy whines.

"Sure, maybe later. Let's head up and see why your mamas left a raw turkey on the counter."

She takes the boy by the hand, and they head up the stairs.

Kell stays with me in the kitchen. I've managed to eat half a chicken and a bag of salad.

"Want some dessert?" she asks with a hopeful tone.

"I can't say no to your apple pie, Kell," I say with a wide grin.

She sighs. "Such a charmer." Then she gets to cutting me a piece. "I'm going to have some too. I think the baby likes apples." She rubs her stomach and smiles.

"It's no fun eating pie alone. Glad you're joining me."

She places a warm piece on my plate, and we each take a few bites before she begins to speak. "I thought you and Sam were getting along well," she says, but I hear the question in her tone.

"We were. I don't know what happened," I admit.

"What happened is that she was happy." She sighs. "I shouldn't say anything, but I love Sam and want to see her happy."

I nod, showing her I understand.

"Do you like Sam, Al?" she asks, looking me right in the eye as if my gaze will hold the answers she's looking for.

"I do," I admit. I want to add that I'm leaving soon so it doesn't matter either way, but I don't know if I'm leaving soon. I don't know what's happening but the thought of leaving this ranch causes anxiety to swell in my chest.

"I mean like-like her, not hook-up-like her," she says, and I place my fork on my plate, swiping at the scruff along my jawline.

"I do, but I'm leaving. I can't stay here. I have to head home, look for a new job, possibly a new apartment," I explain.

"So why are you still here, then? Why are you wanting to spend Christmas in Sam's house with Sam's family?" she asks, and it's a fair question.

I know I'm staring at her blankly. And she sits quietly and watches me. A thought goes off in my head and Kell nods. "Exactly," she says.

I don't know what to say.

"You don't have to admit anything to me, handsome. Just don't go breaking my girl's heart. She's been hurt enough."

"She won't talk to me," I blurt out.

Kell pauses and nods her head. "Everything that girl has ever loved has been taken from her. You can't blame her for wanting to protect her heart from you."

"You talking about her mother? She told me she lost her at a young age," I say, knowing I'm prying but someone has to give me some information. I'll even take scraps.

"There's that too." Kell nods, which tells me there's more. What is it? "It isn't for me to say," she explains.

"I understand."

"No, you don't." she says, surprising me. "But if you want to understand you got to show her you're in for the long haul. First, you need to figure out if she's what you want. If she isn't what you want, then go be with your sister for Christmas. No hard feelings here." Kell nods, takes the last few bites of her pie, and leaves.

Whoa. That's a lot to digest over a piece of pie. I finish my slice and Kell's words ring through my head. I could have left a hundred times over, but I stayed because this is where I want to be. Cleaning cow shit is cathartic, and I like being around Sam. She's different from any woman I've dated before. My mind tells me to leave and get my life back together, but my heart is rooted here on this ranch ... with her. I want her to open up to me, but I can't expect her to be all in when I haven't given her a reason to trust my intentions. Hell, until five minutes ago, I didn't know what my intentions were. I don't want to go hang out with Izzy over Christmas and just wallow in self-pity. I want to stay here with the Belmonts. I want to spend time with Sam, get to know everything about her, and make her mine. I startle from my own thoughts.

It's been a long time since I was this possessive over a woman. I promised myself I would never fall in love again. Not only because things ended badly with Brie but because of the way I grew up. Commitment in marriage was non-existent in my world. In Brie's world too. I thought Brie and I created something special together. We didn't. The ugliness of our world broke our relationship. Loving her was a mistake. One I never wanted to repeat. Until now.

CHAPTER TWENTY-FIVE

SAM

MACK IS FREAKING the hell out that I've allowed a stranger to stay in our house. Autumn is trying to tell her that Al isn't dangerous. She goes off on some rant about his affairs in Chicago, and it doesn't make him sound too good. My sister has always thought I practice poor judgment, and now she has another misdemeanor to add to her list.

"Mack, he's been helping out on the ranch. He's a good worker. With Papa gone this week, he's been a huge help. You have no idea how tiring it is to work here day in and day out." I let out a tired breath and fall back into the rocking chair that's been in her room since we were small. Mama use to rock us to sleep in this chair. When we got older, Mama held a coin toss for who would get to keep the chair. Mack won.

Mack rubs a hand over her lips. "You're right. I don't understand how hard it is to work here because I never worked here. I promised Mama I wouldn't," she says and then flinches. Lord knows why she flinches. She's made that comment more times than I care to keep count. I'm the fuckup. The one who didn't keep her promise to Mama. The one still busting her ass with Papa on this ranch. Mack and Papa have a tense relationship. She was older when Mama died, so I think she understood a lot more about my parents' marriage than I did. Papa didn't treat Mama well. He didn't talk nice or treat her with respect. At least that's what Mack says. She doesn't understand how I've spent all this time out here helping him. He may not have done much while I was growing up, but I loved him because he was my father, and after Mama died, he was my only parent. Even if he doesn't act like it, he's the only blood relative we have.

"Well, Ms. Attorney, kudos to you for keeping your promise." I stand from the rocker. I hate that Ethan is witnessing this fight. I don't see him often, and I would have wanted our time together to be filled with positive memories.

"Ethan, you want to come for dinner to Cracker Barrel?" I ask, smiling down to him.

Autumn takes a step toward Mack and places a hand on her shoulder. "We should all go to dinner together," she says. "If Sam is comfortable with Al being here and helping out, then who are we to judge?" she gives Mack a sympathetic look. I want to walk out of here and slam the door in their face, but they are the only family I've got, so I put up with their judgmental bullshit.

Mack shrugs and I bite down on the inside of my lip, hoping to curb my hot temper right now. "Yeah, okay," she concedes as if she's doing me a favor. She looks up to me. "I'm sorry, Sam. You deserve a lot of credit for staying here and working your ass off. I hate that you do it because ... well, you know why, but I do respect your hard work. You're a fine rancher and Papa should be proud of you. I wanted something else for you is all. I don't mean to come across so harsh. I really don't." She stands from her bed, and her eyes well with tears.

"I know," I answer, my tone soft like butter. Mack has that effect on me. We fight. We butt heads, but at the end of the day she's all I got. I love her. I give her a hug, and she squeezes me harder.

"I want the best for you, Button," she says, calling me by my childhood nickname.

"I appreciate that. I know I've made poor decisions in the past, but I want to assure you that I have my head on straight where Al is concerned. Besides, he's leaving soon, and things will go back to normal around here." I pull away.

"'Kay give us half an hour to take showers and get dressed," she says. I ruffle Ethan's hair as I turn to leave the room. I head downstairs and am relieved Al is nowhere in sight. I was worried he may have overheard the conversation. I quickly shoot Blake a text. There's no way I can meet him now.

Me: **Heading out to dinner with Mack, Autumn, and Ethan.**

It doesn't take him long to answer.

Blake: **Meet me after. I'm growing impatient. Are you sleeping with him?**

Fucking Blake. It's none of his business. I know he hooks up with other women, so I hate that he's acting like my boyfriend now.

Me: **You aren't my boyfriend. I'm not answering your questions. I'll text you after dinner.**

Blake: **Good.**

I tuck my phone in my back pocket and head to my bedroom. Al is lying on my bed, freshly showered in a pair of pajama pants. He's also shirtless. Frustration and want builds in my chest.

"I'm heading out to dinner soon with Autumn, Mack, and Ethan," I say, but I don't invite him along.

He nods but doesn't say anything. It's bitchy of me not to invite him, but it's for the best. We need to maintain distance.

"Yeah, sure," he answers quietly.

I head to my closet to grab clean clothes so I can get dressed in the bathroom after my shower. When I turn around, he is standing in my face. The fresh scent of his shower gel wafts off his body.

"I want to stay here with you for Christmas," he says and pauses. I already know that. That's why he's still here.

"I know."

"No, I mean I want to get to know you better. I like you. I don't know where this will lead, but I'd like to stay and find out." He takes a large gulp and looks to me expectantly.

I feel off balance. I'm not expecting those words to come from his mouth. I swallow hard, hating how much his close proximity affects me.

"Say something," he says, looking deep into my eyes.

"I don't know what to say," I answer quietly, hoping to hide the tumult inside me. My heart beats faster. My blood pumps harder. I want to kiss the hell out of him and fuck him senseless all at once. I keep my poker face. "There's nothing here." I point to the space between us.

The warmth in his eyes turns cold. "I'm calling bullshit, Sam. There's something between us. You know it and I know it. It scares the shit out of me, but for the first time in my life, I don't want to run. I want to stay and see where it will lead because I've never felt this way before." His throat bobs and his stare drops to my lips. He's moving in to kiss me, and I can't let him do that. As badly as I want him to, I just can't.

I take a step back and place my palm on his chest. "Don't."

"Don't?" he repeats and a look of shock hangs over his handsome face.

"I need to go to dinner. I can't do this with you now." I step away from him, and he punches the wall and cries out. This part of the house has cement walls. It must hurt.

"I'm not leaving, Sam. I don't know what you've been through or what makes you scared to take a chance on me, but I'm not leaving," he warns, and his voice is determined and commanding. I leave my room and make my way to the bathroom down the hall. I fear our houseguests have heard him. Why has he had a change of heart? He told me himself he doesn't do relationships. I begin to wonder what he's been through that he's avoided a serious relationship. He has a good heart, he's good looking, attentive...a real catch. I'm thinking that Al has some secrets of his own.

I can't get to the bathroom fast enough, and when I do, the first thing I do is lock the door and break down and cry in silence.

CHAPTER TWENTY-SIX

AL

I CAN'T HELP but overhear part of the argument going on upstairs. Mack seems pretty intense. I can imagine it was hard for Sam growing up in Mack's shadow. She has her shit together, got a degree. She's successful. She also puts Sam down. There must have been a lot of pressure on Sam growing up with Mack constantly on her case.

They all head out to the Cracker Barrel for dinner. I got dressed while Sam was in the shower, and now I'm in the kitchen staring at a raw turkey. I wrap it and put in the fridge since they forgot about it. Her sister and her wife brought a raw turkey and nothing else. With time on my hands, I take Sam's truck and head to the supermarket. They took the rental to dinner which worked out well for me. I realize I've taken her truck without permission, but I hope to be back before they return. Besides, I have good intentions.

I don't know where the hell I'm going, but now that I have my cell phone, I use the app Waze to find my way. I find myself in Grand Junction at a larger supermarket, which probably works out better because the last supermarket Sam took me to was small and didn't have a good selection. This place also has a prepared foods section. I'd like to buy a cookbook and make Sam and her family the best home-cooked Christmas dinner ever, but I'm not talented in the kitchen. No need to pretend I'm something I'm not. I buy a cooked turkey, a ham, and different kinds of stuffing. I figure if the food is fresh from today, it will be perfect for a Christmas dinner tomorrow.

With a cart full of food, I stop by the bakery and pick up a large red velvet cake with festive decorations. I don't know how the Belmonts have done Christmas before, but this year I want them to have it all. My family puts on a show of having a big meal and spending time together, but it's just that—a show. The Belmonts say it like it is, and even though they've had a tough go, the love and dedication is there. It oozes from their pores. Even a stranger can sense it.

On the way back to the ranch, I stop at Chipotle's and order a bunch of things from the menu to go since I worry about Sam returning to the ranch and finding her truck gone. I stop for gas on the way and fill up her tank, and then I'm gunning it back to the ranch since the roads are clear. I pull up to the drive and take all the groceries out of the car, holding fifteen bags at once in my hands along with my dinner. I tuck everything in the fridge and sit in a recliner across from the TV to eat my dinner. I finish eating and throw away the empty containers of food. They still aren't back, so I give my sister a call.

She picks up on the first ring. "Hey, Big Brother. Why does it feel like you've ditched me?"

I laugh. "I haven't ditched you. Besides you have company out there. You aren't alone," I remind her.

"I know. I was hoping we could do Christmas together this year. I also wanted you to meet Tristan," she says. From what she's told me, they've been together two months, which is a long stretch for Izzy.

"I'm surprised the Walshes didn't order you home for Christmas." I change the subject because I can't help but mention them.

Something about this time of year makes my chest ache. Then I remember I was living a lie.

"Dad tried to order me home. I wasn't having it," she answers. When all the shit went down between me and the man I believed to be my father, Izzy was only thirteen. There was a lot about life she didn't understand, and I didn't want to tell her the truth, but then my asshole half-brother, Derek, filled her in on my paternity. It caused a strain in her relationship with our shared brother, my mother, and the man I believed was my father. In a way, Izzy's been running away ever since. I felt guilt about it for a while, but then understood that it was what the family represented that pushed her away.

"Right." I rub at the scruff on my chin.

"Sure I can't convince you to head out here even for a few hours?" she asks, and I hate to disappoint her.

"I'm not making any promises, but I'll try," I concede, unsure how things will play out with Sam. Farmer Joe is also expected back tomorrow, and I'm not sure how he'll take the news that I'm still here.

"Thanks, Bro," she says, and she sounds so young. That's when I realize she and Sam are the same age, only Sam has a maturity Izzy doesn't possess yet. I'm glad that Izzy hasn't experienced true hardship, that she still possesses the purity of a young child unscathed by life. Sam's innocence is gone. Her sad eyes tell a tale of their own. I've seen the sadness disappear for brief moments and a part of me wants to make it my mission to make Sam smile. *And how great men fall.* The words ring in my mind once more, and I internally chuckle thinking of Colton again. I want to call him and tell him I understand now. I wait. I don't have Sam yet. She doesn't trust me. I need to win her trust. I just need to figure out how.

"You there, Al?" Izzy's voice comes through the phone, pulling me from my thoughts.

"Yeah, sorry. Spaced out."

"There's a girl, isn't there?" she asks as if she's got telepathic tendencies.

"Maybe," I admit.

She squeals.

"Okay. Update me soon and Merry Christmas if you don't make it tomorrow. I love you."

"Love you too," I answer, and it's so easy because I love my baby sister, but there isn't a huge list of people I do love. It's small and compact. It makes me doubt myself, which isn't good. I need to win Sam over. If I'm going to do that, I need to be confident. I'm not. I'm fucking scared.

CHAPTER TWENTY-SEVEN

AL

Past

MID-SEMESTER EXAMS WERE BRUTAL. I needed to do my best since I'd applied to the top Ivy League schools back in America. I didn't have much time for Brie. Outside of messaging on our Blackberries, we'd had no contact for three weeks. That was a long run for us. She said she was busy studying, but I got the impression she was in over her head partying and doing drugs.

For some reason my stomach was turning all night thinking about her. I shut off the lamp on my desk and packed my work away. It was late. My Swedish roommate Sven had been fast asleep for hours, although he was an early riser. I figured I'd sneak out under the radar. My need to see Brie felt overwhelming and with Christmas a few weeks out, I didn't even know what she had planned. I wanted to bring her home with me, if she wanted.

I dressed warm and left the dorms through the usual side door. Hoping to look like a ghost in the night, I made my way across a large expanse of empty land toward the girls' dorms. The night chill seeped into my bones, causing a shiver to crawl down my spine. I sneaked into the usual receiving area and went up a back flight of stairs, stopping on Brie's floor. My heart beat rapidly in my chest, and I had no clue why other than the antici- pation to see her excited me. I knocked lightly on her door, knowing she had a roommate. No one answered. I pressed my ear to the door and heard a light thump from music. I slowly turned the knob just in case it was her roommate and not her. The room was lit by a lamp on a desk, the damn techno music I hated thumping in the background. I took a step inside. Her roommate had a guy I knew in bed with her. They were fucking. I was scared to look in the direction of Brie's bed. For some reason the hairs on the back of my neck stood on edge. A glutton for punishment I moved in closer since no one realized my presence. It was then I saw Brie in bed with a girl with dark hair on top of her. My chest squeezed, and a light wheeze left my lips. Unable to formulate words, I walked over to the bed. She was full making out or fucking the girl, light moans and giggles leaving their lips.

"What the hell, Brie?" I boomed. She looked wide eyed for a moment, staring up at me, using her hands to cover a body I had grown familiar to.

Brie and I were better than this. All the students at this school didn't practice monogamy. Even the ones supposedly in a rela- tionship. Brie and I were different. Only now we weren't. I didn't know if it made it worse or better that she was in bed with a girl and not a guy.

She looked up at me and laughed. She fucking laughed, and that was when I saw remnants of white powder on her nose. She was high as a kite. She looked too thin, like she wasn't eating. I didn't know what to do.

"It's a girl, Al. Relax."

The girl she was with looked frustrated. "Brie, come on. Leave that loser alone." She went back to kissing her as if I wasn't standing there.

I couldn't reason with her now. Brie had become everything she feared. She had come to hate her father, yet she followed solidly in his footsteps. I turned and walked out of the room. My heart ached as I made the walk back to the dorms. My head felt spacey, and I didn't care if I was suddenly caught and kicked out of here. If this place could corrupt someone as perfect and pure as Brie, I didn't want to be here anyway. I tried so hard to get caught but I made it back to my dorm room without a hitch. I cried into my pillow that night. The next morning I woke, determined to speak to Brie. She was my best friend. She was hurting. I had to help her only you couldn't help someone that didn't want it.

CHAPTER TWENTY-EIGHT

SAM

AL WAS asleep in bed when we got back from dinner last night. I don't think he's used to the manual labor, and it seems to be tiring him out. I'm grateful to not have to face him because my emotions are running high after he confessed he has feelings for me. He doesn't want to leave Holston. I don't know what to do. I slip out of bed because Mack, Autumn, and I need to prepare the turkey she brought for dinner. First, I check my phone and realize that with all the drama, I forgot to get in touch with Blake last night. Fuck. I don't want him coming over and making a scene, especially with our house guests here.

I shoot him a text.

Me: **Sorry dinner ran late.**

Tonight is Christmas Eve, and I don't spend holidays with Blake, which means he will have to wait.

Blake: **Merry Christmas to you. Be in touch soon.**

I laugh, thinking how his voice would sound saying those words. Grumpy and demanding. Asshole.

Me: **Merry Christmas.**

I answer just to appease his temper. Having Al here and interacting with him makes me question how I spent all these years hooking up with Blake. Yeah, we were young when we got together, but the chemistry between us was never heated like it is with Al. If anything, it's always been more toxic.

I head to the kitchen in a sleep shirt and shorts, rubbing the sleep from my eyes. Mack and Autumn are standing at the kitchen counter, drinking coffee, and Ethan is sitting at the table eating his favorite cereal. He turns his head. "Good morning, Auntie." He smiles, and it's so sweet.

"How you doing?" Mack asks. She overheard Al confess his feelings to me last night before dinner and wouldn't let up talking about him all through dinner. Despite his colorful past, Mack thinks I should give him a chance. I repeat the words in my head because Mack usually doesn't approve of anything I do.

"Fine," I answer. I don't want to get into relationship talks with these two. They don't understand where I'm coming from. They met, fell in love, and it was easy for them. Dad wasn't so accepting that Mack preferred girls at first, but with Mack's fuck-what-anyone-thinks attitude, he didn't have much choice but to accept her or lose her. He chose to accept on his own terms. It isn't like he's this loving welcoming father anyway. "We should get cooking. That turkey will take hours to make," I say, heading past my sister to the coffee maker.

Autumn shakes her head. "Not necessary."

I pour some coffee in a mug and give her a look that says I think she bumped her head when she woke up this morning.

"I'm not following," I answer, my head still muffled by sleep and another hot dream. Fucking Al.

Mack walks over to the fridge and opens it up. I've never seen the fridge so jam packed with food. "We have a four course Christmas dinner already in here. We just need to heat it up," she explains while my jaw remains hanging open. "Seems like your friend was busy while we were at dinner last night. Gotta say, it was awfully thoughtful. We got turkey, ham, and a whole bunch of other stuff. Probably have enough food in there to invite all of Holston for Christmas dinner," she rambles on.

I remain rooted in my spot. Words escape me until his presence looms behind me. I shouldn't know he's there, but my skin feels warm and my breathing accelerates at the thought of him being so near. I'm aware of how screwed I truly am.

"Good morning," he says, his voice deep and raspy from just waking up. The sound moves toward me, making my belly tighten. I haven't even turned around to look at him. Mack eyes me like I'm being rude. I know she wants me to turn around and thank him for the food. I turn slowly on my feet, and when my gaze hits his, my breathing pauses. Why does he have to be so handsome, even in the morning when he's straight out of bed? I'm betting my blond hair is sticking up in different directions right now.

"Thank you for all the food. It was very thoughtful," I say quietly, but I don't look him in the eye.

"It was nothing. I figured it would be easier to pick everything up than spend a whole day in the kitchen," he answers, rubbing at the scruff on his chin. A part of me wants to walk up to him and kiss the air right out of him, but that would be putting my heart on the line. This man can't be a hookup for me.

I don't say anything else to him. I head to the kitchen table and talk to Ethan about school while Al makes small talk with Autumn and Mack, who both seem to be taken by his charm. We spend the day hanging out and playing board games. Ethan and Al seem to be getting along great too. Everyone is getting along except for me and Al, because I keep my words on a need-to-know basis.

At around 4:00 pm, he looks at his watch. "My sister really wanted to see me today. Would you mind if I borrowed your truck?" he asks.

"Nice of you to ask today," I answer. It's bitchy and in all honesty, the words slip out before I can even control them.

He pauses and his mouth hangs open.

I shake my head like I'm trying to instill reason in my brain. "Sorry, I didn't mean that. It was nice of you to buy the food and put gas in my truck. Yeah, go ahead and take it. Will you be back for dinner?" I ask, surprising myself. The question shows him I care, and I shouldn't. He's making the signals in my brain cross again.

"I don't have to," he answers. "I don't want to overstay my welcome."

My foot twists as I try to think of how to answer that.

"I want you to stay." Ethan runs up to Al, smiling. "I like him, Auntie. He's fun."

"I can't argue with my nephew." I grin down at Ethan, but Al doesn't look pleased. He wanted me to say I wanted him to stay.

Al gives me a penetrating look that tells me he's trying to get in my head. He wants to hear if I want him to stay or not. I don't respond.

"Fine, then," he answers. "I'll have the truck back later," he says and heads to the room to grab a jacket. He stalks back through the main room, walking past the Christmas tree where Autumn and Mack have laid out their presents. I also put a few of my own down. He places a small box by the tree and stalks toward the kitchen. My stomach sinks. I know he'll be back to bring me my truck, but will he leave after that? I wrap my arms around my torso. Al grabs the keys from the hook and says, "See you all later. Merry Christmas. Enjoy dinner." He walks out the door and my heart skips a beat.

I'm so fucking confused. When I look at Autumn and Mack, they both look at me sympathetically like they pity me. I can't bear it for a minute longer. I place my mug of coffee on the counter. "I'm going to go get dressed. I haven't practiced riding in a while. I should catch up for next month's competition." I turn to my room. Ethan comes running after me.

"I can't believe you ride a bull," he says.

"Yup, I'm not the only gal around here who does," I answer because no matter how I'm feeling, Ethan releases a tension in my chest.

"That's so cool. Can I watch you train?" he asks.

"Let me get dressed and get warmed up and maybe you can come into the barn a little later," I say, patting the top of his head.

"Great, thanks." He smiles and he's cheerful. Ethan is happy.

I head to my room and get dressed.

CHAPTER TWENTY-NINE

AL

I KNOCK on the family cabin door. I've never been here before. They must have acquired it in the last ten years or so. It's large and fancy. I expect nothing less. I hear the large latch on the door open and seconds later I'm met with Izzy's warm smile.

"Hey you." She reaches up to give me a hug. I hug her back, enjoying the familiarity of being around family. "Come on in. The weather here is insanely cold." She waves me in with a brush of cool air. A butler comes to take my jacket, and I follow Izzy deeper inside the house. "Tristan is passed out. You'll meet him later, and Sasha and Aaron are around somewhere, probably fucking their brains out." She huffs. Yes, my little sister has no filter.

"Right."

"Do you want something to eat? We have the most amazing cook here." She goes on. Truth is I don't feel hungry. I'm too confused to feel hungry.

"Nah, I'm good." I follow her into what looks like a family room. The ceiling is high with large planks of rustic wood. One wall is covered in stone and in the center a fire burns from the fireplace. The place has a country feel.

"Come take a seat." Izzy curls up in the corner of the large sectional couch.

I take a seat across from her on a large recliner.

"What's up? You aren't your usual talkative self," she says sarcastically. I'm never too talkative, but right now I'm silent.

I rub at the scruff on my chin. "You know how I told you a woman helped me out during the snow storm when my car got stuck ..." I swallow hard.

"And you were passed out because you took a sleeping pill." I tried to hide the part of the story that I was passed out from Izzy. I didn't want her to know her older brother took a sleeping pill and almost died like a moron. I ended up telling her anyway because the thought that I did something that careless messed with my head. It scared me, shook me up, and at the time Izzy was the only one who I felt comfortable telling since she wouldn't judge me. "Yeah," she answers, and her eyes look sad and filled with worry.

"I'm fine, Izzy. I mean, I wasn't trying to kill myself. It was a bad decision. That's all." I try to ease that line forming between her eyes.

"Al, if it's more, I need you to tell me. I can help. I want to help," she says, and I think she's a breath away from offering me money or taking me to a drug counsellor.

"I told you it was a mistake. I wasn't trying to end things," I snap, a little on edge from my earlier I don't even know what to call it with Sam because it wasn't an argument. "I'm sorry." I shake my head. "Look. I appreciate your concern. I know I said I was coming out here to clear my head, but trust me, I had no intention of offing myself. The truth is the woman ... uh ... girl ... woman I've been staying with ..." I stutter like a moron, and Izzy's brows draw together.

"Al," she says, stopping my mumbling rant. I pause, wondering what she has to say. "The woman that found you, you like her," she says almost reading my mind.

I stare blankly at Izzy. I stand from the chair and pace the room.

"OMG. You really like her," Izzy says, and when I turn my head to look at her, she is wide eyed and the excitement gleams off her.

"I fucking really like her." I blow out a heavy breath. "But it's complicated. She's complicated. I don't understand her. One minute she's hot, the next she's cold. I know she's had a tough life, but I confessed my feelings to her," I explain to my sister, who is now sitting on the edge of her seat as if she's waiting to watch the climax in a thriller movie.

"And she didn't jump into your waiting arms," she says.

"No."

She gives me a sympathetic look. "I told her I want to stay and see where things will lead, and she said she couldn't deal with me now. She left for dinner ... that was last night. All day today she was basically ignoring me. She can't even look at me." I huff as frustration bubbles through me. "Scratch that. When she does look at me, I can see she wants me ... so she won't look at me. I don't know what to do." I sigh and fall back into the very comfortable recliner, completely defeated. "I've been living in her house. Driving her car. I have to stop doing that if she doesn't want me there. Her damn mixed signals are screwing with my head."

"Holy shit." Izzy gasps. "You really got it bad. I thought this day would never come. Especially after you were pissed about Colton being wrapped around what's her name's finger." My sister reminds me. She doesn't know about Brie. No one does. Not even Colt.

"Evie ... and yeah. I'm completely out of my fucking element. The crazy part is I don't want to just walk away. I don't think I can. I'm in too deep." I pull my phone out of my back pocket to see if Sam called or texted. Why would she? She doesn't even have my damn number.

"Stay for dinner," Izzy says as if it will solve my problems.

"I want to spend time with you, but I need to figure Sam out. I'm running out of time with her." Izzy quirks her lip to the side like she pities me.

"Tell me about the new guy before I leave," I say, not wanting the conversation to be only about me.

"He's just finished his MBA at Harvard. He wants to go work at Walsh, but I'm not sure if that's happening yet," she says, and I already don't like the sound of him. Izzy's got a good heart but can be naïve. Given our family's position, there are always people that want to take advantage and see if they can make a good connection.

A guy comes strolling into the room, and I'm pretty sure it's Tristan. He gives Izzy a kiss on the cheek and extends his hand to me. "Hey. I'm Tristan and you are?" His voice is whiney and spoiled and his attitude is pretentious. I also note a little white powder on his nose, and my blood boils. He looks like the type of guy that would've attended boarding school with me. The thought of my little sister being with someone like him makes my head spin.

Tristan extends his hand to me but I don't reciprocate. My gaze cuts to Izzy. "Isabella where is the kitchen? NOW," I demand as the fiery need to protect my sister from this loser takes over.

"Al, uh ..." Izzy stutters as I take hold of her arm, albeit gently, and force her to guide me to the kitchen. She does as she's told because I'm not playing games. "What the hell?" she asks when we reach the kitchen, and she pulls her arm out of my grasp.

"Don't what the hell me ..." I whisper scream. "That guy is a cokehead, Izzy." I pause and run my fingers through my hair. My insides are going to explode. She doesn't say anything to negate what I've just said. "Holy crap! Are you doing drugs with him?" I give her an incredulous look.

Her eyes turn wide. "Hell no! You know I don't touch that stuff. Maybe a little weed here and there, but I would never touch blow."

"But you would date a guy that does," I retort and she winces.

"It's not like that," she answers.

"Isabella, I'm not walking out of this house until he's gone," I demand, crossing my arms over my chest.

She heaves a sigh. "We're together. I can't just throw him out Christmas Eve."

"You have feelings for him?" I ask because I need to understand how deep she is. Her best friend died of a drug overdose in high school, which left Izzy feeling messed-up for a long time. I know my sister isn't into drugs. I'm surprised she would be with someone that is.

She shakes her head, a clear battle going on inside her mind. "I don't know how to answer that. I like him. He treats me well."

"And he doesn't want you getting high with him?" I cock a brow and wait expectantly.

She purses her lips, and the truth seeps from her features. "Fuck, Izzy. What the hell is going on?" I ask because with all the shit I've had going on in my life, I've clearly been a neglectful brother. The Walsh clan sure doesn't know how to be supportive, which leaves Izzy alone. "I'm sorry." I take a step toward her and hug her.

She hugs me back. "It's nothing, Al. I was lonely. Last Christmas, when I was in Bahamas, I told you I was with friends, but I wasn't. I was alone. My friends were all with their families, and I didn't want to be with mine. Last year I promised myself that I wouldn't be alone this year. You've been busy. I dated Tristan and things were going well, so I asked Tristan to come out here for Christmas. I thought you would join too, but then you got sidetracked."

I release the hug.

"Fuck. I'm so sorry. I need you to be open with me. You're the only family I've got. I don't want to lose you, and I don't need anything bad happening to you."

"I know, and I love you for it." She sighs, and now she's crying.

"He's gotta go." I persist.

"I know." She swipes a tear from her eye.

"You're coming with me," I say, and it isn't a request.

"Where?" she asks.

"To the Belmonts," I answer.

"Who?" She looks very confused.

"The family I've been staying with."

"I have Sasha and Steven here. I can't just leave them." She gives me a look that says she thinks I'm crazy.

Something about the way she says their names does something in my brain.

"You said you had Sasha and Aaron here when I walked in." I tilt my head, giving her a curious look.

She bites her lip. "Busted."

"No more stories," I warn. "I want him gone by morning." I head to the washroom to give her the privacy to go tell Tristan to take a hike. When I return to the kitchen, I hear arguing in the family room. He doesn't want to leave. He's fighting to stay. I don't like it. He asks her about the interview with her father, and my blood turns cold. He's using her. I stomp into the family room and his eyes turn wide. I can see that he's high as a kite, so I don't want to make this worse than it is.

"Tristan, buddy, this is probably isn't a good time for you to drive. I propose that you spend the night here and sleep off whatever it is you are on. I'll be back in the morning to make sure you're gone." I leave no room for questions, and Tristan nods his head and fucks off to wherever he came from.

"Let's go." I look at Izzy. "Go pack an overnight bag."

She stares at me, rooted to her spot.

"Izzy ..." I give her a look that says get moving.

She blinks. "Yeah, let me just grab my things and the cheesecake Amanda made. It looks to die for. I don't like to show up as a guest with empty hands."

I smile. "Sounds good."

I wait for her by the front door. My nerves are worse now than when I walked in here. Izzy finally walks up to the door in a heavy winter jacket and boots, carrying a small bag on her shoulders. She's prepared for the weather.

She stops dead in her tracks when we walk up to the old Ford truck. "Um, Al ..." She gives me a questioning look then looks down to my feet. Then she comes around and analyzes my jeans. "Why are you dressed like a redneck?"

I burst into laughter. "I've been ranching," I say proudly.

Izzy laughs. "I don't know what the fuck that's code for, but I'm freezing. Let me follow you in my car," she says, and I agree.

We head back to the Belmonts, a stranger in their home with a plus one. I hope this will be a Christmas we never forget.

CHAPTER THIRTY

SAM

MACK AND AUTUMN finish setting the table. I get out of the shower after spending the afternoon practicing on Dangerous Rider, our bull. Autumn brought Ethan out to the barn for a few minutes to watch, and now he's looking at me like I'm some wonder woman or something.

"Can I help?" I shake out my wet hair and adjust my shirt. We don't get dressed up around here, so I'm in a pair of jeans and a T-shirt like the rest of the family.

"Make sure the oven is hot enough. I'm worried with all that food in there it won't heat properly," Mack calls out.

"Sure thing." I check the oven and pass my papa in the kitchen. "Welcome back," I say, leaning into the oven. "Hunt anything interesting?"

"Always do," he assures me, but I don't get more than that. I don't like hunting, and so when I decided to forgo my chance at college, I made him promise me to never bring home any animal that he kills. He honors that request.

"Everything good around here?" he asks, looking around. "Is City gone?" he asks and looks a little disappointed.

"Everything's good. Al was a huge help this week with you

taking off like that," I chide, turning the heat up on the oven because at this rate we'll never sit down to eat our Christmas dinner, and I'm famished.

"Figure he'd be. Looks like a fast learner. Where's he at now?" Papa continues to look around, and his interest in Al baffles me a little. He was riding his case all the time. Before I can get in an answer, Papa says, "Want to thank him for this nice Christmas dinner. Mack mentioned he picked it all up." He takes a swig from a beer bottle.

I'm about to say something to answer Papa's question, but there's a knock at the door. It's Al. He hasn't knocked all week, but I figure he saw Papa's Ford outside and thought it'd be best. Autumn answers the door and there's a woman standing by his side. She's pretty and tall with long dirty blond hair and hazel eyes. She's wearing the perfect outfit. Her nails are manicured with red nail polish. Everything about her screams class.

"I hope it's alright I brought my sister over for dinner," he says, kind of staring at all of us and no one in particular.

"Fine by me, Al. It's Christmas." My father takes a step toward him and shakes his hand. I'm confused wondering if he hit the Jim Beam early today.

"Thanks, Mr. Belmont." Al shakes his hand. "This is my sister, Isabella. We call her Izzy," he says, and then he introduces her to everyone, only she doesn't shake their hands. She reaches in for a hug, and I can tell Mack and Autumn instantly like her. "And this is Sam," Al says, and I sense innuendo in his tone, like he's mentioned me. Her eyes warm and she looks at me like I'm a sacred pearl.

"So nice to meet you." I smile.

"Thanks so much for having me. Sorry I'm crashing your Christmas dinner." She giggles nervously. "Al went all big brother on me, and well ..." she trails off. "It's a long story, but I bring the best cheesecake ever." She passes me the cake.

"Thank you. That was kind. My friend Kell is a baker. If this is as good as you say it is, she'll want a recipe," I say, taking the cake and placing it in the fridge. When I turn around, I see her lips have twisted.

"Oh, well..." she bites her lip "...I didn't make it. Our cook did, but I'm sure I can get the recipe if you'd like," she says sweetly.

I wince a little. Right. Her cook. It reminds me how Al and I are from two different worlds. Al reaches over and takes her jacket and hangs it on a hook by the front door.

"Hey, Al." Ethan walks up to us. "Did you know my auntie is a bull rider? I got to watch her today in the barn. She's amazing," he says, and my cheeks turn crimson.

Al gives him a knowing look. "Your auntie is pretty special," he says openly, which means everyone heard the comment. The room falls silent as everyone's attention is trained on Al and me.

"My brother sure knows how to silence a room." Izzy chuckles, rolling her eyes at her brother. She looks like she must be my age. Their sibling banter teaches me more about him. "How can I help?" she asks.

"No need to help. We need to eat now before half the town stops by and we won't get to taste all that food," Papa interrupts with his domineering voice. Every Christmas when it gets later into the evening, friends house hop. It's a fun way to pass the night.

Mack and Autumn put on their oven mitts and slowly unload the oven while I prepare all the cold foods. Ethan helps me by taking the cold platters to the table, which is basically our kitchen table with a couple of added extensions to make it bigger. At least we have the tree in view which makes for nice scenery and a festive feel. We sit at the table and wait for Papa to say grace, which he does only once a year. On Christmas. Only this year he looks to Al and asks him to do it, which throws me off. My father left town riding Al's ass. Now he seems to be buddy buddy with him. What the fuck?

Al looks wide eyed then bows his head and places his interlaced hands on the table. "Oh yeah, okay," he mumbles. "I want to give thanks for the food at our table. I hope this year will be a good year for the Belmont Ranch. I'm thankful to be spending time with a family that loves each other. I want to say thank you for including me in your holiday. Amen," he murmurs then looks up to see who's watching him. We all have eyes on him. Something tells me he's never done that before.

"Thanks, Al." Papa nods. "Let's dig in," he says, and we all enjoy a Christmas dinner filled with laughter and chatter.

My interactions with Al stay to a minimum. When it's time to clean up, everyone chips in, but Ethan wants to play a game on the floor next to the Christmas tree, so I tell Autumn and Mack to go ahead and I'll clean up on my own. Al is nowhere to be seen, and Papa sits on the recliner, drinking a beer and watching them play.

Izzy comes up to me. "Let me help you," she says, and it's sincere. I agree to it and wash the dishes while she dries and stacks them.

"Thanks for letting me hang with you guys. You have such a great family." She smiles.

"Thanks." I smile too and continue to wash while she dries.

"Al went all big brother on me earlier. He didn't approve of my boyfriend, and well ... he asked him to leave my house," she explains, and I can see she's embarrassed.

"He did what?" I ask, surprised. "I mean why would Al do that? It's rude." I shake my head, wondering what kind of man Al is.

"No, I mean well ..." She giggles. "I sometimes don't have the best taste in men. Al saw Tristan for what he is the second he laid eyes on him. I don't always see what I should ... I don't know. I mean ... our family is kind of messed-up. I don't know what he's told you. I don't have a father to watch out for me like you do," she says, and my stomach sinks. Papa has never been a hands-on parent, but he cares in his own way. "Anyway, I'm rambling. I didn't have anyone to be with tonight, so thanks again."

"Please ... don't thank me. It was our pleasure." With all the dishes washed, I continue to clean the suds out of the sink. "What's going to happen with the guy? I mean is he leaving?"

"I don't know. He was high when we left, so he couldn't drive. I hope he'll be gone by morning or else I fear my brother will kick his ass out the door." She chuckles. "I've seen Al get all protective over me before, but he was fuming tonight," she says. I could tell that he was in an off mood all throughout dinner.

"If you need a place to stay, you're more than welcome to stay here tonight. All the rooms are full, but we can set you up on the couch," I offer.

"Thank you. I may take you up on it. It wouldn't be comfortable to head home now if Tristan is still there, which I'm guessing he is." She gives me a sorrowful look. "I'll go join that game." She points to Mack, Autumn, and Ethan on the floor. I nod and head back to my room. I find Al staring up at the ceiling, looking gloomy.

"You're supposed to be happy. It's Christmas." I smile and sit on the edge of the bed.

"You're talking to me," he says, but it isn't a question.

"What of it? I just wanted to see if you're okay. Izzy told me a little about what went down at her place," I say, not wanting to prod too much.

"Yeah, it's pretty messed-up. The guy was high off his ass on coke," he says, and my heart stammers. It's more serious than I thought. "My sister doesn't always make the best choices, and she was feeling alone. I hate to think what she might have gotten herself into had I not come along. I feel like a self-absorbed prick," he admits, and it throws me off a little.

My lips press together. "You may be all those things, but tonight you were her savior," I say, and he just looks at me like I'm an angel or something.

"That's nice of you to say, but I've made mistakes. I need to fix ... certain aspects of my life." He sighs, taking a long exhale.

"Don't we all." I fall back on a pillow beside him. We lie there quietly, staring at the yellowing ceiling while contemplating life.

I hear Kell's voice from the family room. She stops by every year with Gage and Theo.

"Kell's here," I say into the dark room. "I better go to her."

"Yeah, I'll be there in a minute," he says solemnly, and I fall for him just a little more. He isn't perfect by any means. He's got issues, I can see that, but he also wants to learn from his mistakes too, and the way he cares for his sister is endearing. I'm so fucked. "Does it mean you want me here?" he asks, and my heart stops.

"I don't know," I answer honestly, and even in the dark room, I see the disappointment painted on his face. I step out of the room and head back to the family room to greet Kell and Gage.

"Merry Christmas," Kell cheers and she leans in to give me a hug. She places Theo on the floor and Mack, Autumn, and Ethan are instantly attracted to playing with him and making him laugh. I give Gage a hug when I hear what sounds like a beer bottle clambering outside. I give him a questioning look. He stares back apologetically. "Gage what's going on?" I ask.

He purses his lips together before he speaks. "Blake came by our place earlier. Had a fight with my mom and ate dinner with us. He was drunk and Kell didn't trust leaving him in the house. She thought he'd rip things up," he explains.

"So you brought him here?" My heart beats at a staccato. "I hate saying this, but you should leave now." Kell and Gage are like a sister and brother to me, but I need Blake gone. Especially if he's drunk. He can be volatile. In my mind, I'm kicking myself for not getting back to him. This is probably his way of checking out what is going on over here with Al.

"Okay, we're outta here. Kell," Gage says to her and gives her a look that says let's split now. Kell's lips turn down.

"Sorry, I wanted to see Mack, Autumn, and Ethan before they

leave." She grabs Theo off the floor. They are about to leave when Blake walks through the front door.

"You shouldn't be here," I snap. He gives me a look that says he doesn't give a shit.

"I shouldn't be here." He points to himself. "But he should be here." He points behind me, and I realize Al is standing there. Fuck me.

"Blake, please. It's a bad time. Leave," I demand, but he's drunk. He is a messy drunk. His eyes land on Ethan and then on me. He looks at Mack. He hasn't seen Mack for a long time. She hates him.

"Fucking hell, Blake, get out of here." I run at him and begin to push him toward the door like a lunatic. "Go Blake, please go," I beg, my eyes stinging with tears. I need him gone. I want him gone. I push but he's big and strong and he's not listening to me.

"Hey, man, you should leave." Al walks up to him all big strong and alpha male, and I know he's watching me go ape shit, and he doesn't understand. He's only trying to help, but he isn't helping. He's making things worse.

"Fuck you, man," Blake spats and instead of moving toward the door, he's walking back in and trying to get in Al's face.

Papa walks up to him, and Blake shuts his mouth. "Son, leave now. I don't want to have to shoot you."

Gage walks up to Blake and whispers something as he tries to usher him out the door. Blake is swearing and words come sputtering out of his mouth. "No, dammit." My heart stops for an instant, and I fear I may pass out. Blake charges back into the house.

Autumn runs up to Blake. "Grow up, Blake. It's Christmas Eve," she scoffs. "I don't need you making a scene in front of Ethan or Theo." She rolls her eyes like Blake is an idiot, but on a deeper level I see fire in her gaze. I've never seen Autumn look that scary or pissed before. Blake cowers and Papa and Gage walk him to the door. Autumn locks the door once he's outside. I take a breath for the first time in what feels like too long. When I stare back at my family, I don't know what to say.

"I'm sorry." I fall forward and cry as air is sucked from my lungs. Mack is there to catch me. She pulls me by the hand up to her room, and I fall apart in her arms.

CHAPTER THIRTY-ONE

SAM

"WHY DID you bring me up here?" I shout at my sister. Her room suddenly feels like a cage, and I'm a wild animal.

"Because you need to calm down. You need to clear your head, and we need to consider what just happened," she says, and my heart beat continues to soar to a dangerously frantic speed.

"Damn that Blake," I curse him.

"Cursing Blake now isn't going to help." Mack is always the voice of reason. "Truth is, Blake was dumb drunk, but your reaction was batshit crazy. You wanna tell me that you're still sleeping with that sore loser?"

I give her a look that says don't start with me now. I fall back on her bed.

My heart hurts. Maybe that's why I keep going back for more with Blake, because as much as I hate him—and I do hate him—there are parts of me, of him, that will be broken forever.

"Okay." I swallow and stand from the bed. I take a few cleansing breaths.

"Okay?" Mack asks. She looks worried. I don't blame her.

"Yes, I'm fine." I force a smile. I inhale a deep breath and square my shoulders. "We should head back downstairs. Being up here too long will look weird, and I don't want Ethan to think there's something wrong with me. You know he asks lots of questions."

Mack nods. "He's one perceptive little boy. You sure you're okay to head back down?"

"Yeah." I nod and stalk out of Mack's room. I head to the washroom to throw some cool water on my face and use some makeup to cover up the redness from crying. I usually don't wear makeup, but I need it now.

I walk down the stairs, and Ethan comes running toward me. "You okay, Auntie?"

"I'm good, kid." I ruffle his dirty blond hair. "You wanna play a board game or something?"

"I brought Legos. Can we do that?"

"Sure, what are we building?" I ask with a smile because Ethan doesn't have any questions, but I'm sure Al will.

"A dragon," he confirms. I sit on the rug and build a dragon with Ethan. It's as if Blake, Kell, and Gage never dropped by. Papa sits in his recliner, watching us play, while Autumn and Mack mumble to each other in the kitchen. Al and his sister are outside on the front deck since Izzy is a smoker. Everything seems normal, and I can't ask for more than that.

CHAPTER THIRTY-TWO

AL

EVERYBODY'S GONE off to bed. What a crazy night it's been. Even Izzy is passed out cold on the couch. I'm relieved to know she's safe here with me. I head back to Sam's bedroom because I have a lot of questions about what went down with Blake tonight. My imagination soars with all kinds of possibilities. My gut tells me Sam isn't going to give me any answers, and I have to wonder what I'm still doing here. She completely lost it tonight over Blake, like having him in this house was equivalent to a carbon monoxide risk. It doesn't make sense.

When I reach Sam's room, she isn't there. She isn't anywhere in the house either. I put on my puffy winter jacket, the one Izzy says makes me look like a redneck. I chuckle at the thought. I grab the bottle of Glenfiddich that I bought at the supermarket and head outside. It's a little warmer today than it's been, but it's still cold outside. I look around for Sam. Her truck is parked out front. She must be around here somewhere. I head into the bull barn, wondering if she's practicing on the bull again. I think it's insane that she rides a bull because it's dangerous, but given her personality, it doesn't surprise me one bit. She isn't riding the bull, though. She's leaning on the wood fence surrounding it and staring into thin air.

"You want company?" I ask. Her thoughts must have been so intense that she jumps.

"Shit." She holds her heart. "Didn't hear you come in," she says.

"Sorry." I turn the cap on the Glenfiddich and take a long swig. It's a twenty-one-year-old single malt with a hint of rum. It slides down my throat, making me feel warm while awakening my taste buds. "Want some? It's freezing out here." I offer her the bottle.

"The expensive stuff ... huh." She gives me a look that tells me she's going to take it. She does, and she throws back a large gulp.

"Easy there." I smile.

"Damn, that's good stuff." She smiles back but she doesn't give me the bottle.

"You like scotch?""

"Sometimes," she nods. Her mood is solemn, the look in her eyes distant. "You ever wish you could go back in time?" she asks, using the back of her hand to wipe at her mouth.

"I don't know ..." I shrug. "Maybe ... sometimes."

"Would you do things different if you could?" she asks, and she passes me the bottle. I take another long pull on the whiskey.

"Hey ... share," she chides. I give her the bottle, and she takes a long pull.

"I don't think I'd change anything," I finally answer after some long intense thoughts. My words surprise me. My time with Brie, Colton, my family ... I wouldn't change any of it. My family are a bunch of assholes, but walking away from them brought me closer to Colt. I've learned a lot in the time I've spent as his chief of staff, not just professionally. I learned about life, what matters. I would've never learned those lessons if I hadn't stuck by his side. "I wouldn't have ended up here," I say, looking at her. She turns her head, and her blue eyes are smoldering. She leans toward me, and I lean toward her. We kiss. The smooth taste of the scotch mixing with the kiss is hot as fire. Our lips melt together as electricity singes my body, sparking a need to ravish her. She wraps her hands around my neck, and I'm still holding an open bottle of liquor. I continue to kiss her while reaching into my coat pocket for the lid. I find it, twist it on, all while our tongues dance, and I let the bottle fall to the floor. The thick brush of hay protects the glass from breaking. With my hands free, I wrap them around her waist. She begins to move her legs, guiding us to the bales of hay along the wall of the barn.

As we reach the wall, she flicks on a heater. It's the kind that plugs into a wall. The barn is freezing, but the standing heater provides enough heat along with the burning throb in my body, making me forget about the cold air. My hands move up her back and tousle her hair. I grab a fistful and tilt her head back, giving myself access to her neck. I slowly lick and suck her skin, and she melts beneath my touch, her head lolling around. She works my jacket off, and I work hers. She doesn't even bother with my shirt when she reaches for the button on my jeans.

"Make me feel good," she says. Something about her words and the needy look in her eyes has a deeper meaning. This is what she does. She uses sex to feel good. She doesn't create attachments. My body is on fire. My dick is rock solid when I lift her by her thighs so they wrap around me. I lay her on her back in a pile of hay. I continue trying to nip and suck at every exposed spot of her skin, and she moans.

I move my hips against that spot in between her legs, and the passion between us grows. My body burns with need. "Yes, please. Make me come," she pants, and her words are another subtle message. She wouldn't talk to me or pretty much look at me all throughout dinner, but she wants me to make her orgasm. She's low and now she wants to feel high. Sex makes her feel good. As my thoughts register, I stop kissing her. I'm about to give myself the worst case of blue balls ever. I can only imagine how dripping wet she is for me, but we can't do this. Not now. I don't want her using me for sex. Huh! The words in my head make me laugh and cringe and feel sad for Sam, but I've been here too many times, using sex to feel good. Of course we all want to feel good, but I want more with her. She probably won't talk to me in the morning like the other times.

Through ragged breaths, I pull away. I register her confusion. "We have to stop. I don't want to take you like this. The next time we have sex, I want you speaking to me afterward. I want you to let me in," I say, and I'm not deluded. I see the flabbergasted look on her face. She's acting as if I've slapped her. She struggles to straighten herself out, doing up the button and zipper on her jeans. I do mine up too. I give her a hand to help her up.

"Fuck you," she sputters. She's angry. She's had a bad night. I get it, and I'm willing to stick around and wait for her to see the light of day.

"Come on, Sam. I told you I wanted you, but not like this. I want you in a bed. I want to make love to you. I don't want to just make you feel good." As my words leave my mouth, her jaw drops and her eyes look angry, upset, or insulted. I'm not sure which.

"Just get out of here." She waves for me to leave. I leave her alone because she needs the space. I can see it. Whatever went down earlier, she's had a rough night. I back away. I walk back to the main house and head into the kitchen and grab the other bottle I picked up at the supermarket. It's Black Label. Not the best, but the variety wasn't great. I turn the lid and chug it down on the way to her bedroom. It doesn't fly past me that I am still here in Sam's room after she asked me to leave. I don't have a choice but to stay here tonight. I can't go and leave Izzy sleeping on the couch. Besides, maybe after Sam's anger fizzles out, she'll come to bed and finally admit that there is more between us, because if she doesn't then I'm just a sick fuck. An old guy that's been stalking her.

I drink until my nerves have eased, telling myself I will pack up and leave in the morning. I can stay with Izzy at the cabin and make sure Tristan is really gone. I will pick up my car when it's ready and maybe get it shipped back to Chicago. I will find a law firm and get a job and forget that Sam Belmont ever existed. I pass out.

CHAPTER THIRTY-THREE

AL

I WAKE up at the ass crack of dawn because my body seems to have become trained at waking at this hour. It's dark outside, and I will my mind to slide back into the land of sleep, only the bed feels empty beside me. I turn to see that not only is it empty but Sam's side of the bed looks untouched. I laugh at those words ... Sam's side of the bed. My chest stings. I like sleeping beside Sam, enjoy waking up early in the morning with her. She's a force to be reckoned with from the moment her cerulean eyes open in the morning. As I think of her, sadness blankets me. Being here has made the memory of Brie resurface in my mind. Only I'm a grown man now. I'm not a powerless boy anymore. I push myself out of bed worried about Sam. She was upset last night, her emotions running high. My rejection to sleep with her just made things worse in her head. I'm sure of it even though my intentions were good.

I pass my sister sleeping on the couch. The floor creaks, and she opens one eye. "What time is it?" she croaks.

"Go back to sleep," I answer, and she does. I don't see any sign of Sam. A peek out the front door tells me her Ford is parked outside, and relief washes over me that she didn't run to Austin or

Blake for sex. I've never been on the second floor in this house, but I trudge up the stairs. I need to know if she slept up there, wanting to make sure she's safe. Mr. Belmont opens his bedroom door the moment my foot steps on the last step up to the second floor.

"What the fuck you doing, City?" he grumbles, and I startle and pause mid-step.

"Just wanted to check on Sam. She didn't sleep in her room last night," I answer.

"Well, there's no fucking way she slept with Mack and Autumn," he scoffs. I forgot how cheery Farmer Joe is.

"Maybe with Ethan," I suggest, and he walks into a dark room.

"Not here," he mutters. "Fuck." He curses and my heart picks up speed. Where the hell are you Sam?

"We better check the barn," he suggests.

"Right," I run back down the stairs back to Sam's room and grab my boots. I'm wearing a pair of lounge pants and a T-shirt. I grab my puffy jacket. Mr. Belmont is out the door before me. I head into the heifer barn first, but there's no sign of Sam. That's when I hear it Mr. Belmont screaming, "HELP!" It's loud and gargled and filled with pain. I register his voice coming from the bull barn, the one I left Sam in last night, and my heart sinks.

"Help. Help," he screams some more, and I know it's Sam. Something bad happened. I run into the barn, and Sam is on the floor. Mr. Belmont is on his knees, crying. "We got to help her," he says. I register the bull bucking toward us. Sam is on the floor outside of the bull's cage. She has a bump on her head, and she has dry blood oozing out of one ear. It doesn't look good, but she's muttering so I know she's alive even if she isn't coherent.

"I'm going to get help," I murmur and run back to the house as fast as my legs will carry me. I pick up the phone, hoping they actually have 9-1-1 in this backward small town. Someone picks up after one ring. My heart is beating so fast I worry that I won't be able to formulate words but they come. "I need an ambulance. It's an emergency."

"Okay, sir," a woman's voice comes through the phone. "Who is the ambulance for?"

"Sam Belmont," I answer swiftly. "Please. She's unconscious. I think she got hurt riding the bull. I think it's her head." My voice shakes.

"Okay. Try to remain calm, sir. Is she breathing?"

"I think so. I'm not beside her right now. Her father is. She was muttering a little."

"Okay, an ambulance has been dispatched to the Belmont Ranch. We have the address."

"She's in the bull barn," I explain so they don't waste time when they arrive.

"I will notify the driver," she assures me. My hands are shaking and sweaty. "Hang on, they are on their way," she says, and I pray that Sam is okay.

Izzy stands on the other side of the kitchen counter with a worried look. She just heard my call. I don't have time to explain.

"MACK," I scream at the top of my lungs. "AUTUMN." I take the steps two at a time and make it to their bedroom door. I flick on the lights and scream, "Please, it's Sam! Come down fast. I called an ambulance. I'm going to the bull barn. Make sure they come to the bull barn." They begin to scramble, and I run out of the house and back out to the barn. Joe Belmont is on the floor, softly caressing his daughter's hair. He's crying.

"I called for an ambulance. They're on their way," I say.

"Stupid fool. I think she rode him. He must have hurt her, and she crawled out of the pen. At least she got out," he repeats, and my stomach turns. She drank the alcohol last night. She had no right getting on the bull. She needed me, and I thought I was doing the right thing when I walked away from her, but I should have never left her alone in the state she was in. Fuck. I keep fucking up.

It isn't long before we hear sirens. Mack stands beside her dad. Autumn is out front to guide the paramedics over to us. My heart breaks as the paramedics enter the barn and strap her onto a gurney. She looks helpless and fragile, very unlike herself.

Mack gets into the back of the ambulance with her. Mr. Belmont runs to his truck. I rush to the house and grab the keys to Sam's truck. No one bats an eye that I've taken her keys. I'm driving her truck as Izzy bites her nails nervously beside me. Autumn stays behind with Ethan. As I drive, my only fear is that Sam will die. The blood oozing out of her ear has to be a bad sign. She must have a head trauma. Fuck, every movie I've seen about bull riders scrolls through my mind. It's a fucking dangerous sport. People die, people end up with spine and head injuries they don't walk away from. I smack the steering wheel and curse. The twenty-minute drive to the hospital feels like an eternity. Izzy doesn't say a word, and I'm grateful.

When we arrive at the hospital, I slam the truck into park and run inside. I need to know she's okay. I spot Joe Belmont and Mack immediately and listen in while they give the doctors a medical history. The nurse rolls Sam away, and I feel like my life is slipping through my fingers.

CHAPTER THIRTY-FOUR

AL

IT'S BEEN HOURS. We know she's alive. We don't have answers, and I'm losing my mind. Joe Belmont sits on a chair off in the corner of the waiting room, staring at the floor, not saying a word. Mack is pacing in front of me, and Autumn is busy playing card games with Ethan to keep him occupied. And then there's me. I don't know what I'm doing. I pace, I sit, I want to punch the fucking walls. I want to punch myself, but mostly I pray that I get a chance to make things right with Sam. Izzy took a cab back to the family cabin, and I worry about her too, even though she texted that Tristan was gone this morning. She said she'd be back at the hospital later.

"I'm going to call Kell, tell her to feed Snow," Mack mumbles. She seems to always be on top of things. I nod and she walks up to me and squeezes my shoulder. "You care about her. I can see that." She gives me a sympathetic smile. I nod but words fail me because if I speak, I fear I will cry. Crying right now seems wrong. I've only known Sam a short while. I have her dad and sister sitting here with me, and they are keeping themselves together so I should too. I realize just how under my skin Samantha Belmont truly is.

A man wearing scrubs and a cap walks toward us. And we all stand up. He introduces himself. "I'm Dr. Yang. I'm the neurosurgeon assigned to Samantha," he explains. "Cat scan shows she has a minor bleed in her brain. She's very lucky it isn't a lot worse. I'm hoping we don't need to operate since that involves risks of its own. The next forty-eight hours will be critical and we'll repeat the CT scan. Assuming it's the same or smaller, she likely won't need surgery and it will resolve on its own. We'll be doing round the clock neuro checks on her, monitoring her progress. She needs to rest now. I'm going to limit one visitor in the room at a time since I don't want her over stimulated."

"What happens next? What does this mean?" Mack takes a step forward.

"We repeat the CT scan in about 48 hours. Once we get the results, we'll know how to proceed. She's experienced head trauma. It will take time to heal. For now we wait. Like I said, she's lucky the bleed is minor and is not in a dangerous spot, but it's still considered a severe injury. I know you're looking for more definitive answers. Her vitals are stable."

"Thank you, doctor," Mack answers, and she looks to Joe and then to Autumn.

"Is it okay if I go in first?" she asks. Everybody nods for her to go ahead. She's so young, but she definitely acts like Sam's mother.

I exhale harshly and take a seat on a chair in the waiting room. At least her vitals are stable, even though I know that doesn't mean much. A head injury is never a good thing.

About twenty minutes later Mack comes back, and Joe Belmont heads into Sam's room. Mack tells me she's sleeping. She takes my hand and gives it a squeeze again before walking over to Autumn. Autumn embraces her in a hug. I sit and wait. I'm a stranger. I barely know Sam. I barely know the Belmonts, and yet I sit here and my heart aches.

It's been 72 hours since we found Sam unconscious. I've watched every hour tick by at a slow pace. I've been in to see her. She's been sleeping every time. The doctor has been giving her medication to keep her asleep in the hope her injury will heal. The bleed in her brain is improving on its own, which means she won't need surgery and that's a relief.

"They're just taking her for the CT scan now," Joe Belmont says to me. I picked my stuff up from the Belmont Ranch and moved to the family cabin where Izzy is staying. I hate staying in a place owned by my mother and stepfather, but my choices are limited. Besides, I've been spending my days and most nights at the hospital, praying for Sam. It's New Year's Day now. I spent New Year's Eve in Sam's hospital room. I don't say much. I sit and watch her, willing her body to heal.

"Thanks for letting me know," I answer and it still feels hard to breathe, like an elephant has taken up permanent residence on my chest. He claps me on the back and walks away to sit on a chair in the far corner of the room. He doesn't have a cell phone, so he just sits and watches the TV. It looks like he's staring into thin air. Joe Belmont is a hard shell to crack, that's for damn sure.

More hours pass and the doctor returns. "She's awake. Her speech is clear. It will be about an hour for the radiologist to read the scan results. She passed her initial neurological tests with flying colors," Dr. Yang says, and we all let out the breath we were holding.

"That's really good news," Mack says to her dad. Autumn stayed on the ranch with Ethan. She looks to me too. "I really do believe she's going to pull through," she says, and her eyes well up with tears.

"And I'm selling that damn bull," her father chimes in.

Mack huffs. "Good luck with that."

"I don't give a fuck. It's gone," he says with that deep throaty voice of his.

I don't say much. I sit and wait until it's my turn to see Sam. When Mack calls me to her room, my heart picks up speed. I've hated watching Sam looking so fragile, lying in that hospital bed. She's been too quiet, too still. With her eyes shut, I can't see the usual fire burning in the depths of her blue eyes, and it irks me. Only now when I walk into her room her eyes are open and relief washes over me. The bruising on her face looks a little less swollen.

"Why are you still here, City?" she murmurs, her voice scratchy and weak. Her first words throw me off. I don't know what I was expecting. She wanted to use sex to make herself feel good the last time we were together, and I didn't allow it. I left her angry. She got hurt and I've had all this quiet time to contemplate my life and figure out what she means to me. Her words feel like a rough wave has knocked me over, even if I'm glad she sounds like her old self.

"I'm here for you," I snicker, but it's garbled and sad. I look deep into her eyes and moisture pools in my own.

She senses my worry, and her own eyes soften. I haven't seen her emotional before, and I watch her exhale softly. She shakes her head like she's fighting back tears.

"You're supposed to rest, and I'm going to stick around while you do. Gotta say, Sam, I'm relieved you have a hard knocker, but why would you get on that crazy bull? One look in that things eyes and you can see it's one crazy animal."

She swallows hard and the moisture that builds up in my eyes makes an appearance. I swipe at it quick. My words are meant to sound easy and lighten the mood, even though I'm having a hard time keeping my emotions in check. Her lips look dry and chapped, and a stray tear escapes slowly, making its way down her cheek. "You're starting to sound an awful lot like my old man," she says and her lips turn up slightly. It's as if we are both bombarded with such intense emotions, but we are somehow burying what we feel. We are making light of the situation. We are running away. I see the pattern now. It's as clear as day. Funny that I should fall for a woman who has the same personality as me. How could we ever work? My answer is also clear as the light of day. I need to work on myself. I need to act as guide to the both of us because she is young and clearly hurting.

"You going to tell me that I'm almost as old as him too?" I chuckle because I want to make her smile, and she does. It warms my chest. "That's what I thought."

"You're a hot old man." She pouts, and I like those words. I like that she's finally acknowledging that there is something here between us.

"Glad to see you're feeling better." I sigh.

"I fucked up," she says, and even though her cheeks are pale, they still turn a little crimson.

"You're saying that to the man you found passed out in his car in a snow storm?" I remind her, and she gives me a look that says I have a point. "I didn't want to kill myself that night, but I almost did. And just so you know, I wouldn't mind keeping the part about the sleeping pills private. Now that you know who I am, I don't need a media shit storm to ensue because of it."

"My lips are sealed." She presses her lips together and gives me a slight nod. She's still hooked up to all kinds of machines. "Besides, I've made some poor decisions in my life. Some of them good, some of them hard. Some of them just plain hard to live with. I've been holding myself back," she says, and it brings my mind back to the conversation I had with her when I told her about walking away from my family.

"I know all about that." My lip quirks to one side. I take hold of her fragile hand, and my thumb slides back and forth along her soft skin.

"I know you do," she confesses, and her blue eyes turn cloudy. It's that same blanket of sadness that's usually there, wrapped around her and holding her tight. I want to ask her what keeps her trapped here in the sadness. I don't because she's been through too much, and she needs to rest.

"I'm thinking no more bull riding for you," I say, feeling protective of her.

She huffs. "Now you really sound like my old man. I'm going to let you in on a little secret," she says playfully, and I move in closer to show her I'm listening. "I'm not the kind of woman to take orders from a man."

I snicker. "I knew that the first day I opened my eyes and saw you."

"I've been hitting the rodeos long enough. It was the thrill I was after. I hated the way I felt inside," she says, and again she's being vague, but I know better than to push. "I've got to make some changes with my life. I see that now." Her words resonate more than she knows.

"I feel the same way. If you hadn't found me in my car. I could have died. Going through something scary like that has a way of opening your eyes to things, doesn't it?" I smile sadly.

"It sure does." I give her hand a soft squeeze and lean forward to press a soft kiss to her cheek.

"I want you to stay," she says, and I know it's hard for her to admit.

"I want to stay. I think we need to take the time to get to know each other. We've slept in the same bed since the first night we met. I'm going to miss you, but for once in my life I want to do things the right way." I smile to reassure her. Her eyes flutter a little, and I can see that she's growing tired. "I'm honored you're giving me the chance to get to know you. That means no other men," I say, and I can't help the authoritative tone my voice takes because the thought of Sam fucking anyone but me drives me mad.

"There you go again, telling me what to do." She smiles playfully, even though it's weak.

I cock my brow, giving her a serious look.

"I'm playing with you. There won't be anyone but you, old man." She smiles and bats her lashes. The anxiety in my chest eases.

I groan. "Ground rules: you have to stop calling me City and old man."

She giggles at my request and gives me a devious look. Even in that hospital bed with her hair muffled and machines hooked up to her, she looks sexy. "You sure aren't old, Al. You're strong and virile," she says, and my nostrils flare as heat springs through my body. I practically have to remind myself that she's fragile, and I can't maul her like a beast.

"Damn straight." I nod my head in agreement. "It's good to hear your laugh." We sit quietly and look at each other. A few beats pass. "I moved my stuff over to the cabin with Izzy." Sam's face pales at my words. "I'm sticking around. I'm not leaving."

"Good."

Her eyes flutter closed, and her breathing evens out. I sit back in the chair and watch her sleep, and I'm amazed how she's come to mean so much to me in such a short time.

CHAPTER-THIRTY FIVE

AL

Past

It was Friday night there was a school formal for the boys and girls before we broke for Christmas. I decided not to go. The pain of not seeing Brie kept me in my quiet dorm room. I hadn't heard from her in days. A light knock on my dorm room door pulled me from staring blankly out the window.

I stood expecting one of the guys only it was Brie. Her blond hair had soft ringlets on the edges and she wore an off white dress that made her look like an angel. I walked away from the door and fell back on my bed. I couldn't look her in the eye, and she walked in and took a seat on my desk chair, swiveling to face me.

"I'm not here to say I'm sorry. I know it won't cut it," she began. "I don't know if you pay attention to what goes on in Hollywood, but a story about my dad went viral on the internet this week." I watch her throat bob.

"I don't follow Hollywood news," I clip.

"My father had a secret family. He has two children with another woman. Since the story broke, we found out he's been living with them. His oldest daughter is sixteen. That means she was born when I was two."

I shot up to a seated position, my legs swinging off the bed. My instinct was to hug her close. "I'm sorry. That's terrible."

She nodded. "You had to see the pictures. They were this picture perfect family. My dad is smiling and hugging them. I don't have any pictures with my dad. He's never given me that smile. That warmth." Her arms curled around her small frame and she shivered.

"I know how that feels." My gaze cut to hers. "My father has never looked at me like he looks at Derek. I don't know why. I don't know what I've done to him or not done. What I do know is that I want to be nothing like him." I paused because she started to cry, and I stood up and wrapped my arms around her, hushing her cries away. Despite everything, I couldn't help myself. "We promised to never be like them," I whispered.

Her soft cries intensified. "I don't know what's happening. I'm sad and withdrawn. I feel numb most days. I know we promised to never do drugs, but I was curious. They make me feel good," she said, and I pulled her into my lap, her small frame curling into me.

"You promised after you did ecstasy that night you wouldn't touch anymore. We are almost done the year. We can go home and head to college together. Tell our parents to fuck off or whatever. We're adults."

She laughed despite her tears. "I'm so sorry for hurting you." She smiled sadly. "I mean with Catrina. I don't know what I was thinking or not thinking. It was stupid to do the coke. I know it was. I'd pushed so many guys away, wanting to stay loyal to you, but my head wasn't right the other night. I can't explain it."

I wanted to tell her she was high off her ass but swallowed my words.

"What now, Brie? I'm worried about you. You look too thin.

Maybe you should talk to the school counsellor and get some help," I suggested.

"I know I've lost weight. I just don't have an appetite. I can't eat. Besides the food here isn't all that great," she giggled softly.

"It really isn't."

"Mom is coming to get me next week. I think she's taking me to France over Christmas." She frowned.

"That sounds pretty cool," I said only because I hated to see her frown.

"Will you let me kiss you?" she asked. "I know I messed up, but when I kiss you it feels like home. You are the only home I have. My mom takes me traveling. This place is a freak zone. I don't have a real home."

"Shit, Brie." I kissed her so hard my chest ached. I wanted to take her pain. "We're finishing up this spring and you're coming with me. Your parents can't tell you what to do once you turn eighteen. We will be together. We'll make a home. I'll take care of you," I held her close.

She placed her head on my chest, and I held her as tight as I could. "That sounds perfect."

My Brie, my sunshine was broken, but I was going to make everything okay. I was going to give her the life she deserved.

CHAPTER THIRTY-SIX

SAM

It's evening and *The Voice* is on. I sit in front of the television and sing along with one of the contestants. I don't notice Al standing off in the kitchen, watching me. When the song ends, he walks up to me. He looks worn out from a long day. I'm all too familiar with those. I've been home a full week. Mack, Autumn and Ethan left for New York the same day.

"You have an amazing voice." He takes a seat beside me on the couch. He isn't self-conscious about smelling like shit anymore.

"Thank you." I lift the blanket over my legs so it covers my body.

"Did you have professional singing lessons as a child or something?" he inquires some more. I shake my head. "You should be on that show," he says, lifting my legs and placing them on his lap. Another contestant sings a song. Al waits, looking at me expectantly. "Aren't you going to sing that one too?" he asks.

I shake my head.

"Did I miss something? Did the cat get your tongue?" He snickers. "That night after Moe's ... you know the night I wanted to rip Blake's head off?" he starts, and at the mention of Blake's name, my body tenses. I don't know where he's going with this. "I stood outside your room and listened to you sing," he admits. I can't explain why, but I don't sing in front of people. It feels like Al broke into one of my most intimate moments by telling me he was listening in, kind of like now. His features soften, and he rubs my feet a little, massaging in circles.

"Mmm, that feels nice," I moan. He leans forward and presses a kiss to my lips, and sparks shoot down to my belly. Doctor's orders are no sex or anything that will cause exertion. Regardless, Al is hell-bent on taking things slow.

"Don't moan like that. I was serious about the no sex policy," he warns, his lips warm against mine.

I giggle. "I'm pretty sure I could break you," I tease.

"Nothing will make me break the no sex policy," he says, placing soft kisses along both my cheeks and moving to my lids. He makes me feel cared for; he brings me meals and keeps me company, and he's doing my job. I've never had a man treat me this way before. I didn't know men behaved this way. My papa sure never cared for my mom this way, not even when she was sick.

"How 'bout I suck you off," I offer, knowing most men will not say no to a blow job.

He groans. "Don't go saying stuff like that. Now I'm hard as a rock."

"I can suck you off. It's exerting for you, not me." I lick my lips as I say the words.

His head falls back, and then he raises it. "What did I get myself into?" he asks himself.

"Come on." I cock a brow, giving him the most seductive look I can muster.

He groans again, only this time frustration seems to be at the root. "If you aren't getting off, neither am I," he says. "Now don't change the subject. I want to learn more about you. Tell me about the singing."

Now it's my turn to groan. "Fine," I concede, my tone terse, but he knows I'm just playing with him.

"I'll warm up the chicken soup while you talk," he says, and I talk because he's been sweet and caring, and I find it harder and harder to resist his charms.

"I've always loved to sing. My mama used to make me sing every day. She would watch me with warm eyes filled with love and make all kinds of requests. Once I learned to read, I would go on YouTube and find songs with lyrics and just sing my heart out. When I was a little girl, I dreamed of being a singer one day. Then mama passed and I don't know ... life happened." I shrug my shoulders and watch him in the kitchen. "I thought I'd take singing courses in college, but then I didn't go to college. I was offered a job singing at Moe's when they have live music, but it wasn't my thing."

"You wanted all or nothing," Al cuts in.

I nod. "Something like that. Singing was something I did that made my mom proud. After she died, I kind of lost the urge. But it felt like a betrayal to my mother because she always thought my voice would get me out of Holston."

"You should try out." He tips his chin to the television.

My brows draw together as I look at the screen. It's hard to admit that I've had that same thought over a thousand times. "I wanted to. It was never the right time," I finally say, and those words are hard to admit, but Al ... well, he gets things. He's made mistakes of his own. He gets me.

He gives me a knowing look. "That's going on your bucket list."

I snicker. "Sure."

"I'm serious." He gives me a pointed glare.

"Oh! I know you are," I answer. He walks over with a bowl of Kell's chicken soup on a tray and places it gently on my lap.

"Mmm, it's good. You should try some," I say, and he leans over for me to feed him. I give him a spoonful.

"Kell is a good cook."

"Most of the women in this town are good cooks," I retort and it's true. They've been dropping off cooked meals ever since I got home from the hospital. Everything from meatloaf to fried chicken.

"They are something special," Al says. He's been here nightly to sample the food with me. "What happened to you?" he asks with a mischievous smile.

I shove him. "Hey, you jerk. I'm special. That's what happened."

His blue eyes turn liquid. "You sure are, Sam Belmont." And he leans forward and presses a kiss to my mouth, and I melt into him.

"You planning on taking a shower?" It's me who breaks the kiss.

He gives me a crooked grin. "Do I smell that bad?"

I lift my sweatshirt to my nose. It's freshly washed so the smell of fabric softener is strong and dilutes the cow shit smell. "Um ..."

He stands from the couch. "Okay. I better head over to Izzy's and shower," he says.

"I don't want you to leave." I pout. "I still have some of your clothes in my room. Why don't you shower here and head back to Izzy's later?" I ask. He got his Porsche back, and he parked it in the garage at his family cabin. He's been using one of the SUV's from the Walsh garage. It's some fancy truck. A BMW or something. When Papa saw it, he scoffed and said it wasn't a Ford.

"Yeah, okay." He stands and heads to the back of the house, and I eat my bowl of chicken soup. I think to myself how much I like having him here. He awakens feelings inside of me I never knew could exist. He makes me want to conquer my dreams. Dreams I placed on the back burner a long time ago. I finish my bowl of soup and place it on the side table. I pick up my cell and start searching *The Voice* and when the next audition is. I find the information and realize that my bucket list is a lot longer than I thought. There are a few things ahead of a singing career that I want to accomplish.

About twenty minutes later he is freshly showered and wearing a pair of gray lounge pants and a fitted long-sleeve black shirt. He's also bare foot. Papa walks through the door.

"Fuck, City, I thought we got rid of you. Are you back already?" His lips twist in a wry smile. Papa has actually come to like Al—as much as Papa shows he likes anyone at all.

"You can't get rid of me that fast," Al retorts. He's learned how to deal with my father's dry humor.

Papa nods his head and takes a beer out of the fridge and cracks it open. "You kids have a good night." He nods and walks up the stairs.

Al takes a seat beside me. He kisses me on the lips. "Better?" he asks, referring to the smell.

"Much." I kiss him back. Our lips remain pressed together.

"It's late. Let me take you to bed," he offers.

I frown. "I thought you could stay."

"Are you asking me to sleep over, Sam Belmont?" His voice is playful and childlike. It's one of the reasons I like him so much because he has the ability to make me smile with the odd things he says and does.

I bat my lashes. "Take me to bed."

"You're trying to give me the worst case of blue balls known to man." He leans down and scoops me up into his arms.

"You know, I'm capable of walking," I answer. I may be injured, but I can walk.

"Not on my dime, Princess." He smiles and it hits me in the belly.

"I'm no princess, but from what I read online, you are a prince. A prince with a lot of scandal under his belt." I give him a devious glare. I can't help it. Once I left the hospital and remembered he was the governor of Illinois' right-hand man, I had to Google him. The list of exploits was long.

"You are a princess, baby. You deserve to be treated like a princess. And I can't believe you Googled me." He scoffs as we enter my room. He lays me on the bed gently and leans forward to press a kiss to my forehead, and I feel cherished.

"Do I need to worry about the long list of broken hearts you left behind?" I ask, and he climbs into bed next to me.

"You don't need to worry at all. Part of the reason I wanted to get away from the city was to clear my head of all that. I'd had enough of just about everything. I was looking for something different, and I found her. Right here." His glare bores into me, his eyes saying a million words that his mouth doesn't speak.

"Why hasn't someone snatched you up already?" I ask and he stiffens.

"There isn't someone else is there because..." my voice trails off.

"Nothing like that Sam. When I was younger there was a girl." He begins and now it's my turn to hold my breath.

"A girl?" I ask.

"We were young, teenagers but in order for you to understand the story I need to go back further." He gulps hard. It makes me nervous even though a part of me knew deep down that a guy like him isn't single for no reason.

"When I was fourteen I caught my dad having sex with one of my mom's best friends." He begins. "I called my father on it. He kind of threatened me from telling my mom. Over the years there were many more woman I knew about."

"And you didn't tell your mom?" I ask.

"No, he told me not to burst her happy bubble then he shipped me off to boarding school. I didn't know he was my step-father. They told me he was my biological father although when I look back on things now I should've known something was off." He says.

"And there was a girl?" I ask.

"Her name was Brie. We became fast friends. It developed into more. Her dad was a big movie star who cheated on her mother and had a secret family."

"Shit." My eyes widen. My dad was an asshole but you don't hear stories like that in Holston.

"Yeah, Brie and I were kindred spirits cast off by our families. We were the underdog children." He says and my heart aches. "We wanted to be different than our parents. No cheating, no drugs for Brie since her dad was an addict." He explains. "Things spiraled out of control when Brie found out her dad had a secret family. She cheated on me." He swallows and I can see how hard it is for him to talk about her. I don't mean to feel jealous but I do. The way he talks about her shows how much he cared.

"I'm sorry. That sounds hard."

"It was she was my high school sweetheart and I couldn't really do anything to help her." He says.

My hand comes up, and I caress his cheek.

"Now will you tell me what has gone on between you and Blake and the other younger guy?" he says.

"You mean Austin?" He doesn't look happy when I say his name.

"Yeah." He nods, and I know I have a lot of explaining to do, so I start with the basics.

"I began hooking up with Blake freshman year. He was two years older, and he had mischief practically written on his forehead. I got into all kinds of trouble hanging out with him. Cutting school, smoking pot, stuff like that ..." I explain and Al watches me so intently. "Mack wanted me to hang around kids that would be a good influence. She mentioned Austin one day. He came from a good family, and Mack hoped he would be a good influence. We were friends for years before we started hooking up. Austin always had my back," I explain.

"And both of them knew you were hooking up with the other?" he asks.

I bite down hard on my lip. The story is complicated. "Not exactly."

"I'm listening," he persists, and I don't blame him. He's put himself on the line. He shows me how much he cares for me, and I care for him too. He has a right to know.

"Things blew up with Blake at one point, and Austin was there to help me. We didn't hook up at first. That came much later. Blake and I were apart awhile. He went away to college on a football scholarship, but he got injured and found himself back in Holston. We started hooking up again. Austin went off to college, and when he came home for visits, we continued hooking up too," I say, aware of how awful this story makes me sound. I cringe. "We weren't in committed relationships. Austin cares about me, he always has, and Blake is ... Blake." I try to explain even though it isn't much of an explanation.

Al leans over in bed and hangs his arm around my shoulder and presses a kiss to my temple. I don't sense judgment from him. "I can't be a douche and judge you because of some idiotic double standard. You've seen the gossip columns. I've made some bad choices."

"A married woman." I cock a brow.

He blows out a whoosh of air. "I did not know she was married." He sounds exasperated like he has had to defend that action a lot.

I laugh. "Hey! No judgment here."

"Seriously though. One of the reasons I stayed single is because I don't like cheaters," he says and I sense it has something to do with his stepfather.

He pulls me in close. "We're quite a pair, aren't we?"

"You could say that." I nod. I look up to him. "Will you stay the night?"

He wags his brows. "Sam, I'm not that kind of man."

I punch him lightly in the chest. He makes an *oomph* sound. Then his face turns somber, and he goes from playful to serious. "I'd love to, baby." He presses a kiss to my forehead, and then he gets under the covers with me and holds me like I belong to him, and in my heart I feel like I do.

CHAPTER THIRTY-SEVEN

AL

I APPRECIATE the life lesson manual labor gave me the first few weeks I worked on the ranch. When Sam was working out here with me, I thrived on just being close to her. Now I've worked out here for three weeks, and Farmer Joe is the only face I see. Even though he's eased up on being an asshole, he still isn't the person I want to see all day.

I'm out in the heifer barn, preparing the bales of hay, when my phone rings. Colton's name lights up the screen. I drop the bale of hay and answer the call. "Hey, man, what's up?"

His deep chuckle comes through the phone. "You're sounding a lot better. Last time we spoke, you sounded like hell." He reminds me of the night of the snow storm.

I scoff. "I'd never seen such a bad snow storm. What did you expect?"

"I thought I would have heard from you by now," he says, and I can tell he's wondering where I've disappeared to. I sent him a text message before Christmas, wishing his family a happy holiday, but we are used to talking a lot more than that.

"Yeah, man, sorry. I've been staying out here in Holston, Colorado," I say.

"Nice. Never heard of Holston. Is that close to Aspen?" he asks.

"Not really," I answer.

"Vague much?" He snickers.

"Sorry, man." My hands are dirty, and if they weren't, I'd be nervously raking my fingers through my hair. "I ... uh ... met someone," I begin.

"Fuck yeah," he cheers and then blows out a breath. "You fell off the face of the planet. I didn't think you found a woman, so I feared you were dead. Hence the phone call. Your sister wasn't answering."

"Thanks for the concern, but fuck you."

"Yeah, yeah." He pauses. "Who is she? Talk ..." he urges.

"She lives here in Holston. She's uh ... a rancher. I've been hanging out here with her and her family." My words are stilted. I don't know what I'm supposed to say about Sam.

"What's her name?" he asks, and he sounds like a little gossip. I want to laugh at him, but I don't because I know this is him being happy for me.

"Her name is Samantha Belmont. She's twenty-three years old," I say and then regret it.

"Fuck, that's young," he reminds me.

"Age isn't everything, asshole."

"Whoa," he says like he's digesting my words. "Sorry, man. I really am happy for you." He pauses. "Maybe I shouldn't mention the real reason for my call." His voice trails off.

"You mean you actually weren't worried about me?" I feign insult.

His deep laugh booms through the phone. "That's not it. Ainsley Stapleton just gave me a call. He wants to manage a campaign for you. He thinks you've got what it takes to be governor," he says, surprising the hell out of me. I feel dizzy and excited. Ainsley Stapleton doesn't offer to run a campaign. He's made presidents. He doesn't play games.

"What's really going on here, Colt?" I ask, trying to keep my voice steady because Ainsley is the cream of the crop.

I hear his exhale through the phone. "Don't you think I knew when I cut out, I was leaving you high and dry?" he says, throwing me off, but it doesn't surprise me that he's mentioning it because Colton Mathis is the most unselfish man out there. I don't say a word. "Look, Al, I had a lot of shit happen in my life. I know my decisions have affected you. I called Ainsley out to Pine Island. He thinks you have a good chance to make it to the top. With your family name and your resume, you can do this," he says, and his voice is so sincere. The fact that he believes in me means the world to me, even though I hate any mention of my family name.

"Fuck, Colt. This is a lot. I wasn't expecting it."

"And suddenly there is a woman in your life and you don't know what to do," he continues my sentence before the words even formulate in my brain.

"Fuck. Yeah." I let out a sigh.

"I hear you, man. Don't sweat this. Take a few days. Let it marinate and see what you think. We both know that politics is your game. You've wanted this a long time," he says, and it shocks me a little because I don't think I ever showed him that I wanted his position.

"Colt ... I'm sorry if I—"

He cuts me off. "It's not like that, man. I know you would have been happy to get me to the White House, but it wasn't for me. All I'm saying is I don't want you to give up on what you wanted because of me."

Whoa. "Thanks, man. I mean, I appreciate you thinking of me. Let me think on it, and I'll get back to you," I say.

"Sure. You take care."

"Yeah. You too." The phone clicks, and I feel like I've had the wind knocked out of me. I have to stop and replay the conversation over and over again in my head. Ainsley Stapleton ... holy fucking shit. I try to focus on the ranching, but my adrenaline is pumping hard. I finish the work I need to do and walk into the house. Sam is watching *The Voice* again. She isn't singing, but her eyes sparkle when she watches that show, just like I think my eyes sparkle now at the mention of politics.

"Hey there." I pull her from the show.

"Oh, hey." She smiles to me from her spot on the couch. "Leslie brought by some meatloaf. It's in the tray on the counter. It's really good." She smiles, and it hits me in the chest. That smile of hers melts me.

"You got up and warmed it yourself?" I inquire. When she first got home, she was having dizzy spells, so she didn't like to get up for anything other than bathroom runs, which I helped her with—just to the door.

"Yeah." She rubs her temple. "The headache feels like a light thud now, but I don't feel the dizziness. At least, today was a good day," she explains.

"Good, I'm glad. We're scheduled to go into Dr. Yang's tomorrow for a checkup," I remind her.

"I know. I may have bumped my head, but my marbles are still in check." She points to her head and winks at me.

"Oh! I know they are," I assure her, and I scoop up some meatloaf in a separate tray and pop it in the oven. "I'm going to go take a shower so I don't have to listen to you complaining about how bad I smell. I wouldn't want to torture you." I wink and head back to the bathroom.

"Withholding sex is considered torture in some countries," she yells at my back, and I just laugh and shake my head because life is never boring with her around. I do the five-minute scrub down I've become accustomed to. It helps that I don't have much hair on my head; I went into town and got my hair buzzed at the barber shop.

I throw on a pair of my lounge pants and a hooded sweatshirt I bought at a shop in town. I'm looking more and more like a mountain man and less and less like a politician each day, and yet I'm the happiest I've ever been.

"Hey there, sexy." Sam winks.

I walk over to the oven and take out the meatloaf. I plop it on a plate, and it's hot and steamy. I never ate meatloaf back in Chicago. It was never on the menu when I was growing up either, but as I take my first bite, I instantly love it.

"It's good, right?" Sam leans in, and I feed her a bite.

"I already ate my serving, but I love it."

"She makes good meatloaf," I agree, and we sit back to watch the next contestant on *The Voice*. They are doing blind auditions. It's pretty cool. Some of these people have amazing voices, but none of them hold a candle to the woman sitting beside me.

I finish eating and place my empty plate on the coffee table in front of me. I throw my arm around Sam, and she leans into the crook of my shoulder like she's meant to be there. I like these quiet nights just sitting by the TV with her. I never watched much TV before, but I realize I enjoy watching *The Voice*.

"Colt called today," I say matter-of-factly.

"Oh yeah?" She tilts her head up to look at me.

"He wanted to make sure I wasn't dead." I scoff. "And he spoke to a very prominent campaign manager about running a governor campaign for me. Well, at least there's a process, but he thinks I have a real chance. This guy Ainsley, he's out to win. He doesn't take just any candidate. He's made presidents," I say a little too proudly. I can't help it. Just the words themselves are exciting.

She leans away from me a little and looks up to me. "Wow! That's big news. I'm so happy for you. Are you going to take it?" she asks, and her voice is fucking chipper. It pisses me off.

"I don't know if I'm going to take the opportunity. That's why I'm talking to you." I look down at her. I don't do a good job of hiding the irritation in my voice.

"I appreciate you talking to me." She straightens out and pulls

away from me. "But isn't that your dream?" she asks, raising both
her brows.

"It was my dream, Sam. I don't know that it's my dream now. I
don't know what I want to do," I admit. What I don't say is that I
am falling in love with her because her whole pulling back tactic
right now is enough to tell me she would run if those words leave
my mouth, and it irritates the fuck out of me.

"You should totally take it," she says, and I shoot up to
my feet.

"What the fuck, Sam?" I feel like she just punched me in the
gut. "There is something between us. You can't just expect me to
get up and walk the hell out of here." My voice is raised, my
emotions running high.

"Why the hell not, Al? If I were to head to Los Angeles
tomorrow to try out for *The Voice* and I made it ... what would you
tell me? Would you say, 'Sam, don't do it.'? Hell no. You'd tell me
to follow my dreams." She wraps her arms in front of her chest
and gives me an assured nod.

"Yeah, but I would fucking follow you to Los Angeles," I
answer.

"Well, I won't follow you to Chicago," she retorts, and my
mouth falls open just as Farmer Joe walks through the kitchen
door.

"Everything okay in here?" he asks. I grab the keys to the
BMW and grab my coat and shoes at the door. I feel like a jagged
knife cut through my chest.

"Oh! That's fine. Just leave," I hear Sam holler, and I leave. I'm
reeling. My blood pumps so hard through my veins I can hear the
whoosh of blood. Anger pools in my chest, radiating from my
extremities. I just told her I'd basically follow her anywhere, and
she tells me that she won't. What the hell am I supposed to make
of that?

I drive down the street, only I don't head back to the cabin.
Izzy left for New York a few days ago, so the place is empty. My

mother and stepfather don't even know I'm staying there. I don't want to be alone, and the place isn't stalked with liquor. I pull into Moe's instead, fully aware that I am basically wearing a hoody and a pair of jogging pants. I'd never leave the house dressed like this in Chicago, but then again, people in Chicago actually know who I am. I walk into Moe's and the first person I see is Blake. Fucking great.

CHAPTER THIRTY-EIGHT

SAM

"You wanna tell me what the fuck just happened here?" Papa takes a seat in the recliner and waits.

"What the fuck do you care?" I snarl back.

"Fair enough." He pauses. "You could call Kell or Leslie or anyone of your girlfriends, and they will give you the answers you want to hear. I'm going to tell you something different," he says, and okay, he has my attention.

"And that is?" I cock a brow and wait for him to speak. I pull my feet up to my chest and hold the blanket close to my face. My father is a man of few words. Now that he actually has something to say, it both intrigues and terrifies me all at once.

"I fucked up. I was a sorry excuse for a husband and a father." He pauses and holds eye contact. I can't argue with a word he's said. I wait to see where he's going with this. "I know my fucking revelation is too late, but that's just it, kid. It fucking sucks to realize something when it's too late. I almost lost you a few weeks ago. You're my fucking kid and that scared the shit out of me because no matter what, a father isn't supposed to bury a kid. Now I see you working this ranch. You are a damn fine rancher, Samantha," he says.

"I'm dead aren't I? You just called me Samantha," I deadpan, and my father doesn't crack a smile. He doesn't show any emotion per usual.

"Just listen." He scolds me instead. "I'm trying to get you to see the fucking light. I fucked up. I wasn't there for your mother. I wasn't there for you and your sister. Blake wasn't there for you either, but that don't mean that Al is like us. Fucking rich spoiled kid has been working his ass off. He is far from being a good rancher, but he's all heart. Any idiot can see that, and the way he looks at you ... it's like you're the sun. Well, you don't find that every day. And, kid, I may have been completely oblivious for years, but I can see the way you look at him too. You are falling in love with him. Let yourself fall," Papa says, and I'm quiet because I'm in shock. I've been through a hell of a lot in my life, and my papa has never bothered once to discuss anything or give me guidance. He stands from the recliner, tips his hat to me, and walks up the stairs. The slow way he takes the stairs makes me realize how old he's truly getting.

His words sink into my mind. I push Al away. I'm good at pushing him away. I'm not so good at letting him in. He was hurt tonight. The look in his eyes when I said I wouldn't follow him to Chicago rings in my mind. He was more than hurt. He was gutted. Worst of all, he was presented with an opportunity and he came to me for advice. He didn't make a decision and consider me an afterthought. He came to me first. He cared what I thought, and I fucked up.

A relationship with him is proving more work than I thought. I stand up slowly from the couch and walk to my bedroom. I get into the cold bed, hating he isn't here with me. I love the way he holds me, how he takes care of me and makes me feel safe. I love our talks and sharing our dreams. *I'm falling in love with Al.* The words fall from my mouth and they feel right.

I can't drive to him now, and I sure as hell can't call him and dump something like that on him over the phone. I try to fall asleep, hoping he'll be back in the morning and we can talk. I'm emotionally exhausted. Before I drift off to sleep, I say a small prayer asking to have just one more chance with him. I hope it isn't too late.

CHAPTER THIRTY-NINE

AL

"I'M NOT in the fucking mood," I say to Blake as he walks up to the barstool next to me and takes a seat.

I take a long sip of beer and try to ignore the asshole.

"Do you think I care what you are in the mood for? You stroll into town and steal my woman. You spend Christmas with my fucking family." He points to his chest, and I can immediately see that he's far from being sober.

I don't engage.

"Fuck wad," he shouts. I'm angry enough as it is over my fight with Sam; this guy is just pushing all the wrong buttons in me tonight. I won't be so patient and understanding like last time.

"Watch it. I'm not in the mood," I warn because right now I would like nothing more than to turn this guy into my punching bag.

"Don't fucking talk to me like that. Sam is mine. She's always been mine. I was the first guy to fuck her, and I'm going to be the last," he says. That's it. I lose my cool. I stand up from my stool, pushing it back. It crashes to the floor, and I take Blake by his fucking collar.

"Don't fucking talk about Sam like that." I pull him up and into my face as I grit my teeth with warning.

A slow smile spreads across his face.

"Blake, that's enough." Some guy I don't know comes around and tries to break it up. I remember he was with Leslie. He wasn't very talkative, so I don't remember his name. That's when I notice Kell and Gage walking through the door. They spot me holding onto Blake's collar and run over to us.

"Hey, what's going on?" Kell looks up at me, but I'm seething.

"Back off, man," the other guy says.

"Blake you're drunk. Just go buzz off," Gage says to him.

"Fuck no." Blake spits. "He is fucking living with the Belmonts. That is not okay," Blake says. "She is mine." He turns his attention back to me, and he swings a fist. I don't notice because my attention is on Kell. He punches me across my cheek. Even in his drunken state, he is able to land a hard blow. Pain radiates through my face and pulsates through my head.

"Fucking hell." The anger I'm feeling from earlier comes to a boil, and I clock Blake across his face. The asshole is so drunk, he just bounces back up, and now we are sparing.

"You think if you hit me hard enough it will change the fact that she is the mother of my child? Sam Belmont was always mine and will always be mine," he says, holding his fists up in front of his face. His words are like a sucker punch I'm not expecting.

"Fucking hell, Blake," Kell shouts. I look to Kell and then to Gage. They give me a sympathetic look but nothing on their face indicates this asshole just made up a lie. As I pull my attention away, he hits me again—this time on the other cheek.

"Fucking asshole." The pain takes control of me, and I tear into him, pounding hard on him. I get in shot after shot. Some guys around the bar try to stop me. I don't know how many of them it takes to separate us, but the men at the bar finally succeed in pulling Blake off to the other end of the bar while they maintain a circle around me to ensure I don't pounce. Regardless, the fight has been sucked right out of me.

I'd asked Sam what her connection to Blake was. She made their relationship sound like it had been about sex and trouble. Two young kids getting it on just to get off. She did not fucking mention having a kid. My mind spins when Kell walks up to me. She looks at me like I'm a wounded animal that may run away as she nears.

"Can you explain this to me?" I ask. "I feel like a fucking idiot." I don't need to ask her if Blake was lying because I know he was telling the truth.

"I don't know what to say, Al." She shakes her head. "They never married or anything like that. If you want to know more, you should talk to Sam," she says, and my frustration just grows. I wonder if this is the reason she kept pushing me away because in the back of her mind she was holding on to them being a family.

And that's when it hits me. "Ethan?"

Kell nods.

"Fuck. Now Christmas Eve makes a whole lot of sense." I cough out.

"Blake isn't supposed to see Ethan at all. That was the deal," Kell explains, and it confuses me even more. Ethan is Autumn and Mack's kid. He doesn't live with Sam, yet Sam has been fucking the father of her child all this time. Nothing makes sense to me.

"I fell in love with a woman who was never going to be mine to begin with," I stumble back, looking at Kell.

"It's not like that, Al." She picks up her hand and rubs my arm.

"That's exactly it." I turn out of the bar. The men that circled me back away, even though I sense they watch me get into my SUV. I take off, back to my non-family's cabin. When I get there, my mind is reeling. I want to rip the place apart. I can't sleep. I can't even sit still, so I leave the cabin and walk into the woods at the back of the house. There seems to be a long trail leading nowhere. I begin to wonder why the hell I ended up in Holston. I thought it was to find the love of my life, now I realize it wasn't. I learned the meaning of a hard day's work. I fell in love again. It was all meaningless because at the end of the day, I'm back where I started. I reach into my pocket for my cell phone. I remember that I didn't have it at the bar. I trace my steps back and realize I probably left it on the counter in Sam's kitchen. Fucking great. I was hoping to use the fucking compass. I walk and walk and walk, and my life seems pointless.

I figure I'll head back to Chicago and give Ainsley Stapleton a call. Might as well start building my political career sooner rather than later. As I think the thought, I realize that I don't know if politics will make me happy now. I enjoyed working on the ranch with Sam. It was nice working with my hands. No boss except for the sun and the moon and the day's work ahead of me then spending a quiet evening in with my woman. I don't know that I would have wanted to stay on the ranch, but I would have liked to do something low key. Being in a political role means working around the clock. There's no time for quiet evenings in. Every moment of my day is calculated toward a greater goal. More success. Moving up. Where would it have ended? What would it have given me? I know that politics would never fulfill me in the same way as building a life with Sam would. I realize that maybe Colton and I are best friends because we aren't much different from one another. At the end of the day, we want a woman to love, a family to care for.

I kick the snow-covered branches at my feet. The temperatures are dropping, and I begin to shiver from the inside out. I turn around and head back to the cabin, thankful there is a strong light out back that serves as a focal point. I make it back to the cabin and my head spins. I remember Sam told me she wouldn't follow me like I would follow her.

My gut instinct is to call a cab and take the first flight back to

Chicago. The anger bubbling in my chest causes my mind to push in that direction. I should head home and forget about Sam, but when I think of Chicago I realize Colton no longer lives there. And who or what do I have waiting for me there? And worst of all, how can I leave when my heart lives here in Holston? My fucking emotions are like a tidal wave whipping me around. I can't leave without seeing Sam. I need to go to her before I make any rash decisions. I want her to explain why she lied to me about her relationship with Blake. I won't be able to move on.

I walk straight past the cabin to my SUV. I blast the heat because it feels like my toes will snap off. My mind races a mile a minute as I curse the fucking cold weather in Colorado. My thoughts pull me to Sam and Ethan and how she behaved with him. I chalked it up to her being a great aunt. I put the car in drive and head to the Belmont Ranch, needing answers.

CHAPTER FORTY

SAM

"Sam, you gotta wake up, honey." Someone is shaking me. Why is Kell in my dream? I was just dreaming of the summer fair. This doesn't make any sense. "Sam, come on." I feel a hand on my arm, and my eyes blink open. I'm startled at first and turn to see Kell in my room with her jacket on.

"Holy shit. You scared me half to death. What are you doing here? Are Gage and Theo okay?" I ask frantically.

She waves her hand in the air. "They're fine. I have some bad news." She frowns.

"You know it's not okay to sneak into a grown woman's room in the middle of the night and tell her you have bad news," I chide and sit up in bed, blinking the sleep out of my eyes.

"It's only eleven o'clock," she says, looking to the clock by my bed. I guess I crashed early, after all the stress of fighting with Al and then Papa's bombshell lecture.

"Well, what is it?" I ask since there must have been something urgent to bring her this way.

She's bites her lip. "Try not to freak out, okay?" I can tell that whatever it is, she is scared to get me all stirred up because of my injury, but I'm feeling a lot better.

"You're making me very anxious. Can you just spit it out?" I urge her.

"Al went by Moe's tonight and Blake was there," she begins.

"Fuck." Kell bites at her finger, trying to rip off her nail.

"I tried to separate them, but Blake was getting in Al's face, and he seemed to be in a bad mood to begin with, and well ... Blake told him that you're the mother of his child. He kinda said you were his and he wasn't going to let you go," she says, and my heart sinks. I throw the blankets off me, forgetting I'm wearing a pair of panties and a T-shirt. I charge over to my closet and pull out a pair of my warm fleece pajama pants.

I pace my room. "This can't be happening." I flick on the lights and take a seat across from Kell on my bed. "I need you to tell me exactly what happened. To the last detail. I need to know exactly what Blake said." I'm trembling as I wait for Kell to speak.

"I told you exactly what happened. Al knows Ethan is your kid. He put your bizarre behavior on Christmas Eve together and figured it out." She presses her lips together. "It's not the end of the world, Sam. He would have had to find out eventually," she says, trying to convince me.

"He walked out of here tonight. We had a fight and he left," I say, feeling like the ground is about to open up and swallow me whole. I wrap my arms around my torso and the tears start. "Everything is just so messed-up." I shake my head. "Me, I'm so messed-up. That was my secret. A secret I don't share because it hurts too much."

Kell stands from the bed. She embraces me in a hug. "Honey, the whole town knows that secret, which doesn't make it much of a secret now does it? No one talks about it because we all love and respect you, and we know you were trying to do right by your boy, but you've been dead inside for the last five years. Ever since you gave him to Mack and she left for New York, you have not been the same. You gave up on college and you work this ranch as a form of punishment. This small town loves you, Sam Belmont, but we've watched you eat away at yourself too long." She pauses, and I allow her words to sink in. Everything she says is true. I don't have a solid rebuttal.

"He's doing well. He's stable and happy. As a mom, I couldn't ask for more." My voice cracks as my chest pierces with pain. The tears fall of their own free will, streaking my cheeks, and I don't bother to wipe them away.

"As a mom, I understand you want those things for your son, but, Sam, you never gave yourself a chance to provide him with those things yourself," she says, and she doesn't know what the fuck she's talking about.

"Kell, I'm the town fuckup. Do I need to remind you? And what about Blake? He didn't step up to plate. Fucking asshole sticking his nose now where it doesn't belong. He has no right going to Al with this," I shout and tug at the short strands of my hair.

"Blake's been hurting a long time too. You've both been hurting. Fucking him all the time doesn't relieve that burden. Not for him and not for you," she says, and at her words the air is sucked out of my lungs. I just feel exhausted all over again as I fall back on my bed.

I cry into my hands, and Kell lets me cry. She's wrong about one thing, though. Blake made a mistake. He so much as admitted that to me the day he arrived back from college with an injured knee. And I took care of Ethan the first two years of his life, and I was able to do it because Mack helped me. We would never have made it without her. I was always messed-up. My head got messed-up when my mama died, and it never healed.

"Sam ..." Kell's voice is delicate as she approaches me. "You were depressed for a long time, and you had every right to be. I don't believe for one minute you couldn't raise that boy properly. You just don't believe in yourself. That's the problem." She laughs through her tears. "It's fucking crazy too because you're completely beautiful, competent, and smart. I mean look at you..." her hand waves over my body "...if perfection existed, it would be you, but, honey, you gotta feel it in here." She holds her hand to her heart. "You need to believe in yourself. You need to take some risks. We're all scared, Sam. Life is fucking scary. I'm scared we won't have money to feed Theo and this new baby." She rubs her stomach. "Gage is doing the best he can, and so am I, and I have to believe that we're going to make it. You gotta have some faith. You got a lot going for you. You're a fine rancher and you've been dedicated to this place for a lot of years. You haven't given up on this ranch, so for crying out loud, I don't know why you are giving up on yourself. And don't get me started on that angelic voice of yours." She points a shaky finger at me as the tears stream down her cheeks.

"Fuck, Kell." I laugh and a bunch of snot comes pouring out of my nose. "Shit." I reach for the tissue box on the stand beside my bed and grab a bunch. I blow my nose hard because I can barely breathe. And then I look to Kell, and I don't know what to say. "Thank you." I sigh. "Thank you for being there through my dark hours. Thank you for giving me a kick in the butt now. Thank you for everything." I take a few steps toward her and hug her fiercely. She hugs me back.

"I don't want your thanks." She pulls away. "I want to see my best friend happy. I want to see you smiling again." She stops what she's saying, and I can tell she's considering her next words. "I shouldn't say anything. I should let you two figure things out on your own, but back at the bar, Al let it slip that he was falling in love with you."

At her words, my racing heart slows and a calmness washes over me, because I know in my heart of hearts that I'm falling in love with him too.

"Yeah." I nod and sigh.

"Yeah," Kell repeats because I am pretty darn sure that she can read my love for Al in my expression.

"I should go to him," I suddenly spin around, looking for

some clothes. "Will you give me a ride to his family's cabin?" I still can't drive.

She nods. "I'll let you get dressed." She walks out of my room. I throw on a white thermal shirt and put on a pair of jeans. It feels like forever since I wore jeans. Since the accident, I've been living in pajamas. My adrenaline has spiked, and for the first time in my life, I'm filled with hope that Al will forgive me. I know Al isn't the only part of my life that needs to be fixed. I need to do something about my relationship with Ethan. He should know who I am. He should know who Blake is. I also can't continue to work on this ranch. It's not my passion. Kell is right. I've been trying to punish myself and in doing that I've let my mother down, and it's a whole can of worms I can't deal with right now because I need to find Al. I quickly take a brush and run it over my hair so I don't look like I just rolled out of bed. I head to the bathroom and brush my teeth, and then I run out to the main part of the house so Kell can drive me.

"Okay, I'm ..." The words die on my tongue because he is here in our family room, standing tall, looking handsome as ever, his blue eyes sad. I only hope that I can convince this man to take a chance on me.

CHAPTER FORTY-ONE

AL

"YOU'RE HERE," she says, standing frozen in her spot.

"I'll just get going," Kell mumbles while grabbing her purse. She struts out the door fast, and my gaze remains locked on Sam.

She looks like she was ready to head out. "Were you leaving just now?" I grit my teeth, wondering where she would go this late. She's still healing and shouldn't be going anywhere until the doctor gives his okay.

"Yeah ... uh ... I was coming to look for you," she says, surprising the hell out of me.

"Me?" I question. "What the hell for?" I snap, and I know I need to keep my temper in check even with the bombs that have been dropped on me tonight.

"Kell told me what happened with Blake at the bar. I want to explain," she says, and I nod my head.

"Okay. That's why I came," I say as my anger burns through me. I tell myself to rein it in and listen to her. "I need to understand." I rub my hands along my thighs before rounding the couch and taking a seat. I'm still wearing my jacket because I don't expect this conversation to last long. I came to hear her piece and then I'm out of here.

She takes a seat across from me on the recliner, and I hate the distance between us. I take in her shaky hands. I hate that we are here in this position now while she is still on the mend.

She sits up straight, her hands in her lap, when she begins. "I didn't lie to you about Blake." It's on the tip of my tongue to tell her I disagree, but I swallow my words. "He and I were exactly what I told you we were. He was fun. He was an escape. It wasn't love," she says, and her blue eyes cut to mine and my heart aches. "His mom worked at the Walgreens and Gage was never home, so we spent afternoons at his place. We had only started having sex a couple months before I found out I was pregnant. I was sixteen years old, Al. I was a kid," she says quietly and through her words I can only imagine how scared she felt. Her eyes well with tears. "I didn't have a mother to guide me or tell me what to do ... and you've met Papa. He was even more shut down back then ... if that's even possible." She rolls her eyes and giggles, but it's sad, and she swipes at a tear that got away. My heart aches just listening to her. I know what it's like to feel alone growing up, but I can't imagine what it would have felt like to be in a position like that and having no one. "Blake was eighteen. He was in senior year and had a promising football career ahead of him. He asked me to get an abortion. It didn't feel right to me." She looks at me with a deep pain in her eyes. "I thought maybe I would have the kid and give it away for adoption, but as my belly grew, so did my feelings for the unborn child. It got to the point that I had anxiety attacks over the thought of giving him away." A garbled laugh escapes her, and tears well in her eyes. It takes everything in me not to get up and embrace her. I don't because I need to hear this. "Mack was attending college not too far away, and she was just about to finish up her undergrad degree. She offered to take time off to help me out. I didn't know what that would look like until Ethan was born." Her legs bounce like crazy, and I can tell her nerves are frayed. Just watching her tell her story makes me want to kiss her quiet. Kiss away her tears and her pain.

"Mack really stood up to plate. We read books on how to take care of babies, and we kind of got by. I wouldn't have made it through those two years without her. She had aspirations though. I knew her time with us was limited. I was only eighteen when she wanted to leave. She got into Columbia Law School on a scholarship. She worked her ass off for it. I had a decision to make. Mack is gay, as you know, and she loved Ethan like her own. She knew she was never settling down with a man, and so she saw Ethan as her only chance at having a child. I gave him to her, and she became his mom." Her voice cracks as the words leave her mouth, and I see that curtain of sadness that usually hangs over her eyes—the one I thought was there because of her mother's death. The tears begin to fall faster, her shoulders shake from the force of her emotions.

"Hey, come here," I say gently, standing from the couch and kneeling in front of her. I wrap my arms around her waist, pulling her close to me. She buries her head in my neck, and I feel her wet tears seep into me. The scent of her floral shampoo wafts up my nose, and I inhale and savor the smell. I imagine the pain she must have felt when she gave away her child.

She lifts her head to look at me. "I had nothing to offer him. I should've left for college with him and figured things out along the way like Mack did, but Mack and I are so different. Everything she did was gold. Perfection. She put her mind to something and made it happen. I was the loser. I was the girl who couldn't get her shit together. The one that was stupid enough to get knocked up at sixteen." She shakes her head. "My self-esteem is messed-up." She looks up to the ceiling.

"What about Blake? I mean, what role did he play?" I hate asking about him because she's riled up as it is, but I can see she's trying to clear things up between us, so I have to ask.

"I told you. He left. He acted as if Ethan didn't exist."

"Fuck."

"I was alone. Mack took Ethan to New York, then Blake

appeared again. He dropped out of college when his knee injury ended his football career. He felt bad about his behavior. He wanted to see Ethan, but I made him promise to never make contact with him. Mack had met Autumn, and they became a family. I didn't want anything to destroy the little bubble my son lived in. Blake continued on with his juvenile behavior. We somehow began hooking up again," she says, but her tone tells me that she knew it was a terrible idea. "It was like we both felt the loss of Ethan and being together somehow made it easier, but it was never love, and we were never exclusive. I was never Blake's girl." She accentuates it like she's trying to make a point. I'm thinking Kell gave her a word for word breakdown about what happened at Moe's tonight.

"I see," I stand up and scrub at the scruff on my chin. I pace a little, allowing her words to penetrate. I take a seat on the couch. My body feels like it's over heating, so I finally take off the puffy jacket.

"I don't think you do. I push you away like I push everyone away. I don't trust people. I know that sounds shitty. I should probably say men." She chuckles, sitting beside me. "My papa was pretty damn awful to my mother. Mack and I knew it. We hated it. Then she died a lonely, hardworking woman. Blake was also part of the loser department. He didn't stick around when I needed him. I knew there were good men in Holston. The kind that stuck around, but I was pretty sure that there was something wrong with me. That I couldn't find the good ones, or maybe didn't deserve the good ones because I was the woman that gave her kid away. I've been putting my dreams on hold. I've been working myself raw on this ranch, and it's all a form of punishment. You see ..." she says, and her voice cracks on her last words.

I swipe at the tears in her eyes. "I see a beautiful, passionate, and compassionate woman. That's what I see." My voice shakes as I look in her eyes. "You took in a complete stranger and nursed me back to health. You are kind and giving. You even stuck around here because you feel bad for your old man, and he's done nothing to deserve your kindness. You don't even see how special you really are, but if you give me a chance, I want to work on making you see what I see when I look at you." It takes everything in me not to pick her up drop her on my lap and kiss the hell out of her. I can't do that, though, because I need to know where she stands where I'm concerned. I also know that I should confess my own feelings ... something that's never been easy for me. I know I need to put myself on the line because she sure as hell just put herself on the line.

"I haven't been completely forthright either," I say and she tenses.

"What do you mean?" Her brows furrow.

I take a deep breath. "The other night when I told you about Brie ... I didn't give you the whole story." I rake my fingers through my hair. "Truth is I never spoke to anyone about Brie. Sure, my friends at boarding school knew we were a couple, but I never told anyone that mattered about her," I say. Still so many years later it hurts to say her name.

"Brie and I didn't break up because she cheated." My chest squeezes. "I mean she cheated with a chick. She was high on drugs, but we stayed together after that. I tried to help her put her life back together. We planned a future," I say, and I watch Sam's face fall.

"I see." She wraps her hands in front of her chest and curls into herself.

"No, I mean..." I shake my head "...this isn't easy."

Sam nods.

"Brie was doing drugs. She was too thin. Her life was coming apart, and we made these big plans to be together. I wanted to get her help," I explain, and I try to hold back tears because remembering Brie isn't easy. "Her parents were going through a rough divorce and her mom thought it was best for her to go to Europe instead of bring her back to California. She would take Brie on these amazing trips, but all Brie wanted was a home. That Christmas her mother took her to France," I say and look over to Sam. I've never voiced my next words out loud before. I don't know if I'm capable. Sam is patient with me. She takes my hand in hers. "Brie got sick on the trip. Her mom realized she was anorexic and admitted her to a top-notch hospital in Germany. When school let out for Christmas, I went to go see her. She was thin, sickly. Anorexia is a mental state. It's not really about the food or weight," I explain because as a teen I didn't really get it until later when I read up on it.

"Brie wasn't well. She was frail. I spent that Christmas in Germany with Brie's mom, hoping she would get better. Between the drugs she had done and starving her body, she was weak. Too weak," I say, and when I look at Sam, she has tears in her eyes. My own eyes swell. "She died over Christmas break of cardiac arrest. She never made it back to school."

The moment the last words leave my mouth, Sam moves. Her arms wrap around my neck, and she holds me like her life depends on it. A part of me wishes I could tell Brie that I found my home with Sam.

I pull my face away so that I can look her in the eyes. "I'm falling in love with you." I swallow hard. "No." I pause and shake my head. "I already fell. I am so fucking in love with you it makes my head spin, but I feel like I take two steps forward and you take three steps back."

"I'm so sorry." She says and she's crying. "Thank you for sharing that with me. I know that wasn't easy."

"It wasn't."

She pulls away her hands coming up to hold her head. "I know I've been giving you mixed signals." She blows out a breath and blinks away tears. "I wanted the whole thing with Ethan to be this big secret. Something no one talked about. And it's crazy." She laughs. "The whole town knows my story, and no one speaks of it. There is this silent respect. They understood I needed to bury that part of my life. It was a forbidden topic, and when Blake stormed in here Christmas Eve, he broke that oath. When his eyes landed on Ethan, I couldn't breathe. I was sad and angry. It's crazy, I know. Blake and I would have never worked out, even if he had stepped up to plate back then. I know this because of the feelings I have for you. The first time I saw you passed out in your car, I was drawn to you. I can't explain it, but it was like you were this lost soul, and I felt just as lost as you. We started talking and hanging out and things just felt right. You got under my skin in a way that no other man has," she says, looking deep into my eyes. "Trust me, I've tried to convince myself that we were all wrong for each other. Everything from our age to our financial backgrounds was so wrong, but when it's just us and we talk or kiss or ..." Her voice trails off and she giggles. "It's just so right."

I press a kiss to her lips.

"I love you, Al Walsh," she says with her lips pressed to mine.

"I love you too, Samantha Belmont. What I had with Brie was a young love. We were kids. We had similar backgrounds, and I wanted to help her, protect her. With you I feel at home, at peace." I answer, and she climbs into my lap like she knows it's where I wanted her. "You asked me the other night why I never settled down and the answer is because I hadn't met you yet."

"You're a real sweet talker," she chides.

I chuckle. "I don't mean to be."

"Does that mean the no sex policy has ended?" she whispers.

"Absolutely not. You have your doctor's appointment tomorrow. If he gives us the okay, then the no sex policy ends, but if he doesn't ... we wait," I answer and she pouts. I throw my head back laughing.

"What are you going to do about your political aspirations?" she asks. Before I can answer, she says, "I'd follow you too, Al. I need to get my life in order. There are a few things I need to work through, but I'd follow you blind." She presses another soft kiss to my lips.

"You have no idea how much that means to me," I tell her. "And I know you have things to work out. I'm not in a rush to start a political career. I've had some alone time this evening to think on it. I don't know what I want anymore. What I do know is that I want to have time on my hands to be with you and when we're ready, I want time to build a family with you." Before she can get her two cents in, I say, "Relax, there's no rush. We're both very young." I wink, and she rubs her hands up and down my torso. It feels good to have her hands on me again. "I also want you to think about what you want. I can see that ranching doesn't make you happy. We need to figure things out."

Her lips spread from cheek to cheek. "I really like the sound of that. Us figuring things out together."

I nod my head in agreement, and I kiss the hell out of my woman.

CHAPTER FORTY-TWO

SAM

One month later

"This has been a long time coming." I look to Al, and he squeezes my hand as the plane lands. This was my first plane ride, and I'm acting like a child, enjoying the rush of the plane taking off and complaining my ears hurt when the plane lands. Mack and I have had many intense phone conversations this past month. We never discussed making anything formal about her adopting Ethan, even though we've had some informal paper-work drawn up for her to be his legal guardian. I haven't given up my rights. We also never really made specific plans, like if I would ever tell him I was his mother. I've never even gone to New York to visit them. This is my first time leaving Colorado.

Mack's been so good to me. It wouldn't be fair to her or Ethan if I walk in and dump the truth on him. That's why Al and I are moving to New York City. We rented an apartment that we've never seen, through one of his old acquaintances. He got a job working in one of the largest law firms in New York. While he works, the plan is for me to start spending time with Ethan and slowly build a relationship with him other than being the fun and crazy auntie.

"This is going to be great. You are going to be great." He presses a kiss to my hand. The pilot comes on the intercom and makes an announcement. The plane stops, and then the passengers are up and out of their seats, moving quickly to get their carry-on luggage from the overhead bin. I follow suit. Al and I walk off the plane and down a narrow hall to another hall and down an escalator. My heart beats rapidly in my chest, and it's hard to believe this is really happening. We collect my suitcases since Al had his stuff packed and shipped from Chicago. With three large suitcases, we exit the doors to see Mack, Ethan, and Autumn waiting for us. I will myself not to cry, but the emotions swirling inside me are strong. That I've even allowed myself to believe that I deserve to be here and get to know my son is a huge feet. Failure scares the hell out of me, but missing this opportunity would be worse.

Al's played a major part in convincing me of my worthiness. It's a battle I'm afraid I will have to fight continuously since some habits are hard to break.

"Auntie." Ethan wraps his arms around my neck and for the first time since I gave him away five years ago, I allow myself to feel, to hurt, to heal, though I know it will take a long time for me to truly heal.

"Hey, sweetheart. I'm so excited we get to live in the same city now." I ruffle his light hair like I usually do. Mack and Autumn lean in and give me a hug. I can tell they are nervous. I guess none of us knows what the future holds. All I know is that we all love Ethan deeply, and I hope that everything works out the way it's meant to.

Mack drives and I sit up front with her. Al, Ethan, and Autumn sit in the back of the SUV. They take Al and me to our new apartment where we get settled in, and we bid them goodnight. A part of me never wants to leave Ethan's sight now that we are here, but I know I need to pace myself for his sake and mine.

"This place is amazing." I sigh, looking out a floor-to-ceiling window. "A little over the top but wow." I look out at Central Park. When we agreed to move here together, I expected to rent some shitty apartment in Brooklyn or Queens. I didn't expect this fancy building.

"Nothing but the best for my princess." Al swats my ass.

"I'm no princess, Al." I roll my eyes at him, playing with him because he hates when I say that.

"Don't start with me," he warns, pointing a finger at me. He has a serious look on his face, but I read between the lines. We haven't had sex since before the accident. The doctor just gave me the okay to fly a week ago, and Al had all of this organized on a whim. It beats me how everything from the location to the furniture is so fucking perfect, but I guess this is how the other half lives. Even though the doctor gave me the okay a week ago, he still hasn't had sex with me because he says we act like wild animals during sex and he couldn't live with himself if he hurt me. I think there's more to it, though. He knows I used sex to feel good, and he's been trying hard to show me I can feel good without it. He's proven his point. I'm crazy about him, but I still want him bad.

"I lived through the flight and I don't have a headache. I'm thinking it's okay if we fool around a little." I giggle. He slowly unbuttons the shirt he's wearing. The look on his face breathes pure seduction. It's a fancy shirt, nice material, the kind he wore when he first arrived in Holston.

"I'll fool around with you," he says, stalking toward me like an animal after its prey.

"Oh no you don't." I wag my finger in front of him. "I told you I'm not the kind of woman to take orders from a man."

He ignores my words, and when he's worked open all his buttons, he moves the shirt off his shoulders. It pools on the floor.

The breath is sucked right out of me at the sight of his wide shoulders and strong arms. My eyes lick a path down his torso as my tongue moves across my lips. Saliva pools in my mouth. He's so fucking hot. He walks up to me and wraps his arm around my waist, pulling me into him. The warmth of his skin penetrates my shirt and butterflies begin to dance in my belly.

"I'm going to lick that sweet pussy of yours," he says, and I don't argue. I can't argue. He's rendered me speechless. I walk over to the king-sized bed. I still can't believe that I live in this place. The sheets on the bed are white and so is the large puffy blanket that covers the bed.

"Aren't you going to undress me first?" I finally say because I can't show him all my cards. He can't know how much power he truly has over me.

"Lie down," he says, standing so close that I feel his warm breath kiss my skin.

I lie down. I take his orders. I'm willing to beg at this point. I lie back on the bed, and he works his belt then his pants off until he is left in a pair of boxers, his cock fully erect against his strong abs. My breathing is labored as I watch him climb on the bed and crawl toward me. His hands run up and down my thighs slowly, and then he works off the leggings I have on, taking my panties with them in one swoop. The cool air in the room hits my pussy, and I clench. Al's blue eyes look more stormy gray in this light. As he stares at me, he slowly runs his hands up and down my calves toward my thighs, stopping at the apex of my legs. I'm dripping with want and my heart beats fast with need. We haven't been together since we said the words I love you. His head dips between my thighs, his warm wet tongue making contact with my clit first. I let out a long moan. I'm swollen for him as he licks my clit then moves down to my opening and back up again, building a torturous rhythm.

"I want you inside me," I say.

"I want to tongue fuck you," he answers, and I know what he's doing. He wants control in the bedroom. He wants to show me who's boss. Truth is I know who the boss is because he fucked me like a boss from the first time.

I lose my words as his tongue moves faster and he inserts his fingers. I'm so turned on and so needy, I can't control the orgasm that wracks through my body. White lights form behind my eyelids as he works me over, tongue fucking the hell out of me. He doesn't relent, sucking every last drop of my orgasm out of me. And then he's gone. My eyes stay shut and the bed sinks beside me. Soft kisses are pressed along my neck. Goose bumps erupt over my body as he sucks my lobe. My hands run down his back and over his ass, lowering his boxers off him. When his boxers reach mid-thigh, I use my foot and push them all the way down. I take his glorious cock in my hand. Al's body is an art form. Everything about him is perfect. Now that we aren't angry fucking or casually fucking, I take my time and pay attention to all the perfect details of his Adonis-like body.

"Will you let me suck you off now?" I ask as I stroke his cock.

A guttural groan escapes his mouth. I can see his jaw tense. "I need my dick inside you, baby. You can suck me off on round two," he says, and his voice is deep and husky and so freaking sexy that I still can't believe we're here living together in New York City.

"There's going to be a round two?" I cock a brow with a mischievous smile. "I'm exhausted from the flight. From this day." I like fucking with him.

"This is the first night I have you to myself without your dad around. Did you really think I was going to let you sleep?" he asks, and before I have a chance to answer, he captures my lips and French kisses the hell out of me. His hand drops between my legs, and his thumb circles my clit slowly, and I build again. Heat moves through my body, causing my belly to clench in the most delicious way. I'm wet for him all over again.

"Please," I beg.

"Do you want my cock inside you, Princess?" he rasps, and I love that he calls me Princess. He truly treats me like a princess.

"Yes, please. Now."

He laughs. "Always so bossy."

"I don't have time to answer that."

He thrusts inside me, filling me with his thick cock, and I moan at the feeling of him moving inside me, becoming one with him. He holds my hips and moves in and out of me, hitting all the right spots. We create a rhythm all our own as our sweat-slicked bodies move together, both of us working toward our climax. And then he comes inside me and sets me off as my own climax rolls and buzzes through my body, taking me higher and higher. We are a heap of ragged breathes when he falls to the side of me, pulling me close to his body.

"I love you so damned much," he says, looking straight at me.

"I love you too, so damned much." I caress his cheek. It's crazy but I can't get enough of him. I sometimes just enjoy that I can look at him, touch him, and know he's mine. And at the end of the day, when we close our eyes and fall asleep, I know I belong to him and he belongs to me. We aren't alone. We aren't lost anymore because we have each other.

EPILOGUE

EIGHT MONTHS LATER

"I THINK it's cool that I have three mommies." Ethan looks up to me with blue eyes that are so similar to mine, my heart swells. Today is a big day. We've been leading up to this for a long time. Now we sit on a bench in Central Park on this unusually warm fall day, having a cone of soft serve ice cream, while I explain to him that I am his biological mother. A warm wind brushes across my cheek as I smile down to my son. It's been a long hard road to this moment. I had to work on myself to make myself believe I deserved to be in his life because to me he had always been perfect. That meant coming to terms with my past mistakes and realizing that despite everything, I was a good person who deserved love and to be loved. Those words may seem easy to some, but they are something I fought to achieve. Now looking down at my eight-year-old son, I couldn't feel more whole.

"That means so much to me, Ethan." I smile and place a small peck on his cheek. He continues to lick the ice cream. "Autumn and Mack love you so much. I don't want anything to change in our lives. I know all this is a lot to understand, but I'd like you to maybe come over for sleepovers once in a while ... I mean, if you would like to." I stammer a little. Nothing about this situation is easy. I am so grateful Mack and Autumn are open to me playing an important role in Ethan's life. I've been inserting myself into his everyday schedule very slowly. I didn't want to push or overwhelm him. Mack told me that in her heart she knew one day I may have wanted him back. There was never an adoption process. This was my sister owning up to responsibilities I was too young to undertake. Our situation is unique. What I do know without question is that my son is deeply loved and supported. Even Al spends lots of time with him. Taking him to sports games and doing boy things, like pretending to shave with shaving cream in the bathroom.

"You mean I get to sleep over at yours and Al's place?" His is tone filled with an excitement I don't remember having as a child.

"Yes." I nod. "If you'd like." My nerves are frayed. I know I need to take a deep breath and relax. I told him who I am, and he didn't flip out. The depth of this secret has haunted my days and nights for so long that my slow breathing provides no relief. I know it will take time for the news to process in his head and mine.

"I'd really like that. Al is fun," he says, and I realize that the ice cream in my hand is melting over the cone. My stomach is in knots. I stand from the bench and walk across the path to throw my ice cream in the garbage. There is no way I can eat now.

"Good, I'm glad you think so." I sit back on the bench and place one hand on his shoulder, giving him a little squeeze. "Hey! What do you say we try out the kite we bought? I think the wind is just right to make it take off right now."

He smiles and nods his head. Something about him reminds me of Blake. With all his irresponsibility, I know in my heart of hearts that I've been unfair. Ethan may eventually want to meet his father. He has that right. I don't want to take that from him. I tell myself that I will give him more time to adjust to me and eventually we will take that trip to Colorado. I just need Blake to clean himself up. I think he will. I think part of the reason he drinks so much is because he feels guilty about abandoning me and Ethan.

We spend the rest of the afternoon flying the dragon kite. We laugh and play and at the end of the day, I bring him back to Mack and Autumn.

AL IS WAITING for me when I arrive at our apartment. I open the door to see my man is walking around shirtless, his jeans sitting low on his waist—that chiseled V I know leading to a very delicious happy trail—his feet bare and in his hands a bowl of cereal.

"Hey." He stops in his tracks. "How did it go?" He looks as nervous as I feel.

"Really well. He wasn't shocked ... it was more like he finally understood something that he didn't before. It was strange ... I don't know." I shrug. "I was so nervous, but he was just this laid back kid, and he thought it was cool he had three moms." I press my palms to my face. My anxiety is still bubbling inside me. "He wants to come for sleepovers. He really likes you."

"Come here." Al extends his hand for me so I can give him a hug. He wraps his free arm around me, and I squeeze him fiercely, inhaling the scent of his woodsy cologne. I press my cheek against the warmth of his chest. He feels like home. I place a kiss to his nipple and pebble more kisses along his chest. "I thought you said you had a paper to write today." His left brow lifts. "This morning you said we had to practice a strict no sex policy or else you wouldn't finish your composition paper and your professor would dock you marks." He reminds me of my own words. I do need that paper done, but I need him more.

"Did I really say that?" I ask, my voice a little sultry and a little mischievous. "I wasn't expecting to come home and find you half naked. You look ... yummy," I say as my hands run over his chest. I bend my knees so my kisses move lower and lower. I was accepted to the NYU performing arts department this past September, and I am now working toward a degree in vocal performance and music composition.

"Yummy?" He groans, looking down to me, confused, yet his lip quirks up on one side.

"Here, let me take that." I take his bowl of cereal and place it on the floor. I work the button on his jeans followed by the zipper as I look up to him with heat in my eyes. He takes his finger and runs it across my lips.

"Have I told you how beautiful you are?" he asks as his finger finishes its caress.

"Every day," I say, pushing his jeans over his taut ass.

"Fuck, Sam."

I take his cock in my mouth. We are standing in the foyer of our very large Central Park apartment, and I am sucking his cock like it's my lollipop. I don't use my hands as I deep throat him, and his head falls back.

"You keep that up and I'm going to come fast," he warns, and it's exactly what I want. I want to see him come apart at the seams. I want to make him crazy with lust because I love him like crazy. He's given me a life I never knew existed. This man that I found passed out in a ditch on the side of the road has been my savior, my salvation.

His hips thrust in motion with my mouth, and he comes hard. I lap up every ounce of his saltiness. And when I'm done, he extends a hand to help me up off my knees. In one swoop, he lifts me in his arms. I love when he does that.

"Where are you taking me?" I laugh.

"Over to the couch. I want a taste of that sweet pussy of yours. I need to hear you scream my name, and geez, darling, I need to see you relaxed." It amazes me how he can read me so well, how he's able to give me exactly what I need, and right now that is his tongue between my thighs.

When he places me on the couch in our family room, I don't waste time removing my jeans, panties, and socks.

"Bra and shirt got to go too," he commands, standing above me. The only time he does command is when we are having sexy times, and I think he does it because he knows how turned on I get. I work my bra and shirt off too.

He kneels in front of me, and I spread my legs. He doesn't use his hands to touch me when his head dips between my thighs that skilled tongue of his licks my most sensitive parts. My eyes loll shut. I take in the ecstasy. My body relaxes against his touch. His tongue works me over slowly at first, and when he feels me building, he picks up speed.

"Al, please," I moan, and I don't know what I'm asking for, but he does. His hands come up to knead my breasts, and my hips move against his sinful tongue. I come hard and fast. It feels like too much, and I try to inch away from him. He doesn't relent, sucking my clit and drawing out my orgasm longer until my body is sated and my mind is calm. He stands and takes a seat beside me, wrapping me up in his strong arms. He reminds me that he will love me forever. We kiss, and he tastes like me, and I'm sure I taste like him. We mesh together as one.

We lie together, and he brushes some loose hair off my face, looking at me with love in his eyes. "I love you," he whispers, and I close my eyes and fall asleep on his chest.

The phone rings, pulling me from my slumber. I open my eyes to see Al isn't beside me on the couch, but I am naked with one of the throw blankets covering me, so I know that I wasn't fantasizing.

"It's your dad on the phone," he calls out from the kitchen. He walks toward me with a pair of boxers, his strong abs moving with the motion. My cell is in his hand. Papa doesn't call often. He is who he is, but I try to stay in touch at least once a month.

I press the talk button. "Hello."

"Hi, Sam," his deep voice comes through the phone.

"What's up, Papa?" I ask, because there must be a reason for him to call on a Sunday evening.

"I've got news."

"I figured as much," I say, my own voice tired and raspy.

The phone is silent.

"Papa?"

"I sold the ranch," he says, shocking the hell out of me.

"You what?" I ask, surprised. That ranch has been in the family going on a third generation now.

"You heard me. Sold it to the Neumanns. It made sense. You and your sister weren't going to take over here, and my old ass is tired of working. Neumann paid a good price, so I have that to retire on."

"Wow! I mean ... that's great news," I mutter.

"It's the end of an era. That's what the fuck it is, but it is what it is," he says. "Just wanted you to know. You said that maybe you'd be coming back here for Thanksgiving. I thought that'd be a good idea. Told Neumann they can have the place first week of December."

"Okay, sure. Yeah ..." I answer, still feeling a little frazzled by the news. I haven't been home in eight months. I miss my best friends dearly, but they understand that I am trying to make myself a life, and Kell, Leslie, and I talk weekly. "We'll see you Thanksgiving. I'm sure Mack, Autumn, and Ethan will be there too."

"Make sure to bring that man of yours too," he says, and I can't help but chuckle.

"Al will be there too, Papa," I say as if it's obvious.

"Good."

The other line beeps, and Izzy's name lights up my screen.

"Papa, I have Al's sister on the other line. I have to take it."

"Alright. Bye then." He hangs up and I switch calls.

"Hey, Izzy. How are you?" She moved to New York around the same time Al and I did. She enrolled in a design program at NYU,

so I see her around campus. We meet for coffee and she sometimes joins Al and me for dinner. We're the same age, so we get
along well. She's been having guy problems as in she can't find a
nice guy to date.

"Ugh," she answers, and I wonder what that's about. "I just got
on a scale, and I put on fifteen pounds." She groans into the
phone. "It isn't normal to put on fifteen pounds in six months." I
can only picture the sour face she's making. She can be over-
dramatic.

"You can come to the gym with me. I just signed up at this
new place around the corner. It's nice and clean. They have great
classes too."

"I haven't moved my ass since I started school last January. I'll
make a fool of myself," she says, and I chortle. I've never signed
up to a gym in my life, but Al keeps me in good shape with all the
sex we have. I don't share that info with Izzy.

"Come on. I'm in class all day tomorrow, and Al has a late
night at work. Why don't we meet at the gym then grab some
dinner?" I suggest. I really do like to work out after a long day of
classes.

"That sounds nice," she says. "Okay, yeah, let's do it."

"That's the spirit," I answer.

Al walks up to me and taps his watch. "Homework," he
mumbles, and his lips twist in a wry smile.

"Izzy, I'll text you a time tomorrow. I have a paper to finish up
for my composition class, and I'm not so good at pulling all-
nighters."

"Oh yeah, sure go ahead. Let's touch base ..." her voice trails
off, and I wonder what's happened to the call.

"Izzy? You there?" I ask.

I hear what sounds like a muffled cry. "Izzy, what's going on?"

"It's my mother," she cries into the phone.

"Did something happen?" As I ask the question, I look up to
Al and his brows pinch together. He hasn't seen his mother in

eleven years, even though she gives him an occasional phone call.

"She's got cancer, Sam. Breast cancer. The prognosis is good but ..."

"I'm so sorry, Izzy. That's really scary even with a good prognosis," I say, and Al watches me as I watch him. He's wanted nothing to do with his family, but truth is they haven't reached out to him either.

"Mom wants to see Al," she says, and I figured as much. I don't know why Izzy is having this conversation with me instead of Al. The only thing I can think of is that she fears he won't see his mother.

"He's right here. Do you want to tell him yourself?" I offer.

"I was thinking you could convince him to go see her. I know she's made a lot of mistakes where he's concerned, but she's full of regret, and now that she's starting chemo ... I don't know, she just wants to set things right," she says.

"Let me talk to him and if you need anything just stop by or call. Whatever you need," I say. That's one thing about living in New York that I can't get used to: we don't have guests stopping by all the time and getting in our business. The downside to big city living.

"Thanks, Sam. I really do appreciate it."

"Of course." I sigh. "You take care, darling."

"You too." She ends the call, and I look up to Al and blow out a breath.

It looks like he understood a lot from the conversation already.

"It's my mom isn't it?" he asks, and his face has paled.

"Take a seat." I pat the couch beside me. He sits and waits, looking straight ahead. "It's breast cancer. She's starting chemo. Her prognosis is good."

He blows out a harsh breath and nods his head. He runs his hands up and down his thighs, and I want to ease his pain. I know him, though. He needs to process this on his own time, so I give him quiet and space. I wait. A few minutes pass.

"I should go see her. I don't want to regret not seeing her," he says matter-of-factly, but his eyes carry a heaviness.

"Okay." I take his hand. "I can come with you if you want me to."

"I'd like that." He brings my hand up to his mouth and kisses the back of it.

"I'm going to go take a shower." He stands from the couch and walks away. I give him a head start but decide to follow him because I know what it's like to feel like you're drowning. I've had my share of bad times. I enter the bathroom. The glass shower walls are all steamed up. I place my arms around his neck and press kisses onto his back. He turns and captures my mouth, and I let him love me. He pushes my back against the steamed glass and lifts me in the air. I wrap my legs around him and he fucks me hard. His emotions and his frustrations come out in the way he touches me with rough fingers, and I know sex isn't the solution. I know we will be faced with problems in our lives and hard choices. This is about me showing him that he isn't alone, and it feels so different than sex for thrills.

We leave the shower and my eyes widen when I look at the clock on the bedside table.

"Shit."

"You better get your homework done," he says with that deep voice that has an air of command. His lips twist a little, but the smile is weak. I scramble to my feet. "You love to tell me to do my homework." I shake my head at him because he gets some kinky kick out of it.

"You don't like to pull all-nighters?" It's a question. He wraps his arms around my waist.

"To write papers," I clarify. "With you in bed, no problem."

"Glad you cleared that up because I'm still hard," he whispers against my ear, and his warm breath sends goose bumps and shivers down my body.

"Don't. Please. I need to get my work done. I can't focus if I'm thinking of your hard cock." I pout and take a few steps away from him.

"How do you think I felt Friday morning in court when you sent me a pic of your breasts?" he asks.

My eyes widen. "You didn't mention having court." I bite my lip, and my voice is filled with mock regret.

"You knew I had family court," he insists.

I shrug my shoulders. "Okay, I may have known you had family court. I thought it would brighten your day," I say, and it's the truth.

"Oh! It brightened my day alright. I pictured sliding my dick between your breasts when I was cross-examining my witness. I need to come across as assertive, not distracted." He grins.

"You thought of sliding your cock here?" I ask, touching the spot between my breasts. His eyes drop to my naked chest and heat sparks in his glare. Oh dear, I am never going to finish that paper. Or I'm going to finish it at the ass crack of dawn because we can't stop fucking. I used to have to wake up for the cows that early. Now I need to wake up to do my school work because Al and I can't keep our hands off each other. It isn't a complaint. He's my person, my rock, the man of my dreams.

"Come here, Princess," he says. I walk toward him and wrap my arms around his neck and my legs around his waist. I allow him to carry me to bed. I allow him to love me because he taught me to love myself, to respect myself. He taught me what love is, and I want to spend the rest of my life loving him in a way that he deserves to be loved.

ABOUT THE AUTHOR

R.C. Stephens is the best selling author of the Twisted Series, Dick, Halo, Where Promises Die and Mr. All Wrong.

She lives in Toronto with her husband and three children. Loving Canadian winters she could never think of living anywhere else.

ALSO BY R.C. STEPHENS

The Twisted Series

Bitter Sweet Love

Twisted Love

Wild Cards

Standalones

Dick: A Bad Boys Novel

Halo

Where Promises Die

Mister Series

Mr. All Wrong

Mr. So Wrong

Mr. Unexpected (2018)

SNEAK PEEK

Turn the page to read the first two chapters of Mr. All Wrong

CHAPTER ONE

"I thought we were heading to Greensboro Elementary," I say to Albert, my chief of staff, sitting beside me.

He glares at me with his dark blue eyes giving me a sidelong glance, and I sense a hint of guilt in his glare. That's never a good thing coming from him. He straightens his tie and tilts his head to the side. "We have a slight detour." His lips twist into a wry smile.

"Detour?" I cock a brow. "I promised those kids a pizza lunch. They won a contest. I don't need to tell you that I'm a man of my word."

Albert, also known as Albert Walsh the III, winced. "Your father thought we should make a pit stop at Henderson Place. The Bachmakers are having a ribbon-cutting ceremony. They're tearing down Henderson Place and building a strip of condominiums there," he explained as if it all made sense and it did, only I didn't like the reason my presence was needed. I kept quiet, and Al continued. "Mr. Bachmaker believes in you. He wants to give his support for your campaign. Your father thought a quick show-your-face-and-handshake would go a long way in securing the contribution."

For fuck's sake, I mutter under my breath. "I don't know if I'm making that announcement." I shake my head, and a light chortle escapes my mouth as I realize what my life has become. "Al, can you see me running for President of the United States? It would be a fucking gong show."

Al throws back his head laughing at the thought. "I guess most people don't know you stuck your head in a toilet when you were six because you wanted to save poor old Marty," he reminds me of the time I tried to save my goldfish. I had come home from kindergarten to an empty fish bowl. Dad fed me the story that Marty needed a swim and he accidentally got flushed down the toilet by our maid. The truth was, Marty died, and Dad didn't know how to break the news. I went all superhero and tried to save poor old Marty. In my six-year-old mind, it was feasible to look down the toilet drain. Of course, there was no Marty.

"Exactly, I'm the guy who shoves his head down the toilet. I'm not the right fucking guy to run for office."

Al's lips press together, and his head tilts to the side assessing me as if he doesn't get me. "And yet here you are Mr. Governor of the Great State of Illinois." His tone is playful yet reminds me how I became governor. How my father's constant meddling in my life got me to do things I didn't want to do. If it were up to me, I'd be working in the prosecutor's office, or maybe I'd take on some pro bono cases. Lord knows I didn't need the money.

"Yes, and as governor, you would think I would have control to make decisions about the little things in my life like having a pizza lunch with Ms. Fitz's second-grade class while learning about the innovative learning strategies used at Greensboro Elementary." I tried to keep the sarcasm out of my tone, but sometimes my father's meddling was too much.

Al looks at his watch. "This'll only take twenty minutes tops." He gives me a have some patience for my father's meddling look because Al believes I should be the next President of the United States. The polls are agreeable too. I'm the one itching for some-thing different in my life. Sort of a mid-life crisis but since I'm only thirty-five, it probably doesn't classify. It's more like I am having an awakening. I don't like the direction my life is taking. Before I know it, I will be forty and the ex-president of the United States. It's a huge accomplishment for a person whose passion is to become president. It's just not my passion. I sound like a spoiled brat born with a silver spoon in his mouth, but that doesn't mean my life's been happy or straightforward for that matter. It gets to a point where material things are meaningless. Even titles for my power-hungry father become obsolete.

I nod. "Sometimes I think my father hypnotizes you in your sleep. You fucking bend to his every whim." I chastise my chief of staff, who is also my best friend.

He chortles. "I did see a faint old figure hanging over my bed last night."

"Not fucking funny. I love my old man, but sometimes his need to have me succeed gives me fucking nightmares. I should finish this term as governor then go back to being a lawyer," I say, knowing my best friend wouldn't agree. When you're raised with old money your parents and, in my case my father, has ingrained in me a need to achieve more, move higher up in the ranks of power. Money can provide for materialistic bliss but can't buy love. My father comes from the Mathis family. One of America's wealthiest families. They make candy. I know it sounds cool but even getting all the free candy you want as a child becomes old. My father left the family business to become a lawyer and was a partner in the most prominent law firm in Chicago. He planned to enter politics, but there were glitches along the way. He found himself a single father to a young boy instead. Now he lives his dreams through me.

"You know that isn't how life works," Al retorts and I watch as his blue eyes turn dark like he's thinking of something morbid. I've called him on it a few times, but he's a hard shell to crack. His father, a tycoon in the technology industry, wanted Al to come work in the family conglomerate so he could groom him to take over the Walsh empire one day. Just as Al was getting ready to take on the reigns of Walsh Industries they had a big blow out. Al was all hush hush about it. Said some family secrets were best laid to rest. He walked away from his family who then blacklisted him for over a decade even though his mother kept in touch with him secretly behind his father's back, and his little sister also made visits out to see him since they live in Texas. I remember that day like it was yesterday. He was angry, seething and hurt. He had heard my father's plans for me on more than one occasion. That day he said let's go for it. "Let's pave our own way to the white house. You can be President, and I'll be behind the scenes." I huff out a puff of air. He had no clue how jealous I was of him that day. The way he walked away and didn't look back. The way he went after what he wanted. That day I gave my father the go ahead. Told him I'd run for the position of the state attorney. I won. Only the price I was paying was too high. All my life I've felt like I had a noose around my neck. My father's grave baritone voice is constantly ringing in my head, brainwashing me to be the best. I never had the chance to be a kid, have fun. I was always in one extracurricular activity after the next. Most of them were private lessons, so I didn't even get to socialize. My existence was pathetic. Even today at age thirty-five and a long list of accomplishments, I felt inadequate.

"You mean how my life works." I couldn't help but snap. "Say it, Al. I'm a fucking coward. I've let the guilt of my father's sacrifices rule my life but when does it end?"

He tilted his head to the side. "You didn't always let the guilt rule. Africa was you sticking it to the old man. And working in the prosecutor's office," Al reminds me of all the times I defied my father. The list is short. Working in the prosecutor's office was a big one, but I didn't want to work in his law firm as a defense attorney. And Africa... while attending Harvard, Al and I decided to join the Peace Corps while we were on summer break. We loved it so much we went back for another two summers. My father had other plans for me. He wanted me to spend some time in Washington making political allies.

"Yeah, there's Africa and the tattoos running up my arm," I chortled thinking of my tats, then tilted my head to the side and considered Al's words. I was young and rebellious. The tattoos are a constant reminder of my brief freedom which ended once we started law school. By then my father's method of lathering on guilt had thickened. *Boy, I could have been president* or *boy sometimes I wondered why I didn't just give you up, find a new wife and conquer my dreams...* I know... that last comment was particularly rough. It made me feel low, made me realize how much I owed him even though he was an asshole for saying it. He was the only parent I knew, and quite frankly I didn't have a better frame of reference since I didn't hang out with other kids and their parents.

"Yup, Africa, and tattoos." Al nodded, his gaze seemed miles away like he remembered the good ol' days.

"But where did it get me? He only became more determined after that," my lips twist.

"Fuck Colt, you're depressing me today. What the hell is going on with you?" Al's humorous tone changed to a look of concern. Nothing like having a heart to heart with your best friend in the back of an SUV with your security detail possibly listening to every word. That was it. I was sick of everything.

I gave Al a long hard look. "Everything is wrong." I let out a strangled laugh. "Look at you, man. You like what you do, and you enjoy the political games. You took life by the balls. You couldn't understand me," I huffed out.

"My life isn't perfect, Colt. There are things you don't know. Things I can't discuss with you. Still..." he paused and swiped a hand over his mouth. I looked at my watch quickly, wondering if we would be late for my visit to the school. Al had secrets. I knew that. Everyone has a secret or two they don't share with anyone. A secret you keep locked inside because it's either too painful to reveal or too it would hurt many people. My secret was simple. My mother walked out on me when I was five and didn't look back. That shit has messed with my head all my life, and caused me to have insecurities that made me feel inadequate. My father turned a blind eye to how I felt, and then made me feel worse by telling me there was no room for my feelings in the game of politics. Only the tough prevailed and so I put on armor that made me look tough. I was living a life I didn't want and for some reason, just recently, it began to gnaw at me like termites chewing on a tree, slowly degrading it to nothing, and now I'm at my wit's end.

"Still..." I repeat Al's word because he still won't say what his secret is. I worry my lower lip. "And here I am still..." I emphasize the word. "Eating the shit my father shovels."

"You're the governor, and Colt...life could be a lot worse." Al retorts and I know he doesn't mean to, but he's feeding me the same line my father does. I need to appreciate what I have. Problem is I want something completely different. I just don't know what.

"Yup, heard that one before," my tone bleeds sarcasm. Al gives me a knowing look,

and rolls his eyes at me. As I said, he likes political life; he doesn't understand my discontent. "Snap out of it. You know how this is going to go down. The way I look at it, the presidency is your destiny. People love you, you worry about the common good. You're the right man for the job and we both know it."

"Give me a break. We can get my father to feature you in his campaigning. You can do everything that I would," I quip.

"Man, you're a saint and I'm the devil incarnate." He wiggles his brows. "There's no way the American people are voting me in. I have no morals." He guffaws, and that sentence is only half right.

"You're no different than me. The only problem is you get caught and I don't," I scoff.

"If you're talking about Sheila Angel, man, I didn't know she was married or being followed by the paparazzi," he tries to feign innocence.

I roll my eyes at him. "Everyone knows Sheila was married to Gord Mabely," I state the apparent common knowledge giving him a *you should have known better* look. Gord's wife is hot as hell and so the media is glued to their lives reporting on their power couple status.

"Man, I watch football because of football. I don't pay attention to the little stories about football players and their wives or families," he shrugs me off.

"Well, you should start," I snicker. Maybe Al wouldn't get himself into trouble then and be outed as the asshole that broke up the Mabely family even though Gord's affairs were public knowledge. For some reason though the media didn't find that story entertaining. It also caused heat in the governor's office that my chief of staff was caught with his pants down. So, to speak.

"And you hitting on that princess...where was she from?" Al taps his chin...his voice stalls. He damn well knows where she's from.

"Princess of Monaco, fuck wad. And I didn't know she was to be betrothed to the Prince of Sweden. She didn't mention it when I was balls deep—"

Al cuts me off. "Shut up. I don't need to be hearing about your balls." He lifts a hand and turns away. Hopefully, I've shut him up on the topic.

"Just saying I'm no saint. If I go through a presidential race, the media will be taking apart my past. It'll be everywhere. There'll be no escape," I say, and my chest tightens at the thought. It's an aspect of being a political figure and public person I can't get over. I hate the attention. Hate that reporters think they have a right to know about my personal life. Growing up a Mathis, I should be used to it. My cousins happily pose for pictures as opposed to ditching paparazzi like me, but I also guess that the paparazzi aren't very interested in their dull lives. Married with kids and running a candy conglomerate doesn't scream scandal the way my escapades do. My looks just help things right along.

Al lets out a mock exasperated breath. "You know I love you man, and you also know that if Pop wants you president, you'll be president." He reminds me how I bow to my father's every whim. He doesn't chide me about it, he's just stating a fact I can't deny. He's right, and I'm my father's puppet. Me bowing to his every whim is my penance. "Don't I know it. I'm just getting frustrated. I've had enough of his bullying tactics and the thought of announcing my candidacy is causing me to wake up sweating in the middle of the night."

Al cocks his head to the side. "We could take off. Head back to Africa." He gives me a challenging look. Knowing I'd love to take him up on his offer, but he also knows I don't have the balls to do it. Besides, I still have commitments as governor.

I scoff, "Yeah, Right." In my fucking dreams.

The Escalade pulls to a stop, and both Al and I exit in front of Henderson Place. "Isn't it a shame that they're ripping this place down?" I ask Al while wondering why I'm here to support the destruction of this beautiful landmark. My forced presence serves to remind me how I don't have control over my own life. I don't have time to overthink it because as I leave the SUV, my security detail guides us to the podium. The funny part of us walking with my detail is that Al and I both stand around six-foot-two. We're both built and in dark suits which means it's hard to tell between our security team and us.

Al turns to whisper using his hand to block his mouth. "It's a landmark so, yes," he shrugs. "But Mr. Bachmaker is going to make good on this new investment so who the fuck cares about maintaining a historical landmark." His tone is sarcastic. It's one of the reasons I respect Al. He isn't only about the bottom dollar. He cares even though he doesn't like to admit it too often. He'd rather people think he was an asshole. I never did understand that about him.

I chuckle and shake my head. We walk toward the podium set up for the ribbon-cutting ceremony. The press is front and center ready to snap the perfect shot and come up with their next headline. I walk up to Mr. Bachmaker and shake his hand. "Congratulations, Mr. Bachmaker." I give him my million-dollar smile.

"Governor Mathis. Glad you could make it." Mr. Bachmaker's grin is wide. He's a good five inches shorter than me and at least fifteen years older. "Your father tells me you have some big news breaking next week." He waggles his thick black grey brows.

I smile. I think. It's more like I'm pinching my lips together. "Yes, news," I repeat because I'm now seriously considering taking off on a plane to Africa next week. If it weren't for my commitments as governor, it would be the game plan.

"Well, I'll tell you. I have a niece. A pretty girl. She's coming to town tomorrow. Maybe you two can get together. She'll be working at Kincaid and Landry, moving here from Texas. Sweet girl... my sister's daughter. I'd appreciate you showing her around. And hey, you need a lady by your side to run for office, you know? My niece Madeline may be the one." He winks, and I groan internally. Another attempt at a setup. Blind dates weren't my thing.

If my father were here, he would be all over Mr. Bachmaker's attempt to set me up. According to dear old dad, a candidate can't run and win without a woman on his arm. At thirty-five and looking the way I did, snagging a first lady was a walk in the park. Only it was a walk I wasn't ready to take. My sexual needs are more than met. No complaints from me in that department.

I forced a smile, hoping I didn't look constipated as opposed to happy. Mr. Bachmaker sure wasn't the first person to try and set me up with a family member, and he wouldn't be the last. Occupational fucking hazard. "Thank you Mr. Bachmaker, and your niece sounds lovely. Kincaid and Landry is an excellent firm, very reputable. My schedule is incredibly busy right now. I'm sure you can understand with my upcoming news and all, I don't think I'll have time to show her around." I reply hoping I dodged that bullet. I hated lying through my fucking teeth.

"Well, now I'll have to talk to your daddy. Maybe we can all get together," Mr. Bachmaker replies, his Texan accent coming through. He's apparently unwilling to drop this idea. Why he thought that talking to my father would help was beyond me. I'm a grown man, and I decided where I stuck my dick, not my old man.

"Sure, Sir, let's set something up," I concede knowing the old guy isn't going to let up. The contribution he's offering came with a price tag, it usually did. Now I had a week to tell dear old dad I wasn't running for the presidency. The public saw me as this sharp, powerful figure fighting to get things done, laws passed, but that wasn't who I was on the inside. I was a fucking grown man who was scared. Yes, I can use that word in my head only. I was scared to stand up to my old man. Fuck that was a difficult internal confession to swallow.

The ribbon cutting ceremony began. The press took their positions and Al took his spot beside me. "You think his niece looks like him?" he whispers in my ear.

I kick him in the shin and he lurches forward. "Shut up," I whisper. Cameras are on us. I didn't want to come across as a juvenile. My opponents liked to argue I was too young for my role. I didn't want to give them bait. There was also the issue that Al was a bit of a prick when it came to women and he had many which could bring unwanted media attention. I wasn't a prick. I was always honest, upfront. I didn't want to leave a trail of broken hearts behind or bring scandal to my office.

Mr. Bachmaker stepped forward to cut the ribbon. In the distance, I noticed a long line of protesters making their way to the front of the podium. They were holding large signs and screaming "Save Henderson Place," repeatedly. I had half a mind to jump off the podium and join them.

"Don't even think about it," Al elbows me in the ribs and speaks from beneath his hand. He knew me well that was for damn sure. I gave him a knowing glare.

He tilted his head to the side and gave me a look filled with caution. "Don't," he said to emphasize his point. He was right. As much as I supported free speech and the right to assemble, this was not the time to stand up for what I believed. Now was the time to shake the hand of the man that was going to rip this beautiful building down. A structure that added character and vitality to our city. Instead he was going to build high-rise condominiums that would result in more traffic jams, use of too much hydro-electricity, and generate inequality due to the expense of making such a tall building.

I smiled and took a step forward to shake Bachmaker's hand. Yes, I was a fucking hypocrite but don't judge. At least not until you hear my whole story.

I spoke a few words into the microphone, but I honestly don't think anyone heard me over the shouting of the protesters. I focused on the police cars positioned on the edge of the parking lot where the ceremony was taking place. I noticed the police setting up a blockade. After my brief speech, I stepped off the podium and shook Mr. Bachmaker's hand once more.

"I'll be in touch about that date with my niece," he nodded assuredly.

"Yes, looking forward," I smiled and straightened my tie which suddenly felt a little too tight around my neck. "Good luck with this project," I said, then turned to leave. My detail is hot on my trail as I walked back to the Escalade since the protestors had moved up closer to the podium.

"You planning on getting hot and heavy with what was her name again?" Al tapped his chin fucking with me. "It started with an M." He pressed his lips together. As we walked past the protesters, I picked my head up to look at them. Although they were a rambunctious crowd, they weren't putting up with shit. They were standing here voicing their opinions, standing up for what they believed in, and me? I was a fucking joke. I knew it and it was eating away at me.

"Governor Mathis?" I heard the voice of a female shout my name. I picked my eyes up to make eye contact. When I spotted the female with the shouty voice, she had a cream pie flying at me faster than I could think. It slammed me in the face. The cool feel of whipped cream practically blinding me. Al burst into laughter beside me appreciating the sight when not a moment passed and he was met with the same fate. Pie is making contact with his smug grin.

"Not so funny, now is it?" I shook my head. He could be so juvenile at times. As we both used our hands to wipe away the excess cream from our eyes, one of the men on my detail offered me a handkerchief while shielding us from any more protesters. I noticed the police charging toward the crowds while I kept my gaze locked on the woman who called my name and then had the nerve to whip a pie in my face. Her red hair flailed in the wind as I saw her taking off in the opposite direction. The red-haired vixen got away. I chuckled to myself. Can't say I blamed her for the courageous act. I had just openly supported the destruction of a beautiful historical building.

"We have to cancel the school visit," Al said, looking down to his suit. The whipped cream had oozed down his neck and was dripping on his suit jacket. I was in a similar state.

"We aren't canceling. We're heading there as promised. We can clean up in the school bathroom," I said, and it wasn't a suggestion. I was a man of my word, and those kids were waiting for their pizza.

He rolled his eyes at me knowing I wasn't going to concede. On the way to the school, my cell phone rang. My father's name lit up the screen. James Mathis was a force to be reckoned with.

"Father."

"Colton, what on earth...." His list of expletives followed. "The media is all over the fact that you had a pie thrown in your face. What happened to keeping a low profile before the announcement next week?"

My father ran my campaign and he took his job too seriously.

"Don't shout at me. You're the one who set up that media op anyway. I played along as usual. Don't blame me if it backfired," I hissed, biting my tongue because what I wanted to tell him was that it turned out perfectly. I didn't want to run for president.

"Did they at least catch the son of a bitch that did it? No one throws a pie at the Governor of Illinois and gets away with it." My father was pissed and his long drawl came through the phone.

"They didn't catch her. Fine by me though."

"Her?" my father asked, perplexed.

"Yes, it was a woman that threw the pie," I responded thinking of her pretty face. She was more than lovely; she was beautiful, the way her blue eyes danced with mischief as she ran away from the police was now ingrained in my brain maybe forever. She was a free spirit and her smile breathed sunshine.

My father huffed. That's what he did when he was at a loss for words which didn't happen often. Then I heard a few heavy breaths before he continued. "Just great. I need to go. I have to find a way to spin this incident," he mumbled to himself before I heard the phone click. No goodbye. I wish I wanted the things my father wanted for me because he was so driven and together we could probably do it together, that was the irony in all this. So many people envied my position. In my head, though it felt more of an instance of the grass being greener on the other side. To me the simple people who lead ordinary lives had me intrigued. They did what they wanted and didn't have to answer to bossy parents who were power hungry.

After cleaning ourselves up, we spent a good hour eating pizza with Ms. Fitz's class. Well, it was more like I ate the pizza while Al flirted with Ms. Fitz. We discussed learning and the kids asked me questions about government and making the world a better place. I never wanted to have children of my own. It was something I just never craved, but I loved how real and altruistic children were.

"Mr. Mathis. Can you help end poverty in our city?" a young boy named Mathew Murphy asked.

Man, I would have loved nothing more than to make sure each person was fed and had a roof over their head, but Chicago is a dynamic city with many people. The budget wouldn't cover that reality.

"Mathew, I'm working on all kinds of reforms. I want to end poverty. I want everyone to have a nice place to live and food on their table. I'm doing the best I can, buddy." I forced a smile because I wanted to do more. More needed to be done. It was obvious. It was times like this that I wanted to pack a bag and head back to Africa. At least there I saw the difference I could make. Here in Chicago making a difference took a lot longer.

Mathew smiled at me and nodded. "Thank you, Mr. Governor, I'd appreciate that."

His words pulled at my heartstrings, reminding me why I allowed my father to convince me to run for state attorney and eventually the governorship- so that I could influence change. I learned the hard way that change wasn't so easy. I was a grass-roots kind of guy to my core, that's why I fit in the Peace Corps. In the villages, small changes helped improved agriculture and drinking water. It was a group effort. Here in the US, bureaucracy bogged things down.

We wrapped up in Ms. Fitz's classroom and I'm pretty sure Al scored her number. Then we headed back to the office. My dad always tried to sell me on the idea that I was different than other politicians, that I was special and that I could be a driving force for change, for creating good and equality. Heck, there were times I bought his rhetoric, just not this time. Years in politics taught me change was hard to come by and that little incident this afternoon with Mr. Bachmaker reminded me that money didn't sway me. I wasn't the guy who would concede on his values for an endorsement; I wasn't the right guy to run for president.

Back at my desk, I pressed the call button and my secretary Susan picked up.

"Yes, Mr. Governor?" her voice came through the speaker.

"I need you to search for a boy named Mathew Murphy."

"Can you give me a little more information, Sir?" Susan asked.

"Yes, he's a student at Greensboro Elementary. Find out where he lives and what his parents do," I said through the phone, knowing this wasn't a conventional request for a secretary in a governor's office. Susan was used to these types of requests from me. She was very good about keeping things confidential. Even things that may be borderline illegal, like this request.

"Okay, Sir. And once I have that information what would you like me to do?" Susan asked because she was good at her job, always thinking a few steps ahead. That way she didn't need to bother me when she found out.

"Secure the home address and let me know where they live and any family background you can gather," I responded.

"Getting right on that, Sir," Susan responded.

"Thank you," I pressed the speaker button to end the call. I had to know why Mathew was so concerned with poverty. His old clothes and worn out shoes told me that maybe his family wasn't fairing so well. I couldn't save the world with my trust fund but I liked to make a small difference when I could.

CHAPTER TWO

"Would you stop consulting with Albert on his latest conquest and mingle a little." My father leaned into my ear and shout-whispered. There was never a moment to myself when he accompanied me to functions, and this one was no different. *Mingle Colton, make connections Colton, maybe find yourself a wife while you're at it, Colton.* I swear I was sick of my name. I clenched my fists at my side feeling my jaw tense. I had wanted to give my father a piece of my mind so many times in the past and held back. Lately, the urge was growing stronger and gaining fuel. I didn't know what fire was causing my fuel to burn but I was embracing it for once.

I gave him a side-long glance while gnawing at the inside of my cheek hoping it would curb the words threatening to spill from my lips. Without answering him, I returned my attention to Al, who just asked me to tweak my speech tonight to include a vague comment about old age pension since we were trying to capture the senior vote. Assuming I was still announcing my intent to run for President. I tended not to share my intimate thoughts on the matter with Al anymore even though he was my best friend; he always wanted me to run. He believed I was the right guy for the job. "Will do," I replied, not wanting to stir the pot before I made a final decision.

"Don't ignore me, boys," my father cut in. It's funny that he still liked to call us boys. We were far from boys. I left my father's home when I went off to college and never returned. Al and I also paid our bills and fucked around with too many women to be considered boys.

"With all due respect Mr. Mathis. Our boy," Al grinned salaciously, "is nowhere near ready to settle down. He may not have a bride by his side, but our boy," he accentuated again, "is well liked." Al responded to my father understanding his hidden meaning in the words *mingle*. I knew there was a reason I kept Al close.

I blew out a breath, straightened my tie, gave my father a cheeky smile and said, "Time to mingle." I just wanted to remove myself from my father's presence before he took on the role of matchmaker and dragged me around the room to meet all the potential lifelong partners in the place. I'm not exaggerating; he'd done that before. It wasn't pretty. It usually ended in him finding me a lady whom he felt was, and I quote, *the perfect match... proper upbringing, education and wanting to commit to the role of the first lady*. Gah! The problem was the many holes in his tactics.

Firstly, most of the single women he came across wanted to date me or at minimum bed me. These females took in the scent of power that the governorship gave and wanted in. I was good looking, built, had a trust fund, and a sleeve of tattoos down my arm. Most women were intrigued by the tattoos. Few men at my political stature had them, at least from what the public knew. It had become an intrigue for a politician to have a tattoo. I blame the Canadian Prime Minister who visited Washington last year. The media was all about publicizing his tattoos and somehow they latched on to me too, reporting on my muscular arms and colorful sleeve. The media attention added to the frenzy on me even though I'd already been established as Chicago's most wanted bachelor.

I scanned the room in search of some interesting conversation. This was the second year I was attending the Veteran Affairs Gala. I respected our veterans wholeheartedly. Before I applied to Harvard, I wanted to join the military. My father had been against it. Said I was all he had and if something happened to me, he wouldn't be able to live with himself. I didn't enlist naturally but I've always felt like it was something I should have done.

Just as I'm about to have a seat at one of the tables next to some older veterans that have tags on their suit jackets saying they fought in Vietnam my father stops me. "Son, glad I caught you. Mr. Bachmaker wants to introduce you to his niece." My eyes widened and I blew out a long puff of air. Is that guy here tonight? Dammit! For some reason, I had a feeling my father would orchestrate a meeting. I just didn't think it would be so soon.

"Not tonight. I was hoping to speak to these men." I nodded to the gentlemen sitting around the table exchanging war stories. My father pursed his lips together a telltale sign he wanted to get his way.

"Don't you see that this is for your own good?" I was losing the battle to meet the niece, so I caved like I usually did. I couldn't be the only one raised by a single parent who was intrusive and borderline obsessive about my personal life. I just couldn't be. "Wouldn't it be nice to have a woman standing by your side when you make your announcement?" My father's dark brows furrowed together. His deep brown eyes, so different from mine, darkened while he waited in anticipation.

I tilted my head back and a deep chuckle escaped my throat. "I don't need a woman beside me when I have a different one under me every night." I winked because my father was the one who taught me how to be a lady's man. I learned from the best and now he was all for me throwing my bachelor status and fun out the window.

"Not here, Colton. You can't think with your dick when it comes to campaigning. Thinking with your dick will have you falling for the wrong woman." And even though he didn't say it, I knew he was speaking of my mother.

"You can't surely believe I could meet and have time to fall in love with a woman in a span of a couple of weeks? You know me." I scoffed, shaking my head at the notion. I've never had a relationship last longer than three months. My old man hasn't had a relationship with a woman last more than a few weeks since Mom left. How he thinks I can fall in love so quickly was ludicrous.

"You're my son. I'm fully aware of what you are and are not capable of. That's why you need a nudge from your father." He tilted his chin urging me forward.

I turned my head so that our eyes were level. "Did you ever consider that maybe I have no interest in being president?" The words escaped my mouth before I could stop them.

My father clenched his jaw and got a daunting look in his eyes. I usually didn't take such a rebellious stance with him but sometimes desperate measures called for extreme responses.

My father's face fell and his skin paled. "Is that what you want, Colton? Truly? Because I've dedicated my life getting you to this point," his voice trailed off and his words settled on me like a thick honey coat of guilt.

"Just introduce me to the niece," I conceded feeling even more defeat. Like my face was pressed into the sand and I was unable to breathe. I extended a hand for him to lead the way a hollow version of myself following.

He glared disappointedly before passing me with the silent instruction to follow. And even though my breathing was labored, my usual guilt roiled in my stomach. The blame he used to get me to do anything he damn well pleased.

"Mr. Bachmaker, you remember my son, Governor Colton Mathis." My father smiled proudly making the introduction. Mr. Bachmaker's family was in the oil business down in Texas before they began to spread their wings across the country and buy real estate when the market crashed many years back. My romancing his niece would result in a substantial contribution to my campaign. I felt like a prostitute. I wasn't going to sleep with her even if she was pretty just to prove that I stuck my dick where I chose and not where I was told. Why did I feel so childish thinking those words? My mind had been warped somewhere from the time my mother took off until today.

"Hello, again Mr. Bachmaker."

"Pleasure is all mine, Colton." He grinned before turning to the young woman sitting by his side. He gave her a nudge and she fumbled to stand. "I'd like to introduce you to my niece. Madeline Huntsworth." The woman smiled a toothy grin. I couldn't help but rake my eyes over her body. She didn't look like Mr. Bachmaker at all. She was blonde, pretty green eyes, smiled a lot. Wore a dark blue dress that was simple and sophisticated. I wouldn't be surprised if she came straight from her office to the gala. She was average height, nice full breasts. In short, she was doable. As the thought entered my mind, I chided myself for sounding so much like Al in my head. Was I considering sleeping with this woman? What had my life come to? I felt low, dirty. It's the one thing I promised myself I would never feel like as politician and here I was for the first time in my life feeling utterly defeated. And it was only a matter of time before I would make an announcement that would change my life forever. Fucking hell.

I extended my hand with a smile because Mathis men are always gentlemen. "Madeline, it's a pleasure." I paused to look at my father. He had such a pleased look on his face. That overwhelming feeling of not wanting to disappoint him swept over me once more. "Colt," I finally said and my father let out a loud cough like he was choking. Only him, Al and a few close friends from college ever called me Colt. He was probably worried I was about to sabotage his efforts.

Madeline's cheeks turned pink as I said my nickname. It wasn't something new for me to see a woman blush in my presence since most women had that reaction to my looks. It was my ocean blue eyes. Women feel like I can see right through them because of the bright coloring. I never argue that notion because it gets me laid, but it's a crock of shit. They also tell me I could be Henry Cavill's twin with my large built frame, wide jaw bone and high cheeks. My response is usually, "You mean he looks like me." Okay, so I may be a little conceited but I still am a nice guy, I swear. On some level, it's my self-deprecation about my looks that makes me brush them off too. I know I don't look like my father which means I look like the woman that gave me life and left me behind. A part of me hated having her look back at me when I looked in the mirror.

"Nice to meet you." She shakes my hand firmly and I felt the reverberations down my arm. Not surprising. I suspect she had to earn her place in a courtroom as a defense attorney.

"Which law firm are you with?" I ask just to make conversation because her dear old uncle already told me. Off to the side, I noticed my father whispering something to her uncle probably campaign stuff I didn't care to know about.

"Kincaid and Landry," she replies while smiling from cheek to cheek and batting her eyelashes. She must be a second-year associate at best. I was much older than her but I get why her uncle would think that the possible next president of the United States would be a good match. She's precisely the type of woman my father refers to as proper upbringing, education, and family name.

"Yes, of course, I'm familiar with the firm. I used to practice in

Illinois myself. I heard Kincaid Senior is about to retire," I say feeling the need to pull teeth to make conversation.

"Yes, I heard that too," she confirms. Again, she ends the potential for further conversation. Feeling like I've been staring at her awkwardly for a few seconds longer than I'd like, I allow my gaze to wander to either side of the room. Father was in deep conversation with Mr. Bachmaker to my right. I scan the room for Al, hoping I could eye motion him to save me from this situation but instead I notice a woman briskly walk past me, her long red hair catches my attention and the scent of strawberry she leaves behind makes me want to follow her like a dog in heat. My gaze remains trained on her as she pauses and smiles at an older man. I watch their animated conversation. How they look warmly at each other. Like a grandfather would his granddaughter and suddenly I'm so intrigued I forget where I am and who I'm speaking with. I can only see her profile, pale skin, blue eyes, lush red lips, a spattering of freckles across her cheeks. My eyes roam down her body unashamedly to the curve of her behind in that slender red gown and my dick stiffens. Oh, fuck! I'm the first to admit that my body readily reacts to a beautiful woman, but this lady...she blows everyone else out of the water. My breath catches and my chest warms, I'm not sure what's happening but before I know it, my feet are moving. I'm following her and the older man she's with, but I'm at least a few feet behind them. I'm pretty sure I hear my father call out my name from behind me but I don't turn around because I'm too enthralled with the lady before me. She pauses in the middle of the dance floor where she and the older guy begin to dance to "Unforgettable" by Nat King Cole and Natalie Cole and for some reason this moment is unforgettable as I watch them, her face pressed to the older man's chest. He looks like he must be a World War II veteran, maybe her grandfather. Before I can think my legs are carrying me toward them. My eyes glued to her. This mystery woman who has captured my breath with one glance.

"Excuse me. May I cut in?" I ask. Her back is facing me and she doesn't move from her spot or turn her head. The older man stops dancing and she lifts her head to look in his eyes.

"That would be up to her," he replies. He looks at the beautiful woman in his arms and she turns to look at me but her stare is blank. Her blue eyes sparkle in the dim light of the dance floor and some crystal stones on her dress glimmer off the chandelier lights.

She doesn't answer me, so I repeat my question and extend a hand. "May I have this dance?"

She smiles and it's brilliant. It also sends a pang of warmth into my chest. She looks at the older man for a moment. "Sorry, I'm busy," she replies. It's completely unexpected. I wonder if she knows who I am. I know it sounds cocky but seriously, given my looks and position women are putty in my hands.

She continues to dance with the older guy.

I'm stuck standing in my spot, my mouth hanging open. I'm speechless for a brief moment when I realize I don't want to take no for an answer. I want one dance, one conversation, at least the chance to know what she's like. It's an odd sensation for me because I've never been genuinely interested in a lady past a good lay, but I'm intrigued.

I take two steps and tap her shoulder since her back is to me. She turns to look at me like I'm a nuisance, her mouth opens to speak but I interrupt her. "Sorry to intrude again, but..." I pause as the memory of the Bachmaker ribbon cutting ceremony replays in my mind. I get a fluttery feeling in my chest, my brows furrow and my curiosity becomes even more heightened because looking at her up close tells me that my memory isn't mistaken and she's the pie-whipping bandit. For some reason, I find the situation amusing and my eyes drag up and down her body. Geez, she cleans up nice. She's fucking stunning, classy, elegant. Nothing like the wild, free, and apparently angry woman that threw the pie.

"I'm sorry can I help you?" Her brows are dipped together as she asks the question. She also seems a little nervous like maybe she knows I've recognized her.

"I'd really like a dance." I persist hoping she doesn't get turned off by my perseverance but now that I see it's her, I want the dance even more.

She shakes her head.

"Why?" I insist. I'm a little pushy but my ego is hurt and now I also want to know why she's a pie-wielding vixen in her spare time.

The older man gives her a little nudge and with unspoken words with a blink of an eye and a tilt of a chin tells her to dance with me. She blows out a puff of air and stares at the old guy, her eyes narrowing to slits. I'm pretty sure she's about to tell him off or me where to go when she says, "Fine. One dance."

Ha! My ego is taking a real beating tonight. I feel like I'm treading on uncharted territory. In my past relations with women when things got too serious we broke it off. It was an arrangement I always set up off the bat. No complications, no spewing my undying love. Just raw animalistic sex. Simple.

I tilt my head almost in a bow and extend my hand. She takes it and I place one hand on her slender hip. My hand making contact with the silky fabric of her dress. She smells delectable; I'm enthralled. I can't understand it for the life of me. We dance at a distance from each other and as the music continues, all I can think is that this woman is unforgettable.

"Are you going to give me your name?" I finally ask, breaking the silent stare between us.

She bites her lower lip and tilts her head to the side like she's assessing me. "I guess I could," she replies but she doesn't give me her name while her lip curves in one corner. She continues to smile devilishly as we softly sway to the voices of Nat King Cole and Natalie Cole radiating through the hall making the moment feel surreal.

"And it would be," I coax her into giving me her name.

"Evie," she says sweetly looking deeply into my eyes. She has an accent I can't place.

"Evie, that's a beautiful name. I'm Colton," I grin.

"I know, Mr. Governor," she replies her tone terse. It throws me off a little as I wonder what her deal is. My intrigue wins out.

"So, beautiful Evie. What brings you to the Veteran Affairs ball tonight?"

"My uncle is a vet, World War II. He raised me; I respect him very much. So, I'm here." She shrugs her shoulders. It felt like she wanted to say more and stopped herself. Her accent has me very curious but I don't want to be rude and ask. I have to be careful with this woman because my sense tells me one wrong word from my mouth and she's taking a hike. I'm not used to this, being the one to chase. It gives me an unexpected thrill.

"And you Mr. Governor. Why are you here?" she asks throwing me off my tracks. Isn't it obvious why I'm here? To support the veterans, of course.

I smirk and bite my lower lip while I contemplate my answer for a moment. "I thought my presence would be obvious."

The song changes to another slow song. I'm worried my time with her is up, but she doesn't pull away from my embrace. "You mean to secure your support with the war veterans. I heard you're about to announce that you're running for the presidency." Her words are more of a statement than a comment which causes my chest to tighten and my breath to hitch. I know there's speculation whether I will run, but I hadn't realized it was common knowledge.

"Ouch, that isn't fair. I respect our military. I respect the men that have given up so much of their lives to fight our wars, to protect our freedoms." The words bleed from me with the utmost conviction.

"You seem passionate about the subject," she retorts with a hint of surprise in her tone. I can't help but notice how she watches me so intently when I speak grabbing onto my every word. Watching my mouth, looking into my eyes. This woman is so different. Different, good.

"You sound surprised." I grin, hoping to win her over with my smile. My smile has always been a sure thing.

Her lips slowly spread and I feel like maybe I'm winning her over.

She shakes her head. "Sorry, I don't know why but I had a different picture of you in my mind." I want to say yeah, a picture where my face is covered in cream pie, thanks to yours truly? I keep my mouth shut. For now.

"Really? Do you mind sharing exactly what you mean?" I'm pushing a little but I can't help myself. She seems to be a critic. I need to sway her.

"I just figured you were this spoiled rich kid who had the governorship handed to him on a silver platter," she answers, and my jaw drops.

Fucking hell. She has no filter and yet I find her sexy as hell.

"That isn't fair. I worked damn hard to get top grades at Harvard Law School. I worked a hundred hours a week in the prosecutor's office before I even ran for state attorney. I may have been raised with money and I may have a topnotch education, but I've worked hard all my life. I set goals and I achieved them. I shouldn't be blasted for hard work," I scoff. I don't mean too, but I need to set her straight. Besides I've been blasted with such accusations in the past. I have this speech ready at the tip of my tongue. The only difference is I've never defended myself to a woman I wanted to bed so badly. And a woman who I seem to repulse.

She squints her eyes, not relenting on that deep stare she seems to give me. It looks like she's unsure if she should buy my argument. I need to change tactic. "Enough about me and my uninteresting life. Tell me about you. What do you do?" I ask as we move to the music. We've been dancing for a while; I hope the DJ continues with the string of slow songs.

"I work in a clothing shop and on my free time, I volunteer with Habitat for Humanity. It's—" I cut her off.

"I know what it is. Jeez. You must think I'm a real schmuck."

She eyes me curiously.

ACKNOWLEDGMENTS

I started writing this book the day I got back from my friend's funeral. I know its depressing and her death shook me to my core. I couldn't stop thinking of the four kids she left behind and how they would grow up without a mother.

I don't have her name in the dedication but the quote at the beginning of this book is dedicated to her and her sweet children. I hope they soar and follow their dreams knowing their mom is looking down on them from heaven.

I wrote this book fast is the truth only because I lived and breathed these characters.

I have so many people who helped me tell this story. Thank you to my beta readers. Your comments and feedback not only put a smile on my face during my read throughs but helped me take this story to the next level. Karen Isopi, thank you once again for taking the time for this project. Your input is so valuable to me.

To T thank you for going through the developmental edits with me more than once. I appreciate your dedication to detail.

To Max my editor, thank you for your patience with all my grammar faux pas and putting up with my tight timeline on this project. To James, thank you for proofing the MS for me. You saved my sanity from having to read through the story another time.

Thank you to my lovely agent, Stephanie Delamater Phillips thank you for all your sound advice and all your amazing work.

Thank you to Sarah Hansen for another beautiful cover. I never have to tell you what I'm looking for you just go and create the perfect covers.

To all the readers and bloggers that have read this story, you have my heartfelt thanks. I am very aware of all the wonderful books out there and it warms my heart that you have chosen to dedicate your time to this story. I hope it was as meaningful to you as it was to me.

XOXOXO

R.C.

www.ingramcontent.com/pod-product-compliance
Lightning Source LLC
Chambersburg PA
CBHW020909200626
46814CB00001BA/251

* 9 7 8 0 9 9 5 3 4 9 9 7 1 *